ASSAULT

MICHAEL KELLY

Assault

Harcourt, Brace & World, Inc., New York

Copy IV

B. 1.68

Library of Congress Catalog Card Number: 68-12578

Printed in the United States of America

For
John and Sarah Talbot
and
Valda J. Stamp

CIE	Companion of the Order of the Indian Empire
CIGS	Chief of the Imperial General Staff
DSK	Dansk Sukker Kompagniet, Danish Sugar Company
ETA	Estimated Time of Arrival, Air Navigation
GAF	German Air Force, British abbreviation
GOC	General Officer Commanding
ID	Identity Card
MC	Military Cross
MEAF	Middle East Air Force
OKW	Oberkommando der Wehrmacht, High Command of the German Armed Forces
PIAT	Projector, Infantry, Anti-tank
PR	Photo-Reconnaissance (aircraft)
RDX	Cyclonite, Hexogen, T4, Plastic explosive
RLM	Reichsluftfahrtministerium, German Air Ministry
SAP	Semi-Armour Piercing ammunition
SOE	Special Operations Executive
SS	Schutzstaffel, bodyguard. An *élite* Nazi corps
V-Mann	Secret Agent

Private	Gemeiner
Lance Corporal	Gefreiter
Corporal	Obergefreiter
Sergeant	Unteroffizier or Feldwebel
Company Sergeant-Major	Oberfeldwebel
Second Lieutenant	Leutnant
Lieutenant	Oberleutnant
Captain	Hauptmann
Major	Major
Lieutenant-Colonel	Oberstleutnant
Colonel	Oberst
Brigadier	————
Major-General	General-Major
Lieutenant-General	General-Leutnant
General	General-Oberst
Field Marshal	General-Feldmarschal

FÜHRER ORDER, MOST SECRET
Senior Commanders Only

All enemies on so-called Commando Missions in Europe or Africa challenged by German troops, even if they are to all appearance soldiers in uniform or demolition troops, whether armed or unarmed, in battle or flight, are to be slaughtered to the last man. It does not make any difference whether they are landed from ships and aeroplanes for their actions, or whether they are landed by parachute. Even if those individuals, when found, should apparently be prepared to give themselves up, no pardon is to be granted to them on principle.

I will hold responsible under Military Law for failing to carry out this order, all commanders and officers who either have neglected their duty of instructing the troops about this order or who acted against this order where it is to be executed.

ADOLF HITLER

CHAPTER ONE

'HOLD back. Hold back I say!' They obeyed him, grouping under the leaky awning. 'Hans?' One nodded in the darkness. 'Remember—you must be the last in. You've the grenades?' Another quick nod. 'Then be ready to cover us out with smoke.'

'Will do!'

'Sven? Bjorn? Anders?' He damped his lips. 'Don't crush the fuze pencils till I give you the word.' He paused to swallow hard. 'We'll only have 180 seconds once they begin to run.' He stopped again, squeezing the pulpy satchel of RDX slung over one shoulder like a sandwich bag. 'If there's any trouble inside, stuff these under the vacuum plant.' His voice cracked. 'You all know which one that is?' They nodded again, less confidently, catching the infection of his nervousness. 'Good!' He tried making them an easy laugh; it choked at birth; he coughed harshly.

'Good; but don't get split up by the others in the clocking hall; follow me close.' He coughed again and watched the thickening shuffle of workers hurry past, heads bowed against the night rain.

'Fine!' He fumbled back the windbreaker cuff and cupped his watch's phosphorus dial. 'Zero six twenty-seven.' He glanced up. 'Time the morning shift clocked-in.' The rain must have found a crack in his boots; both feet were dead with cold. He stamped the paving slabs and tried to think of another question, but it wasn't possible to stall off any longer.

'All OK?' His lips scaled; he licked them damp.

One after the other they filtered into the crowd, twitching their collars high against a thin, dawn wind tip-toeing off the Baltic.

The morning shift slowed about ten yards from the wire mesh and started getting out the grey, pasteboard Workers' Passes— photo stapled on one side, police and German garrison seals on the other. They filed in through the narrow gateway, bending left into the Time Office. But there was a new man on Pass Control this morning, sharp-nosed and awake. Scrutinising each photo, carefully matching it with the man, curtly waving him past to the clocks. 'Come on! Hurry it up!' His cindery voice kept the queue meek and obedient. 'Herr Hendrikssen?' His eyes and mind focused on the first man's pass.

11

'Yes...?' Hendrikssen tried to sound unconcerned; he hoped his fear didn't show.

'Herr *Otto* Hendrikssen?' The Pass Controller seemed to caress each word before reluctantly letting it escape.

'Yes! That's me. Says so there, doesn't it?' The Pass Controller blandly ignored him. 'You've newly signed on the strength of our Company.'

'That's true.' He sounded righteously impatient. 'What's it you want now?'

'Pay Accounts; a routine matter concerning your Insurance cards; be so good as to step into the office one moment.' He nodded over to a nearly shut door by the clocking machines. 'It won't take long.'

Unwashed sweat slicked Hendrikssen's arms; he started to obey, then abruptly hesitated; the watchers' nerve sheared; the door exploded open, men in belted leather coats pounced out, coshes swinging. 'RUN!' Hendrikssen spun down, blindly reaching his pistol.

Nailed boots skidded from cover outside. 'HALT!' A blast of tightly packed shots chopped low, aimed to cripple. The dazed workers hit the floor as Militia troops viciously clubbed the staggering men, reluctantly taking them alive. They nearly succeeded.

But the last man in had cleared his Colt and begun firing, bent double, scrambling for the grenade; one of his slugs blew away a booted knee before they trampled him, rifle butts flailing. He jerked away, covering his head, blood pouring as he forced the Colt's hot muzzle between his teeth and snatched back the trigger.

After a while they stopped pounding the body; there was no fun. Instead, a couple of them took an ankle apiece and bumped him over the Time Office doorsill, dumping him beside the other four, shackled wrist to wrist, sprawled face-down on the dirty floor.

'Filth! Stupid dungheads!' Militia Leutnant Rolf hysterically bawled out his troops. 'Filth! Dung! Idiots!'

'Silence.' Rolf swallowed his tongue. A tall civilian in green loden, knickerbockers and brogues slowly paced into the light. 'Thank you, Leutnant.' He brushed Rolf to one side and frowned at the seeping blood. He glanced round. 'Leutnant?'

'Herr Hauptmann!' Rolf worked hard on his German accent; an ambitious young man could go far these days if he knew on which side his biscuit was buttered. Sepp Bethmann didn't notice, or care. Instead he stubbed a gloved finger at the floor. 'Get some sawdust on that.'

'Immediately, Herr Hauptmann!' Rolf jumped to obey, yelping orders right and left. One of his Militia troopers doubled back from the boiler house with a bucket of hot ashes and threw them over the head. Bethmann sighed and looked away, it was hardly elegant but it probably served the same purpose in the long run. God! What cretins he had to work with nowadays! One of his own Stuttgarter Police was worth a score of these Danish blockheads. He searched a tooth with the tip of his tongue and nodded casually at Rolf—sprung rigidly to attention, face set, almost as if the Führer himself was about to decorate him for this messy scrimmage. Bethmann soured. 'Take them all away!'

'Immediately, Herr Hauptmann!'

The German abruptly turned his back, flicking their dismissal with one hand while he reached for the outside telephone.

CHAPTER TWO

'CONCLUDE with "The arrests were ably carried out under my personal supervision by SS Oberleutnant (Acting Hauptmann G/3) Bethmann assisted by a detachment of local Militia forces stop." Put in my usual signature and cypher group, have it sent via SS Communications North, Lübeck.'

'Jawohl, Herr Oberst!' Kierzner rubbed his eyes and eased back in the chair. A sudden flurry of rain dashed across the window behind him. The pale eyes jumped into focus again. 'Where was I, Fräulein?' The voice matched the eyes, matched the man—accurate and guarded at all times.

'You have just finished the telex to SS Führer-Headquarters Berlin, Herr Oberst!'

'Of course, Fräulein, of course.' Kierzner nodded, thoughtfully toying with a service issue pencil; rolling it between the flats of his hands; casting round a well-ordered mind for exactly the right theme. He must be careful to choose well for this next piece of dictation; he started humming a passage by Mendelssohn, something he was transcribing for the cello.

Kierzner suddenly realised what he was doing, and shut up tight. The new secretary might not be nearly so stupid. She might easily recognise a Jewish composer and hurry the word back, to others. He began smiling kindly at the puzzled girl. 'The telex to Führer HQ you said?'

'Yes, Herr Oberst!' Kierzner skilfully tested her answer before relaxing again. He turned off the smile.

'Personal and most confidential to SS Reichsführer Himmler, Reich Security Office Berlin; copy to SS Obergruppenführer Heydrich; two file copies...' The stenographer's pen swooped along her pad's faint lines.

'Usual introduction. Begin. "I have the honour to submit a more detailed report of the recent Action"' (he liked that word, it rang well), '"referred to in telex such and such reporting the successful elimination of an English terror unit parachuted into the Danish Protectorate, stop."' He examined a thumbnail with sudden concern, lost interest and went on.

'"SS Security-Intelligence immediately put them under close surveillance and classified their contacts among the civilian popu-

14

lation—from which further arrests may be expected at any time. The target of this terror raid was easily identified, being the Mercur radio valve and tube assembly workshops referred to in Special Security Order," ' Kierzner turned over a green file cover, ' "Order A/7—Schwarzwald." New paragraph, Fräulein.' He went on.

' "It was immediately decided, at Staff level, to allow a limited freedom of action before concluding the arrest. This was deliberately chosen to cancel out the possibility of escape always inherent in House Raids; my confidence was amply justified by the results obtained." ' Kierzner stopped short and began analysing the whole phrase, carefully weighing each word. 'Correction. Fräulein. That last sentence must read "your Excellence's confidence in SS Security-Intelligence Copenhagen was amply justified by the results obtained..." ' She struck out the bad line; he went on smoothly telling lies.

' "The subjects have been removed from Militia custody and are being interviewed by specialist SS interrogation officers; their findings will greatly increase your Excellence's knowledge of the English espionage/sabotage networks and their objectives in the Reich Protectorate. This department will, of course, submit immediate and detailed reports." ' Kierzner stretched his legs and leaned back. 'Read it over from the beginning, Fräulein.' He listened intently to the beautiful tapestry of half-truths they were stitching together for Himmler's delight. Satisfied with their progress so far he went on.

'Continue. "I am honoured to inform your Excellence that, in connection with the complete neutralisation of these terrorists"— no—gangsters, make that "gangsters", Fräulein. "With the complete neutralisation of these gangsters that greatly strengthened defences are being deployed round the named installation to prevent any further attacks, either by land or by air." ' Kierzner paused to admire this letter to his leader. It must be respectful— natürlich!—and flattering to the reader, yet supremely confident; it must shore-up Berlin's high opinion of Oberstleutnant Kierzner. He frowned. 'Read back, Fräulein.'

She bobbed her head, squinting at the hurried loops and curves. 'Excellent!' he approved. Crude flattery and subtle self-praise, all strung together on a thread of in-jargon and official form. 'Close with the usual subscription and full signature block this time...' The stenographer looked up at that. 'Yes, full signature—Maximilian Ruprecht Kierzner; SS Oberstleutnant; Divisional Head of SS Intelligence; the Danish Protectorate.'

'Jawohl!'

15

'Have the letter, and copies, ready for my seal and immediate despatch by special courier.' She sprang to attention, hands flat down by her sides and marched away to the Correspondence Section.

Kierzner wearily rubbed his eyes again, stifled a yawn and flipped open the massive, ebony cigarette-box by his wife's framed photo. He carefully selected a cork tip, screwed it into the long holder and waved a match under the slowly twirled end, inhaling deeply, letting the grey reek trickle down his nostrils.

Another close squeak; more saboteurs landing to attack a top security site in his charge; another fright like this wouldn't have the same happy outcome. He'd been very lucky this time, but luck isn't the sort of thing on which a long and happy life should be based, not luck alone. Kierzner-the-fortunate could so easily become Kierzner-the-who? His climb through the SS grades had been spectacular. His descent, if he didn't watch it, would be breath-stopping. More trouble in Denmark and he'd be damned lucky to get off with a posting to the Eastern Front—and that was no sinecure nowadays. His cigarette smouldered while he carefully juggled with the problem of how much money to award the Englishmen's betrayer.

After a long time he sauntered back to the question of sabotage; he must be very alert; no second bite at this cherry for the English! Kierzner crushed the cigarette in a brass nosecap from a 150-mm shell, reached out to his inter-office speaker and stubbed a contact. 'Bethmann!'

'Herr Oberst?'

'What's happening down there?' Bethmann mouthed a foul word at the harsh voice which always talked down to him; he padded his armpits dry with a square of grey rag. 'Well?' Bethmann nodded over to his assistants. Another wavering shriek exploded from the man racked across an iron frame. Kierzner frowned at the microphone. 'Is that all?'

'It's enough to be getting on with.' Bethmann in his own kingdom—the cellars—was quite different to Bethmann at other times. 'I'm still correcting him.' He paused to chuck the rag at his locker before glancing back at the speaker box. 'There is one interesting tit-bit ...'

'What's that?'

'They're not English; they're all Danish traitors.'

'Hardly a master stroke, my dear Hauptmann.' Kierzner sounded impatient.

'Perhaps, Herr Oberst, but their Shock Tolerance is still very

16

low; the Militia thugs were too rough this morning.' Another gagging scream wrenched from the tormented Dane.

'Now that's more promising!' Kierzner's amplified words bounced off the concrete walls. 'But take it easy, don't use them up too fast.' Then, helpfully now. 'Why not try scopolamine injections?' Bethmann sneered at this one.

One of his assistants glanced away from the rack and scowled, shaking his head. Bethmann felt very tempted to tell Kierzner just what he could do with his scopolamine injection, but he didn't. 'Of course, Herr Oberst, if that's what you order me to do—but I think we shall see results my way ...'

'Very well—I'm only interested in the answers obtained. So, my dear Bethmann, is Berlin.' He paused. 'Remember that! I want the questionnaire filled in, and quickly!' Kierzner cut the line, stubbed another contact and alerted his car and driver down in the Transport pool.

He thrust himself upright, stepping round the desk, striding across his suite. He slowed half a beat for cap, gloves and leather switch before marching into the corridor, his public face setting into dark, vertical lines. Non-commissioned and ranking staff were completely ignored as they jerked to attention, backs flat against the wall; subordinate officers received a cold acknowledgement as he strode past, heel irons beating a harsh drum roll on the flooring.

They all breathed out as he broke step in the long entrance hall and carefully squared off his steep-fronted cap, badgeless except for the plain silver deathshead. SS Feldwebel Dorfer, Kierzner's servant and driver, stood ready by one of the tall glass doors, deferentially holding his master's leather topcoat folded over one arm. He stamped forward and rammed his heels together like a pistol shot. 'It still rains, Herr Oberst!'

'So I observe.' Kierzner was on form. He paused just long enough for the fellow to drape his coat like a cloak before continuing his progress. Waffen SS troopers on sentry duty presented arms like exquisite marionettes as he marched across the rainswept pavement and ducked under the canvas hood of his Mercedes. Dorfer heaved the door shut and trotted round to the driver's seat. He sat to attention, rain trickling down his face and collar, mutely waiting for orders. 'VI Korps General-Kommandantur!' Dorfer toed-in the clutch, running the Mercedes V6 to full power, steering wound hard over to give his chief the police raid exits he demanded.

The camouflage drab staff-car lanced along Copenhagen's misty boulevards while Kierzner permitted himself to relax in the deep,

17

richly polished upholstery. A look of dreamy contentment eased his face back to normal as the Mercedes' tyres droned on wet asphalt.

So far life had been calm and very well ordered here in Denmark; a few carefully selected hangings should work miracles with the remaining diehards and agitators; provided the English kept their noses out. Kierzner watched his profile in the side window, getting the expressions just right. His head tilted back. No mercy for anyone working with the English—none! Prove once and for all that the best interests of the Danes lay in service and obedience! He wouldn't tolerate any of that nonsense they were getting in France nowadays—none! None at all!

The Mercedes slowed, wheeling sharp left off Grøningenvej, aiming into Kastellet Park. Shaggy, uncut grass and weeds grew waist high along the cobbled road, shattered by heavy loads pounding up from the docks and disembarkation areas. Dorfer had to ease past an artillery limber and 88-mm gun which a sweating Wehrmacht section was still unwrapping from a chestnut bole.

The staff-car wheeled left again and rolled along a short causeway over the Fortress' moat, braking only when the radiator nudged a red-and-white striped hurdle. Two infantrymen sprang to attention as Kierzner's pennant of rank came abreast of them, smacking their rifle stocks, marching forward—capes glistening, helmet covers sodden with rain. His nose wrinkled at the whiff of damp serge and oilskin as they respectfully bent to inspect the reserved, SS Pass. Both men ran to drag the hurdle aside, saluting woodenly as the Mercedes nosed past, its beautiful motor pulsing, exhausts burbling, accelerating towards the Wehrmacht garrison area.

Kierzner wound down the window to get a better view of things; VI Korps was changing fast, putting on muscle! Columns of field-grey tramped past a full Panzer Regiment's transport, parked hub to hub under the old ramparts. Workshops glittered with oxy-acetylene sparks where mechanics winterised the Tiger III's. Double lines of field cannon crouched under tarpaulins, barrels cranked to maximum elevation. Mounds of stores; cubes of ammunition chests; pyramids of shells. All the precision-tooled might of the world's finest army! Invincible legions of fire! Bunching its fist to crush the barbarians for ever! Kierzner's mouth froze, his shoulders came back, spine erect, the intoxication of the moment driving blades of pleasure through his bowels. God, but it was so good to be a serving part of this all-conquering force!

18

Dorfer didn't share the moment as he drove the staff-car to a halt on a yellow rectangle painted near another, but larger Mercedes flying a General-Leutnant's metal pennant from the bonnet. He jumped out, wrenched open the door nearest Kierzner and crisped a salute as the Oberst moved up the gravelled path to VI Korps Kommandantur.

More dumb sentries braced themselves rigid, shouldering the heavy oak doors apart. Kierzner didn't notice them either as he stepped into the overheated headquarters, shrewdly glancing round at the paintings and old weapons brought in by the present Commander, Army Korps VI. Kierzner approved. He approved of tradition and this was tradition; old tradition going back to the first Pannenburg in the times of the Teutonic Order. He liked tradition; he would have tradition himself one day.

An aide-de-camp, Duty Officer for the day, hurried in from a side room and clicked his heels with just enough punch—but no more than necessary. 'Herr Oberst?' Kierzner turned and casually looked over the ADC while he loosened his gloves. 'Kierzner; SS Security; to see the General-Leutnant von Pannenburg.'

'Immediately, Herr Oberst.' The ADC snapped his fingers at an orderly cruising by, signalling him to come and take Kierzner's things. 'One moment!' The young man faced the SS Oberst again, nervously blinking his one good eye.

'Herr Oberst?'

'You are new here.'

'Yes, Herr Oberst.'

'I'd say.' He frowned, studying the black eye-patch; the palsied neck and face muscles; the Ritterkreuz with swords and oak leaves. 'From the Eastern Front.' A short, hostile silence.

'Yes, Herr Oberst.'

'I see.' Kierzner lost interest, turned and tossed his cap, gloves and coat at the waiting orderly. He glanced back. 'Well? That's all; get along with you!' The ADC spun and clicked away, swallowing his temper before rapping on a door of von Pannenburg's suite. 'Herein!' He stepped through and crashed his heels together. 'What is it, von Prim?'

'An SS Oberstleutnant Kierzner, Excellence!' General-Leutnant the Graf von Pannenburg glanced up from his papers. 'Kierzner?' His voice matched his tunic and face—dark grey. He looked tired. 'Kierzner? The so-called guardian of the Fatherland?'

'Yes, Excellence.'

'What's he want now?'

'It isn't known, Excellence.'

'I see,' a lengthy pause, 'it isn't known. Very well, I suggest we let him cool his feet. Yes, let Kierzner wait!' Von Prim's eye glazed with admiration. 'I'll tell you when we're ready to see the fellow; let him wait.' The ADC carried his head a degree or two higher as he marched away with the good news.

'What's a Kierzner?' Von Pannenburg ignored his new son-in-law and hunched over the porcelain bowl hidden from sight in a desk drawer. He hawked, spat distastefully and tiredly wiped his mouth clean with cotton gauze. 'Herr General—Excellence!' Manstein ran over to the old man. 'I must call the garrison Lazaret immediately!'

'What d'you say?' Von Pannenburg sounded frosty as he looked up at the other man, a Major and only half his age. 'Permit me, Herr General!' He seemed genuinely bothered. 'This cannot be allowed to continue unchecked; Elizabeth and I, we are both concerned to see you like this; it doesn't grow better!' He paused, blinking through gold wire frames. 'Surely you will see that it needs some attention?'

Von Pannenburg slowly balled the gauze and dropped it from sight; surprisingly enough he didn't seem to mind so much now. 'Franzl, you're both very kind to me—but *you* are a very poor judge of health.' He coughed dryly, having some difficulty with the familiar 'du'. 'In any case, Colonel Professor Hahn is already prescribing a new course of treatments for me, though he says they're bound to take a little time before beginning their work.' Von Pannenburg lied with some skill, glancing pointedly at the zinc oxide strapping across one side of Manstein's shaven scalp. 'Anyhow, those desert boils can't be too comfortable, eh?' The tired old man tried hard to sound a little less the General commanding, and a little more the father-in-law. Manstein smiled politely and shut up.

'Tell me, when do you have to fly back to Hochwald?' The General couldn't bring himself to describe the place as Supreme Führer Headquarters; Hochwald was too near his own home in the east. The thought of that jumped-up Lance Corporal polluting the windy heaths and dunes of Prussia made von Pannenburg coldly angry with recent history. He scowled. 'When d'you go?'

'Tomorrow midday at latest—it's the longest break von Bülow can wangle for me while they're getting the despatch bag made up.' Manstein shrugged. 'Of course, I'd like to stay longer, but it seems my leave entitlement is weak just at the moment...'

Von Pannenburg wasn't paying attention; he was lost in thoughts of another age, almost. 'So things are really beginning to

20

happen in Libya; I suppose that in your place I'd be itching to hurry back as well.' He sounded wistful about something.

'You would?'

'Yes, I would. I would.' He toyed with the blue enamelled cross at his throat. 'In war the only place for a front-line officer is the front line! In peacetime, Franzl, advancement comes so very slowly. You will have to seize every chance as it comes. You will have to seize every and any chance, be it in Libya or at the North Pole.' Von Pannenburg coughed abruptly and went quiet. After a moment he glanced across at Manstein. 'Ah well, I suppose I'd better get this Kierzner finished. When you go through to Elizabeth ask her not to delay lunch, I'll be as short as I can.'

Manstein stopped and looked back from the door leading to the General's private apartments. 'I'll be interested to learn more.' He smiled wryly. 'SS?' Von Pannenburg looked sour. 'Yes, Kierzner is SS—an absolute nobody, nothing, null, zero become something only by sucking up to our all-wise leader and his party!' Manstein looked worried as the older man swept on with the recklessness of inherited power; von Pannenburg still had one foot in the thirteenth century, the other in the twentieth; it made him careless at times.

'All that I say is true, and nothing will change it! Without the betrayal of 1918—and all it meant to us—creatures like Kierzner would have remained where they belonged; they would never have been permitted!' Von Pannenburg coughed harshly. 'Without the Treaty of Versailles, so-called, Kierzner would still be cringing behind the counter of some dreary little draper's shop in Middle Germany, bowing and scraping for a couple of Groschen!

'He's a classic example of scum floating to the top—along with all the others of his mark. SS, huh!' Manstein looked worried by the General's lack of caution. 'They undermine the true authority of the Army with corrosive little tales for you-know-who!'

'I know, Excellence,' the younger man murmured discreetly. 'Fortunately we've been spared their company in Libya, so far. I don't think that General Rommel would welcome the addition of Waffen SS Divisions to our Expeditionary Force, even if they were offered.'

'Then count yourselves very lucky!' von Pannenburg snapped peevishly. 'They become SS Colonels and SS Generals without ever hearing a shot fired; their promotions are based purely on Party influence and greed; they're bad people, very bad!' Von Pannenburg hawked and tiredly aimed down at the bowl again. After a difficult moment he went on. 'If there weren't so many of them they'd appear ridiculous; I'd clap the whole lot in one

Penal Battalion and pack it off to Smolensk. But I can't, it wouldn't be allowed.' He began reaching for the buzzer. 'I can't. Do you know that I can't touch a single member of the SS? A General-Leutnant of the Army cannot even discipline a Gemeiner of the SS; they're a state within a state, a law unto themselves.'

'And this Kierzner?'

'Oh *that*! Ask Elizabeth—he gatecrashes the Music Union with that damned cello under one arm, spine curved, a sly smile pinned in place; ask her, she'll be able to tell you far more than I feel inclined to do!' He scowled back at the main door where von Prim now stood waiting for orders. 'Send him in!'

The ADC escorted Kierzner into von Pannenburg's suite, bowed and left without regrets. 'Be seated, if you wish.' The General nodded by way of reply to the SS Oberst's curt salute, sighting a finger at a very hard-backed chair—his unwelcome guests' chair with an inch sawn off the two front legs. 'Thank you; the Herr General is always most gracious.' Kierzner deliberately misread the finger and settled in a seat next the stove; von Pannenburg now had to turn himself to watch this man. 'What trifling service can the Army do for its—uh—colleagues the SS?'

Kierzner looked mildly surprised, giving the older man a warm smile, gently shaking his head. 'The Herr General is possibly mistaken, for once.' His hands spread apologetically. 'Indeed, it pleases me to report that, this time, *we* have been able to perform a trifling service for our—uh—colleagues the Army.'

'Glad to hear it.' Von Pannenburg's eyes stayed alert under their puffy lids; he waited for Kierzner to make the running at this stage. But the SS Oberst was in no hurry to oblige. Instead he leaned forward and fiddled around with the stove's mica doors before warming his fingers with delicate concern. The silence stretched out; the older man's ill nerves gave first. 'Well? Astound me with your news!'

Kierzner smiled with real charm. 'Oh, it's nothing so dramatic as all that—just the English terror raid we mopped up this morning.'

'WHAT TERROR RAID?' The old fool lashed out; his aim wasn't too good either. Kierzner went on smiling. 'You weren't kept informed? But surely you must have been? No? Then it's obvious to me there's been a very grave administrative mistake.' Kierzner wagged his head. 'The Herr General may rest assured the guilty ones will be most severely punished.'

'Thank you.'

'My honour, Herr General.' Neither, of course, believed a word

22

the other said. This rubber went to Kierzner and his SS; someone's head would roll unless that someone took more care, von Pannenburg memoed himself without pity. He glanced up, deliberately taking his time. 'Oberstleutnant, you still haven't told me where this terror raid took place—do so now!'

'Of course, forgive me,' Kierzner apologised. 'Very simply, Herr General, the terrorists tried to enter and sabotage the Mercur installation.' Von Pannenburg looked hard. 'Schwarzwald?'

'Yes.'

'Damage?'

'None.'

'Prisoners?'

'Four were taken.' Kierzner was quite relaxed.

'And how many weren't?'

'Only one.' He eased himself in the chair.

'What a pity!'

'Yes, wasn't it?'

'But you knew of this attempted sabotage, didn't you?' The General heaped his shoulders and crouched across the desk. 'You knew! Before it took place!' He was guessing, but he recognised the authentic SS touch in Kierzner's handiwork. The other man looked genuinely surprised at the General's lack of self-control. 'Of course. A most valued contact gave us exact information, so we acted upon it...'

'That being the case, and since the proper Army authorities were not informed at any stage, I shall consider your personal conduct to be treasonable, Oberstleutnant!' He paused heavily. 'It will not be forgotten.'

'Will the Herr General be kind enough to remember that I am only responsible for SS Security-Intelligence—internal state security, nothing more?'

'Exactly so!'

'Whereas the Commander Army Korps VI has been entrusted with the much greater responsibility of national security which is, and here I must quote, "the neutralisation of armed incursions, invasion and external interference in the affairs of the Danish Protectorate".' Kierzner's smile began to fade by degrees. 'Thus, since he was unable—or unwilling—to prevent the landing of these gangsters, by any definition an armed incursion I think you'll agree, then it automatically became my special responsibility...' Von Pannenburg felt the walls inch forward a little; he counter-attacked. 'Who else has *just* been informed?'

'Berlin.'

'OKW, of course.'

23

'That will no longer be necessary now this affair is SS, General.'
'I REPEAT! WHO ELSE HAS JUST BEEN INFORMED!'
'Reichsführer Himmler.'

'*That* I might have guessed!' The crisp tailoring began to leak from von Pannenburg's uniform; such backstairs intriguing wore him out; he deserved better than this. Neither man spoke while Kierzner pushed the stove doors farther apart, turned and straddled his legs in front of the blaze, balancing himself like a boxer. Von Pannenburg scowled malevolently at the black, pinch-waisted silhouette; he turned away, disgusted. 'That being the case I can see no point in continuing this interview!' Kierzner gently shook his head. 'I am reminded of a request the Herr General can grant.'

'I doubt it very much!' Kierzner abruptly smashed the remark, striding away from the stove, bending across the desk, fists doubled on the waxed mahogany. 'Wrong! I want a full strength company of Sappers, with materials, immediately!' Von Pannenburg sneered; Kierzner didn't notice. 'You're going to detail two Infantry companies for the close defence of this factory until I receive Totenkopf SS reinforcements! You will counter-sign orders bringing all Luftwaffe Flak Regiment batteries under my direct command!'

'Oberstleutnant!' Von Pannenburg's hand whipped towards the buzzer; Kierzner roughly slammed his open palm across the older man's corded wrist, pinning it to the blotter. 'GENERAL!' He leaned hard on the bone and sinew. 'You would do better to remember that the Führer himself ordered the special defence of Schwarzwald sites! The Führer, General!

'It is not unknown in Berlin that the brother of the Herr General's late wife is, even now, trying to arrange the Herr General's appointment to the command of a Panzer Army—it is not unknown to us, either.' He paused for effect. 'But nothing is settled quite yet, is it? It's still not too late for a decision to be reversed, forgotten, lost, eh? What do you think might happen if the secret radiographs of the Herr General's rotten insides were unofficially brought to the attention of OKW?' Kierzner shook his head. 'No Panzer Army; no Marshal's baton; no victory parades; no place in our national story; nothing. At best an indefinite period of sick leave, strictly confined to one of his smaller and less accessible estates; at worst...' The SS Oberst suddenly paced backwards a short step, abruptly clicking his heels. 'So,' the voice was quite neutral, 'make your choice.'

24

CHAPTER THREE

A USED man slept under the tangle of sheets and khaki blankets, mouth sagging, living another night of shallow, ugly dreams. A weak blue nightlight stared down with interest as the hours sifted past. Abruptly his muted telephone began to nag, arrogantly drumming its base on the uneven plywood locker. The sleeping man jackknifed sideways, snatching the overhead light toggle, dragging hard. 'Deane.' He coughed. 'Special Operations.'

'Good morning, sir,' the earpiece squawked apologetically. 'Morgan here.' Deane slumped, tiredly rubbing the sand from his eyes. 'Well?'

'Can you scramble, sir?'

'One moment.' Deane thumbed the green switch on his telephone rest. 'Right, go on.'

'Bad news, sir.' He hesitated a fraction. 'Knightsbridge failed, blew out.'

'Oh, God, no!'

'I'm afraid it's been confirmed, sir.' Deane breathed out quite slowly. 'When did it happen?'

'It seems they had a go at the place yesterday morning, sir.'

'When did they confirm?'

'Three minutes ago—Dansection sent it over.'

'I sense finger trouble!' Deane was getting into his stride again. 'A day's too long to know nothing; what's happening out there?'

'Shall I read their transcript, sir?' Morgan countered, reaching across his littered table to scoop up the yellow form.

'All right.'

'It doesn't say much.' He twisted the paper to get a better light on the type. 'Begins—"Knightsbridge betrayed stop target undamaged stop four taken stop intense enemy countermeasures stop Dansection."' Morgan put it down and leaned back in the shadows, switching the phone to his other ear. 'That's all we have so far, sir. I thought, because it's Knightsbridge, you'd want to hear straight away . . .'

'You were quite right to call me, Harry, quite right.' Deane sounded worn out, even on the telephone. He pulled himself together with a little difficulty and reached for his watch on the locker-top, snapped his thumbnail under the silver dial cover and

25

squinted at the figures. 'It's now just over five—I'm coming across.' The voice in Morgan's ear was getting brisk and incisive again. 'You're to alert the planning sections; shuffle Hoskins and his crystal gazers together, get them working on an immediate autopsy!'

'Yessir!' Deane clamped down the receiver and kicked his legs clear of the blankets. 'Roberts!' His batman was already dressed and waiting outside the door; he stepped in deferentially. 'Good morning, sir.'

'My Number Two's—and have a car ready!'

'Gieves took them in yesterday, sir.' Roberts was final; no Number Two uniform. Deane scowled, remembering that no man can be a hero to his valet. 'Very well, the One's, but hurry up!' Roberts glided away while the Brigadier padded over to the minute shower-stall and wash-stand.

Deane let his pyjamas slip and went on scowling at the face in the mirror—hardly the answer to any maiden's prayer. He stood to attention and let the icy water lash his thin shoulders, driving the blood, turning himself corpse white under the snuff-coloured souvenirs of India's sun. He was beginning another day in an evil mood.

The War Cabinet was going to howl for more victims once they heard about this latest setback! There was no lack of chopping blocks for unlucky Generals either, as the Allied war avalanched into defeat—Greece, Crete, North Africa and the Far East as well. Deane clenched his teeth and jerked round to let the soap rinse off. And now Knightsbridge went into the fire with the rest of their hopes! The Old Man had seen it as another Gallipoli— though on a different scale and with different methods, of course —but Gallipoli in the sense that it was a chance to shove the Huns off balance where they least expected it. Typical of the whole political vipers' nest; damnfool people!

The Brigadier stepped up to the mirror and began rasping the skinny hollows and ridges of his face with a dull blade; skirmishing with the thin, wartime economy lather along the clipped border of moustache. 'DAMN!' His chin oozed lazy red beads. 'Order, counter-order, disorder!'

'Sir?' Deane turned and flung his towel through the back of a chair, narrowly missing Roberts' timid question. 'My uniform ready yet?'

'Quite ready, sir.' The batman deftly fussed around, conjuring up everything as it was needed until Deane had knotted his tie and turned, elbows bent for his tunic to be slipped on. Roberts muffed his fingers in white cotton gloves and carefully fastened its

26

gleaming brass buttons, flicking his brush at imaginary flecks of dust, particularly along the meagre row of campaign ribbons—only saved from total mediocrity by Deane's C.I.E. 'Just one moment longer, sir.' He whipped out a small pair of scissors and snipped away a fuzz of worn threads along one cuff. 'Getting a little beyond it now, sir,' Roberts commented professionally, stepping back to get the Brigadier's Sam Browne. 'I know.' Deane sounded bitter. 'Hurry up, man!'

A khaki drab Humber waited for him, engine running, headlamp slits throwing pale bars of light on the damp gravel. Deane slid in behind the duty driver. 'Kensington!' The staff-car ran him across a silent, blacked-out London to SOE billeted in a tatty mansion overlooking the park.

As it braked alongside the kerb a Commando sentry, loaded Tommy-gun loose and ready stepped out from behind a sandbag blast screen and flared his torch at Deane's face, then his pass. The man snapped back, cutting a salute as the Brigadier marched into his Headquarters. There were two more identity checks before he reached the Planning Area housed in a deep, concrete bunker. Deane curtly acknowledged the clerks and orderlies before stepping into his own office, set in an alcove behind an unpainted beaver-board partition.

'Good morning, sir!'

'I'll take your word for it, Sarn't,' he commented dryly, snagging his cap on a nail driven through the screen. Deane turned and carefully sat down at his work-desk under the chilly, white fluorescent tubes. One of them was fluttering to the end of its useful life. 'Get the bricks and works people to come in and change that damned thing!' Deane scowled up at the dying tube.

'Yessir!' The Sergeant coughed behind his hand. 'I thought you might have missed breakfast, sir. I had the canteen send this down.' He looked at the chipped cups, an enamel teapot and a plate of grey, chewy toast on a cheap Woolworths' tray with most of the flower pattern rubbed off. 'Thank you.' Deane pinched the cartilage between his eyes and rubbed them for a moment. 'Thank you, that was very thoughtful.' He looked up again, slowly massaging his forehead. 'Sarn't?'

'Sir?'

'Be so good as to ask Colonel Morgan to step over right away.'

'Yessir!' He marched away, boot studs painfully loud on the bunker's cement flooring, threading his way between the banks of tracing tables outside. Morgan rapped at the beaver-board a minute later. 'Come in.'

27

The younger man stepped behind the screen and threw up a salute which tried hard to be military. 'Sit down, Harry.' Deane nodded briefly. 'I'm just starting breakfast. Care to join me?'

'No thanks, sir.' He paused. 'Would you mind if I smoked?' Deane nodded again, all the while looking at the jet of dark, stewed tea arching from the pot. 'You're probably well advised,' he grunted sourly, feeding it a level spoon of sugar and tilting in a dash of watered milk. He took a trial sip, then wearily set the cup down and fiddled with a piece of toast instead while Morgan went through the motions of tamping a little tobacco in his briar, probing with an index finger as he patted all the wrong pockets looking for matches.

The man was still indelibly a schoolmaster and would always remain that way, Deane realised, his eye picking its way over the blue parachute wings and ribbons of an MC and Croix de Guerre stitched under them. But schoolmaster or not, Deane reminded himself, this man had been an outstanding operator in the field before being moved up to Lieutenant-Colonel and coming on the staff. An excellent brain, too, with a Double First at Cambridge— whatever that was exactly.

Deane abruptly broke his line of thought, got rid of the horrible toast and sat forward. 'What was Dansection's temper when they had to send over the news?'

'Officially, no comment.' Morgan hesitated. 'Unofficially I'd say they're pretty near to mutiny at the moment, sir.' Deane didn't like the word, and showed it, but Morgan was carrying on in the same objective voice. 'You see, I've had to work with Dansection quite a bit during the last couple of weeks—I've come to know most of the team quite well, I think. But an hour ago they'd have lynched me as soon as look.'

'They've taken it badly?'

'Can you blame them, sir?'

'No, I can't.' Deane looked sour. 'The Danes have had a basinful recently, soldiering right at the end of the queue, only getting the scrapings off others' plates, others with higher priorities.' He paused. 'Small wonder they're undermanned and uncertain of their place in the world while this fiction of a Danish Protectorate keeps going.' He glanced up at Morgan, still impassively sucking the briar's stem. 'God knows I did my level best to get them off this Knightsbridge fiasco; I did my best, my very best! Such an operation never had the shadow of a chance, rushed through regardless of time or opportunity!' Deane pulled himself up short. After a moment he went on with more control. 'Even with really trained operators I didn't see it scoring better than seventy to

28

thirty on; it remained for us to compound such folly by throwing in new men, straight from the school!'

The Brigadier paused to discipline himself again, he must remember who he was and where he was. The deaths of five very young and eager men were already nothing more than a statistic, they had failed. But their target remained, and so did the Cabinet directives ordering its destruction. Deane cleared his throat, slowly joining his hands together, lacing the fingers tight. 'So now we find ourselves faced with the task of forming and despatching another team—any suggestions, Morgan?' The man looked politely incredulous. 'Another team?'

'Correct.'

'But the whole idea's blown wide open to the enemy, sir!'

'While their factory remains intact, Morgan. I've just reminded myself of this fact—I commend it to you as well.' Morgan snatched the pipe from his mouth and crouched forward, nervously excited about something. 'Then let the Air Force get off its arse and do some work for a change! The bloody BBC is for ever braying about the hundreds of tons of explosive the RAF drops every other night.' His voice went up sharply. 'Let 'em try something simple for once!'

Deane was surprisingly patient with Morgan, he felt the same way about things. 'The Cabinet says it can't be done, and you know it.'

'That housing estate nonsense?'

'Glad to hear you've remembered it.' Deane was back in control. 'Over or undershoot the target by a few score yards—and Air House says it's easy enough to do at night—and we'll knock down those civilian houses. Civilians, Morgan, that we're trying to woo over to our side in this war.' He paused. 'Blow off a couple of roofing slates and Goebbels' propaganda artists will have a festival blackwashing us.'

'I suppose you're right, sir.' Morgan looked down and twiddled with the angle of his briar's mouthpiece; he looked up after a moment. 'But I still think the Cabinet will have to risk it.'

'Oh, how come?'

'Well, sir, I had a little chat with Personnel Selection just before you arrived—quite unofficial, of course. I asked them what the manning position was in Dansection, now.'

'And?'

'There won't be a new intake from the School for another three weeks—and they say that's pushing things.' Deane shrugged curtly. 'Then use what they have in stock; fatten 'em out with swaps from other sections if you have to.'

29

'Oh, come off it, sir!' Morgan was careless after a long night of watch-keeping in a badly ventilated bunker. Deane bristled. 'You have your orders!' Both men began to stare down the other one, but Morgan knew to within fine limits just how far he could go with the Brigadier, he pressed along another tack. 'In pity's name, sir. If five men—no matter how badly prepared and briefed—if five men who were at least natives of the city were betrayed so quickly—then what hope is there for anyone else? What hope can we offer another team now that Jerry is wide awake and knows that we care about his bloody factory?'

'Morgan,' Deane was starchy, 'the hope of which you speak belongs to the Chaplains' Department—not mine!' He paused for effect. 'My only concern is for the Cabinet's decisions, and the Cabinet has decided that the Mercur factory must cease production, soon. And so it will. It *will* cease, Morgan, understand?'

'Yes, sir.'

'You understand me perfectly?'

'Yes, sir, I understand you,' pause, 'perfectly.'

'Then go away and plan me another, better version of Knightsbridge. Go away and find me a team of specialists that can walk on water, dematerialise, fly on the wind!' Morgan tiredly got to his feet. 'And Morgan ...'

'Sir?'

'You don't have much time to do it in.'

'No, sir.'

'Apart from all the normal considerations, remember this moon period ends in just ten nights from now, after that date no parachute operations are feasible.'

'I'll remember that.'

'A month's delay, till the next one, is no longer possible either.'

'I'll remember that as well.'

'Just see you do,' Deane commented tersely, dismissing him with a curt nod as he reached across to his red, external telephone. 'Give me Kingsway Seven. Yes, Air Commodore Hallam if he's still on duty.' Deane closed his eyes for a moment and leaned on the receiver, listening to the click and whine of connections being made on the Priority Net. 'Oh, Hallam? Deane of Special Ops here.'

'What the devil d'you want at this hour?' Hallam wasn't feeling so bright, either. 'What's it you want now?'

'You're going to lend me an aircraft.'

'No dice.' Deane blandly ignored the man. 'They tell me you've a squadron of the new PR Mosquito forming at Lakenheath.' Hallam grunted non-committally; Deane went on with the pain-

30

less extraction. 'Reliable gossip in this part of London says they're well into the 400-mph class—though I must say it all sounds a bit exaggerated to me. Anyhow,' he coaxed, 'I'll bet you couldn't get one of those machines over Copenhagen and back by lunch...'

'What's the bet?'

'A fifth of Haig's?' Deane had to wait a moment. Hallam sounded doubtful. 'That's a lot of trouble, even for a bottle of Scotch.' He turned to get a better look at the wall clock before starting lightning arithmetic on the back of a Player's packet— juggling fuel loads, speed and endurance with wind force and a dozen other variables. Deane cut in again. 'I'm sorry to give you such a bum steer, Hallam, but believe me a very great deal depends on it now.' He was no longer fooling. There was a longish pause while the Air Commodore back-checked his figures. 'What time do you start lunch?'

'One-thirty, if I'm in luck.'

'Make it two—just to be on the sure side.'

'You're on; I'm sending over the target co-ordinates straight away.'

'We'll be waiting for them.'

'See that you are, f'Godssake,' Deane grunted, ringing off to start the shake-up of his own specialist departments. The Air Force moved just as quickly once Operations had pin-pointed the exact building on an old high altitude mosaic shot and related it to the last known AA defences.

Cold dawn light flooded the fens, silently drowning night as a factory-new photo-reconnaissance Mosquito lifted into the cloudy murk and set course for an airfield in Yorkshire. There was a break of just over eleven minutes while ground crews scrambled along the knife wings, brimming each overload tank with 100-octane, resetting the camera heaters and lens muffs before jumping clear, waving off the loaded machine.

It was a bum steer, racing low between the green wavecrests, radio silent, the pilot and navigator staring ahead through salt rimed perspex, calculating their first landfall after England. The navigator, prone on his couch in the nose, made it first.

The Mosquito went starboard a fraction, lifted a dozen feet to clear the low sand dunes and dropped over the top, boring ahead at full boost, stunted trees and lonely farms lashing astern either side. Neither man spoke without cause; they were flying on mortgaged time; the Luftwaffe was already scrambling 109's to hack down the intruder; minutes trickled by.

Abruptly they were clipping across more rooftops; curtains of

31

grey rain whisked aside; the navigator searched for landmarks, mind spinning on jewelled bearings, face sweat-sore under his oxygen mask. 'Left at the next cross-roads!' He wasn't being facetious. The Mosquito swerved up a quiet suburban street at rather more than 390-mph.

'Now right!' The machine went hard over, charging along a main railway line, silvery metals ruled straight into Copenhagen.

'Right again!' The pilot dragged them round a cluster of camouflaged gasometers south of the main harbour and began jigging left–right–left, straining the mist to pick out the exact street corner.

'STEADY!' His navigator punched the camera switches as they blasted over a small industrial estate; staggering in a near stall turn; sprinting back to clear the factory's roof by fifteen to twenty feet. Some lonely soul opened up with a light flak cannon, but he was pumping tracer at empty sky.

Deane got his photos by half past one. An Air Ministry courier drove to Kensington Gardens and signed them over to him personally. The Brigadier slowly turned the bulky manila envelope over and over in his hands before breaking the yellow seals. He set out the spirit-dried prints in four rows across his desk and carefully adjusted the Anglepoise lamp, going over each photo with a reading glass. He tiredly scooped them together and reached out for the phone; it was Morgan's turn to be woken up. 'Step down here, Harry.'

A few minutes later, unshaven and still looking frowsty, Morgan came down from the Duty Officer's quarters. 'How are you coming along?' Deane asked, nodding to a seat. 'Still fighting, I think,' Morgan answered, without much dash. 'That's fine,' the Brigadier was studiously non-committal. 'You'll be pleased to hear that the Air Force has just nipped back from Copenhagen with some snapshots of the Mercur place.' Morgan looked up sharply. 'Was that such a good idea, sir?' Deane shrugged. 'I don't think our interest in the place is much of a surprise to anyone now.'

'No, perhaps not, not now.'

'Care to take a look at them?'

'All right, sir.' He sat forward and began sifting the bundle of prints, holding them under the stronger light, focusing the reading lens on each one in turn. Suddenly Morgan's face creased with pain. 'Oh, that's bloody wonderful!'

'Which one have you got there?' Deane craned his neck to spot the print in Morgan's hand. 'Yes, that is rather well done.' Morgan

32

didn't comment. Instead he went back to the print, studying it inch by inch—noting everything, missing nothing.

The Mercur factory—a squarish, ugly building on the intersection of two small streets facing some minor railway sidings—was lying at an odd angle in the photograph, but the banking aircraft had caught two sides of the factory block with absolute sharpness. What Morgan saw made him feel ill.

A squad of troops was drilling up paving slabs and hammering in what seemed to be ten-foot posts while more troops followed close behind, stapling on brace wires. Someone, he could see, was reacting with exceptional speed. By the time they were finished with it the factory would be surrounded by chain-link fencing, triple strands of barbs along the top, lights and, inside, double concertinas of wire. The only way in, or out, was past an already finished guard-hut walled round with sandbags. For all practical purposes Mercur was spy-proof. The Brigadier was still looking across at the print; he was speaking; Morgan tried to pay attention.

'I'm rather puzzled by these little efforts, Harry. Here, here and here.' He stretched out and flicked at them with his fingernail. Morgan glanced at the heaps of logs piled up outside the wire on three visible corners of the building. 'Yes, I've noticed them too.'

'Any idea what they could be?'

'Yes.' Morgan was flat and sad. 'There's someone in there who doesn't think all the wire, and lights, and guns will be really enough; our friend is going to put up pill-boxes too. These little things in the photo are railway sleepers, nine by six chunks of wood. They're going to put a pill-box on each corner for the guards to dive out of trouble. Safe behind that wood they can enfilade with machine-gun fire any attack ever thrown at any side of the place!' Morgan halted. 'I had a similar set-up waiting for me at the Sud Aviation annealing plant, near Toulouse.'

'These pill-box things?'

'Yes.'

'How did you tackle them?'

'With twenty picked men, Bangalore torpedoes and a box of Gammon bombs.'

'What happened?'

'Nothing. To the factory, nothing. Not a thing; not a bloody thing.' He paused. 'We blew up a few feet of the wire before they beat us off. I lost nine men.' His voice sharpened. 'A few railway sleepers—only a few railway sleepers and sandbags—don't sound much, do they? But stand a machine-gunner inside and watch

33

how quickly an attack fades under the cross-fire!' Deane coughed with embarrassment. 'Then, in the light of your experience, how would you plan an attack on a similar place, with only five men?' Morgan didn't trouble to hide his sneer. 'So, once more into the breach, dear friends, with Knightsbridge!' Deane was barely patient. 'Let's forget Knightsbridge, or anything else just for the moment; let's treat this as an abstract problem, shall we?'

'I can't, sir.' Morgan pushed away the prints like a beggar's palm and nervously scratched his bristly chin. 'The next team to go won't even have the marginal advantage the first lot had—not that it was so much use in the event.'

'Save the pessimism till I ask you for it!' Deane started the short climb to anger. 'Within twenty minutes I must go over to Horseguards and—damn you! I'll need something more constructive than just wet eyes to show for the day's work!' He halted, breathing a lot faster than usual. 'You, Morgan, were seconded off operations to be my G-1 Planning, well, plan!'

'Planning a massacre isn't my forte, sir!'

'That's your problem, not mine!' Deane shouted. 'I want the answer to this problem inside twelve hours; a workable answer with a high chance of success! I want it within that time because it's all the grace I shall win once the Cabinet and its cronies get really vindictive!' He paused just long enough for Morgan to get the point. 'And by Jesus Christ they're going to be savage once they learn we've let this operation grow cold!' He began to round off. 'So, now we understand each other quite clearly, let's see that list of men you've found me for the next attempt.'

Morgan hid his tight lips by bending and picking up his brief-case. He dragged it open with shaking hands and tossed out a thin file cover which landed on the desk between them. Deane fingered up the front and scanned a sheet of typewritten names with their service numbers. He glanced back at Morgan. 'Where are the rest?'

'There aren't any.'

'Don't get funny with me, Morgan! I can have you command-ing a tiny patch of heather in the Outer Hebrides if I want to!'

'There aren't any more; no more suitable volunteers, or even conscripts; no-one else.' Morgan shrugged with indifference. 'I've scraped the barrel clean; there won't be any more till the next course is ready at the school. That list you have there contains every single person known who stands even the remotest chance of survival in Denmark—take it or leave it.'

'But, dammit, hardly any of them are Danes!'

'So that's an index of just how undermanned Dansection is.'

34

'How the hell am I supposed to suggest this as a serious basis for operations, tell me that?'

'We use them or we use nobody at all.' Deane began to look beaten and old; he didn't speak for several long seconds; then he looked up again. 'This is absurd! I shall press for an air attack.'

'You think there's a chance of getting them to agree to that, sir?'

'No, I don't,' Deane grunted, gently hissing between his teeth. He browsed around, mentally trying on all the alternatives for size. 'No, there's very little hope that we'll be let off so easily. I'll lay you good odds I come back with my arse in a sling.'

'Do you want us to carry on planning, sir?'

'Yes, and make it good.'

'Very well, sir, I'll make a start by getting out the telegrams to the chaps on this list.'

'Do that.' Deane glanced at the paper again. 'Though it hardly counts as a selection procedure where you have to perm any four from four numbers, is it?'

'No, sir.'

'Who are you considering as a possible to lead them in?'

'Madsen?' Deane nodded. 'Not much doubt about that, I suppose. The only officer in the whole boiling and one half of our operational Danes.' He looked back at Morgan. 'What's he like?'

'I can't say much from personal experience, sir, but he's said to be very good. An engineering graduate—at Göttingen University too; fluent German, of course, as well as his Danish; done his parachute scheme at Ringway; has a very good rating from the School; still unmarried—something which might not be such a bad thing under the circumstances.'

'You make him sound interesting, Morgan.'

'He was also the long-stop for our first team; very nearly went instead of Hendrikssen.' Deane couldn't remember; he was thinking about something else. He looked up after a moment. 'Very well, he sounds like our man. Get him over here straight away and start grooming him for the job.'

'Movements say he's on leave in the West Country just now, sir.'

'Get him!' Morgan saluted and left very quickly.

35

CHAPTER FOUR

HE went down to Personnel Movements soon after breakfast and elbowed a way into their small, overcrowded room. 'How are those people getting on? The ones you called in yesterday?' The clerk on duty was impassive; he ran a finger through the register. After an awkward moment he looked up, deliberately avoiding Morgan's flitting eyes. 'Corporal Meyer—129, and Sapper Shepherd—402, have both signed in at the billet, sir. Warrant-Officer Erikssen's reported to be on his way up from Devon, he should arrive this morning, I've arranged transport from Paddington.'

'What of Captain Madsen?'

'Reading Royal Infirmary rang through about him, sir, last night, after you'd gone off duty.'

'Yes? What is it, man?' Morgan's voice grew more sharp and unfriendly by the second. The clerk swallowed. 'They say he's been killed, sir. His motor-cycle hit a tractor or something. They want to know what to do with his things.'

'Killed?'

'Yessir. They want to know what to do about his Special Services papers.' Morgan didn't hear. He turned stiffly and walked away, sending a chair flying across the floor. The clerk looked up anxiously. 'They want to know soon, sir!' But he was already talking to himself.

Morgan sat alone in his shared office and slowly tore several sheets of paper into very small pieces. Some time later he reached for the phone; Deane answered immediately. 'Can I come in for a few moments, sir?'

'Yes, come over straight away, I was expecting you to call.'

'Thank you, sir.' He crossed the planning room and stepped inside Deane's office. The Brigadier eased back in his chair and nodded. 'Sit down, Harry.' Morgan began without preamble. 'Madsen's dead.'

'Yes, I know.' Morgan frowned at that. 'Oh, I see.' He paused, hoping for Deane to go on. He didn't. 'What does one do now?' Morgan's voice was oddly scratchy and off-key. 'Looks as if the Air Force has this one whether they like it or not, doesn't it?'

36

'Your guessing's poor this morning, Harry.' Deane spoke calmly, ignoring Morgan's mood, repeating a lesson learned by heart. 'The Cabinet Office didn't have much to say to me yesterday. After only a short wait I was informed there can be no question of the RAF bombing the place—yet. Neither will they ask the RN to risk getting a submarine through the Skaggerrak minefields just to land a Commando Assault on Zeeland. Mercur's still ours,' he added bitterly, twisting at the waist and holding Morgan full face, 'so draw your own conclusions!' There was a long and uncomfortable silence. 'Knightsbridge goes on?'

'Yes.'

'Without Madsen as the master mind?'

'We still have three left.'

'We had at the last count—but God alone knows what might have happened in the last hour!' Morgan was getting careless. Compared with this stunt, the miracle of the loaves and fishes was routine sleight of hand. He glanced back at the Brigadier, still sitting impassive and oriental as ever across that desk of his. 'Then I suppose I must pick Madsen's replacement from the three left?'

'No, *we* shall pick him, Morgan.' The man began to frown again, then had the sense to kill it. 'I'm taking over from here till it's finished.' Deane stopped short and leaned forward, eyes bleak. 'You're tired; I think the first attempt took a lot from you; nothing personal, you understand.'

'Perfectly!'

'You'll get a chance later. You'll get another chance later on.' Deane paused. 'The PM wants results, and he wants them quickly. He demanded them nearly a couple of weeks ago and, frankly, my old age pension won't survive any more shocks like this.' He looked back at the younger man. 'Have you seen the Intelligence Digest yet?'

'No.'

'They've got out the corrected bombing statistics for September/October; they're awful.' He tapped a pad of duplicated pages stapled between blue cards, top classified material with a very short circulation list in front. 'Bomber Command has crossed the fourteen percent chop-line at last, and the graph isn't showing any sign of flattening, either.' He sounded tired as he went on. 'Air House is screaming and pulling wires to be let off the Ruhr targets; they'll probably get their way soon.' There was no need to dramatise, the percentage tally of missing aircraft did it much better than he could manage; both men knew this was the point in time when defeat in the air, and on the ground, became dead

37

certainties. Morgan jerked round to the only alternative to an impossible sabotage raid. 'Then they must let the factory be bombed!'

'Oh, they may well order it yet.' Deane was dry. 'But I very much doubt if either of us will be sitting down here to appreciate the fact.'

'I see, they're getting like that now.'

'Yes.' The Brigadier waited long enough for it to become an awkward silence, then leaned into the light. 'But no self-pity, not yet. Instead, let's get on with the thankless task of putting Humpty-Dumpty together again, shall we?' He flicked the inter-department speaker. 'Records? Send down the dossiers on those Dansection volunteers telegrammed yesterday. No, not Madsen's.'

Records brought down three slim files and Deane set about putting them in line, glancing critically at the ID shots pasted inside each cover. He looked up at Morgan for a moment. 'Let's begin with the logical choice for a team leader—Erikssen.'

'Seems the best bet, sir,' Deane began squinting at the first dossier, holding its forms at near arm's-length before, a little furtively, taking out a pair of regulation, metal-framed glasses from his tunic pocket. He tried again, summarising the facts as he read aloud.

'"Erikssen, Lars Christian. Born 17th May 1903 at Gentofte, Copenhagen, Denmark; emigrated to Canada late 1920 and worked at various farm jobs in Manitoba and Ontario till 1925. Enlisted in Princess Patricia's Royal Canadian Highlanders, Toronto depot, 21st October 1925."' Deane stopped and looked up from the papers. 'Does that suggest anything to you, Morgan?'

'Trafalgar Day?'

'No, try again.' Morgan knew the tone; he became serious. After a moment's hard thinking he looked up again. 'The Depression?'

'Yes, Canada got it very badly. The way I read him this man was recruited by hunger—nothing more, nothing less. It could be significant.' He turned back to the forms. '"Corporal, 1930; Sergeant, 1934; Sergeant-Major, 1937; awarded BEM, Coronation Honours List; Warrant-Officer (1), 1939; volunteered for special duties when his regiment landed in the UK. After parachute course transferred with substantive rank to Danish section of the Royal Kents and"—here we are—"turned down for commissioning earlier this year."' Deane skipped through the usual facts of Erikssen's Conduct and Bearing—both excellent. He looked up. 'Now, what sort of fellow does that suggest to you, Morgan?' The

38

younger man thought hard for a longish time before finding an answer. 'The eternal NCO?'

'Anything else?' Morgan tried to read Deane's mind again before giving up the riddle. 'No, sir, except that he seems to be a fairly typical thick Regular.' Deane bridled at that but kept his tongue between his teeth. 'You're right, up to a point, Morgan, but you miss the essential fact.'

'Which is?'

'He's coming to the end of his Service. In four years he'll be eligible for half-pay; you can be sure he'll want to be around to enjoy it.' Morgan thought about that one for a moment before replying. 'Even so, sir, he *has* volunteered for Special Duties.'

'One moment—I don't doubt his motives, or their purity. Erikssen probably still has a family of sorts back in Denmark and, well, after so many years a Canadian he may have grown even more Danish than if he'd stayed at home, odd though it sounds.' He paused reflectively. 'You know, Morgan, I've often found that the most English of the English haven't set eyes on the place in thirty years. Like many things it improves as the square of its distance and age. Anyhow,' he went on a shade more acidly, 'the extra florin a day parachute money must be useful. And, for the "typically thick Regular"—as you so delicately put it—the chance of an MC to put under those wings would be quite a powerful inducement, eh?' Morgan didn't like that. 'You make it all sound rather sordid and commercial, sir!'

'No, I just know what makes God's children tick inside.'

'But he *did* volunteer, that you can't ignore! Nobody forced him to join Special Ops!'

'Erikssen doesn't know what he's letting himself in for.' He paused, brooding about something hidden from sight in his own mind. 'Neither do the others. Besides,' he went on with sudden decision, 'he's too old for the job.'

'You'd let that weigh against him for the leadership?'

'Dammit, Morgan, this isn't a question of weighing for, or weighing against anyone!' Deane brought himself under sharp control. 'No, I'm simply trying to visualise any one of these men *leading* an attack—by cunning or brute force—through that wire and into Mercur. I'm trying hard to visualise any one of these men lying out there in the darkness; the damp soaking up, chilling his belly; the enemy alert and watchful; the "Go" decision his alone to make.' He paused again, becoming even more sombre.

'At that point, when it comes as come it must, the actual energy and force that will get them off their faces and moving forwards

39

can only spark from one man, the leader. This work of ours isn't a shop stewards' committee, or soldiers' soviet, and you know it. In the minutes of waiting alone with your fear, the urge to foul your breeches or wriggle away unseen is very strong, very strong indeed—and only a leader, a heart and soul leader can check that.' He went on slowly, hoping to make plain something he sensed by instinct rather than knew by rote.

'There's a lot more to being an officer than just wearing pips and watching other ranks duck in shop fronts, though it may seem that way most of the time.' He groped for the right phrase to use. 'At a moment like the one we have in mind he must soar above himself, and his worries, actually *giving* strength to everyone else around him. D'you understand me?' He paused, almost shyly.

'There's far more to this business of ours. It's not a simple matter of waving a sword, or blowing a whistle, or shouting the advance—that's for cinema audiences, and you should know it by now. No, this is something which has to surge up from deep inside, and God alone knows it's hard enough to find when no-one's watching to see it's done. When no-one is sitting on our man's shoulders, giving him the push in turn.' Deane's head cocked to one side as he looked at Morgan's thoughtful frown. 'You *do* see what I'm driving at?'

'Yes, I think so, sir, though I've never had it put to me quite this way before.'

'I don't suppose you have. Anyhow, bearing that in mind, can you see Erikssen—no matter if you promote him Field-Marshal— generating the necessary boost when the moment comes? Frankly, I can't. I can't, no matter how respectful and keen they appear to be at first. Comes the big push and he'll go cautious, he'll always have a good reason for not going, it's the way of older men.' He coughed harshly, probably seeing himself in the same light. 'And a cautious man, Morgan, isn't going to find the way into that factory—now or ever.'

'You've made it seem that Erikssen's just about useless, sir.' Morgan was openly critical of the whole argument. Deane leaned back and scratched his knee under the desk. 'You're not thinking too well today, I can see that, Morgan. Erikssen will go wherever he's told to go. He'll keep fighting till he drops dead. He'll also keep his head no matter what panic and confusion is brewing round it. After all is said and done, Erikssen has the better part of sixteen years of Service, in a good regiment, and he's won Warrant-Officer's rank which is no mean achievement, I can tell you! But he won't lead, Morgan, he won't lead as I want him to

40

lead, I'm very sure of that.' Neither spoke while Deane pushed away Erikssen's file and picked up the next in line.

'Let's try Corporal Meyer for size, shall we?' He scanned the record sheet for a moment. 'At least he doesn't lack a certain variety—no matter what else may, or may not be there.

' "Meyer, Solomon. Alien's Registration Order G.136/1939. Born, Heilbronn in Würtemburg, 12th February 1910. Educated, Leipzig Realgymnasium before winning an open scholarship to the Berlin Conservatoire, studying keyboard and composition." ' Deane glanced up. 'That's piano playing, isn't it?' Morgan nodded intently. Satisfied, Deane went on reading the sheet aloud.

' "Doctorate from the University of Basel for a thesis entitled J. S. Bach: Die Praxis und Theorie von sein Klavierwerke; Schumann Memorial Prize for 1935; fled from Germany, 1935 (attached appendix refers). Night-club work in Alexandria and, later, Buenos Aires as request pianist doubling as an illusionist's assistant." ' Deane softly shook his head. 'God, but don't we get them? An illusionist's assistant no less.' He glanced up. 'What's that exactly? Sawing the lady in half?'

'More probably sawing the pianist—chained inside his own piano, of course.' Morgan was dead-pan. Deane nodded thoughtfully, trying hard to imagine such a freakish act on stage. 'You could be right, but let's press on.' He went back to the record sheet.

' "Enlisted in XIth International Brigade, third battalion (the Dabrowsky), 1937, serving on the Ebro and Madrid fronts, rising to the command of a Tercio, two body wounds (see appendix II)." ' Deane nodded to himself and quickly turned up the second appendix. He glanced back at Morgan's consciously impassive face. 'In plain language that means he was a sort of major to some mixed artillery and machine-gun companies.'

'Sounds promising.' Morgan was non-committal. Deane coughed and went on reading. ' "Landed in United Kingdom with the defeat of Spanish Republican forces and found employment with a firm of wholesale fruit importers in Covent Garden. Faced with the alternative of internment as an enemy alien at the beginning of war, volunteered for service with the Special Identity Unit of the Pioneer Corps—transferring to Royal Signals for radio training, and earlier this year, the school and Ringway for his parachute course. Foreign languages, Spanish and English." ' Deane sniffed. 'Meyer would also seem to be a natural comedian, something we could use right at the moment.' He glanced up. 'What d'you make of that one?'

41

'He appears to have at least one of the basic requirements, sir.'

'That bit about his majority?'

'Yes.'

'I'll need a lot more evidence than just this sheet of paper, Morgan.' He put the file down with the others. 'Beaten armies have an old habit of suddenly spawning field-officers by the million, after the event, like so many Southern Colonels. Makes you wonder, at times, who did the actual shooting.'

'Well, sir, discounting that for the moment, I doubt if he can bear much love for the Germans now.' He paused. 'It could be a pretty powerful force to use if we have to get aggressive with Mercur...'

'You really think so?'

'You *don't*, sir?' Deane ignored the question. 'Meyer the fruiterer; Meyer the Major; Meyer the magician; Meyer the musician, what's the difference? The essential difference?' He looked at Morgan a moment, challenging him to step over and get it. 'None, they remain the same man under everything else. Oh, I don't doubt you're right, he probably doesn't have *any* love for some of them, but does a right hand war against its left?' Deane shook his head. 'No, Meyer is a German, only this time we're all on the same side for once.'

'And yet he has volunteered, sir. He has volunteered, and I shouldn't think it's to get a free ride back home.' Deane considered this carefully. 'True, so what's he want out of it? What's he hoping to find?'

'Two bob a day extra?' Morgan sneered casually.

'Could be, could be.' Deane was light years away at the moment. Morgan went on a little more persuasively. 'Honestly, sir, I think you underestimate the phenomenal power of hatred. I'd bet anything you like the first appendix, the one you have there, could reveal a lot about Meyer's...' He watched Deane slowly turn over the papers in the file.

'A very shrewd diagnosis, Morgan, I'd say you've already taken a peep.' Deane shuffled the papers in order before reading out the appendix for his own benefit.

'"Subject arrested by Magdeburg civic police for distributing left-wing propaganda at the Siemens factory. Handed over to the Gestapo. Sentenced, after interrogation, to fifty years' penal servitude in the Gleiwitz lime quarries. Escaped over Czech border,"' Deane hesitated unconsciously, '"after strangling some guards. Detained in Cyprus as an illegal immigrant *en route* for Palestine."' Deane looked back at Morgan. 'Would seem to be some-

42

thing of a card, our Mister Meyer. I wonder how many guards make "some"?'

'Well, sir, isn't this just the sort of material we can cast and use in this raid?' Morgan was fighting hard for choice number two. 'Meyer strikes me as being resourceful; tough; a whole universe above average if we consider intellect—they didn't award him the Schumann medal for playing Chopsticks. He's seen action too, and as a commander, no matter the side or the motives; he's a hard man with a proven record of survival under conditions that flatten ordinary people. Frankly, sir, I think Meyer's got what it takes.'

'You do, Morgan?' Deane fidgeted a moment. 'I'm still chary about his essential qualities as the leader. The *leader*, Morgan, of this assault.'

'I really can't see why, sir.'

'You can't; I can.' Deane eased himself in the chair and began searching round his desk drawer for a quarter of wine gums. He looked up again. 'Care for one?'

'No thanks, sir, though I'll use my pipe if I may.' Morgan took the chance to load his briar. Deane selected a gum, Claret, and popped it in his mouth. 'You're keen on Meyer, aren't you? Met him before?'

'No, sir.' Morgan carefully blew out the match and made a large smoke-ring in the still air between them. 'No, sir, I've not met him yet, but I like the sound of him, he's good.' Morgan took time off to hang another grey, misty doughnut in the air. 'My number two man, in France, was from the same stable, and he was superb. Got us all away after the Toulouse fiasco—I'd stopped one and couldn't do much except look after myself.' Morgan puffed smoke and went quiet for a moment. He looked up and carried on in a slightly altered voice. 'Marc, my number two, did everyone's job during the week they hunted us up and across the Pyrenees; that's why I like the sound of Meyer, he's tough. He's Jewish tough, and that's really tough—one has to be to survive four thousand years of history, I suppose. And he's varied enough in background to have ideas, good ideas, when things start going wrong over there, as they probably will.'

'A valid point, Harry.' Deane was still being objective, still reserving judgement on Meyer.

'Seriously, sir, I definitely think he's got what it takes—to ram home an attack, that is. And another bonus point, the school tells me he's one of the finest radio operators they've had. So much so, they want him back in one piece, after some field experience, to teach the newcomers. It must be something to do with his music, I suppose.'

'That's valid, too.' Deane was still unaccountably cool to the subject. 'One thing's nagging me, Morgan, how come he's been smuggled into Dansection? With all these talents I'd have placed him almost anywhere else.'

'True enough, sir, but I believe he can be palmed off as a German—in Denmark—one of the Todt Organisation types.' Morgan shrugged. 'After all, he's been at the production end of the slave labour force, hasn't he?'

'You think he could keep it up?'

'Long enough for this, yes.'

'I'm still not sold on him, not for the leadership, Harry.' Deane sounded a little saddened by the decision.

'Why on earth not?'

'Because I see Comrade Meyer in a different kind of light. No less flattering than yours, but quite different.'

'I don't see how, sir.'

'I do.' Deane looked tired. 'The way I read his papers, Meyer hates—as you said in the beginning—but nothing in particular now, just raw hatred. He's stuffed up to the ears with hatred, I'll lay you a fiver on that.' He paused, expecting Morgan to weigh-in with arguments, but he didn't. Deane went on.

'Imaginative—undoubtedly; brilliant—in his line; politically dedicated—sometimes we can warp this force to our own ends; almost certainly a fanatic in any cause he decides to support— but *he* makes the decision. The Meyer I see is probably very bitter towards the people who've turned him into a fruit importer, and Egyptian magician's hack. His bright, sunny morning at the Conservatoire has become, as it does for so many of us, a wintry afternoon fading into early, premature dusk.' Morgan looked politely surprised, he'd never heard his chief open up before, he grabbed the chance to learn more. 'What do *you* think this means, sir?'

'It means that we, or I, can't depend on Meyer just when we have to. Just when it's most important to keep calm and in control of a lunatic situation like this, he'll crack.'

'Go off his head, you mean?'

'Not exactly that.' Deane paused, going back to his sweet packet for another Claret. 'No, he won't start foaming at the mouth, or biting the air, or anything so obviously odd as that. But that famous hatred of his will blind him to any alternatives once he's made a final decision about, say, the attack route. It'll set like plaster of Paris, stone hard till you shatter it. He won't be

44

able to maintain an open mind right up to the moment of impact, evaluating the situation, controlling it as everything goes to bits in his hands. He won't manipulate events; they'll manipulate him. He'll claw at the first chance offered, toot the advance and off we'll go to another monumental balls up.' He paused. 'You *do* follow my reasoning, don't you?'

Morgan shook his head slightly and scratched another match over his briar, sucking flame into the bowl. Deane looked fretful, but went on outlining the obvious. 'I see our friend Meyer as a person no longer at home in any land, or place. He no longer fits with Germany, or the Argentine, or Spain, or really, with us. So he must be looking for something else—question is, what?' He paused, moodily playing with the problem. 'A chance to escape this world too? Just possibly he's looking for a grand chance to escape everything, to make the dramatic exit, and maybe he hopes to find it via our gang of desperadoes?'

'I wouldn't know the answer to that one, sir,' Morgan commented impartially. 'I do know this war is bringing some very peculiar sorts to light, but whether or not our Meyer is the fellow you think, that's something altogether different.' He weighed the problem for a second. 'No, I'm disinclined to agree on that point, sir.'

'That's uncommonly decent of you!' Deane bit hard.

'Don't misunderstand me, sir, but the possibility of suicidal tendencies does seem a bit unlikely! Anyhow,' he went on, a fresh idea sprouting in the past couple of seconds, 'is that such a bad thing? I mean, if he wants to earn some kind of salvation— fighting his own people—what's to prevent us using that drive? Isn't he just the man who *will* get off the ground and over the wire, regardless?'

'You've taken a damned long time coming round to my point of view, Morgan, that's just what I fear the most. He frightens me almost as much as the no-goer; both men will leave the target untouched. Only, one will walk away to tell the glad tidings; the other, Meyer in this case, will be found draped across the barbs, thankfully quit of the world's cares! I've met them before, though it's usually trouble with the wife, or bad debts, or girl problems that drive them to it in the end.' Deane paused to take off his reading glasses, rubbing them clean with his tie. 'Frankly, Harry, this collection you've brought together *is* rather scabby, isn't it?'

'I'm sorry you feel that way, sir!' Morgan was getting huffy. Deane completely ignored him, paying far more attention to slipping his glasses back in place. He glanced at Morgan through

45

them. 'There's no use in taking umbrage, it won't get us anywhere. Now, let's try selection number three—Shepherd.'

'I was beginning to wonder if you'd forgotten him, sir.'

'No.' The Brigadier picked up the third file and flipped it open. He began to read in flat, scissored tones. ' "Shepherd, Francis Xavier. Birth registered 23rd November 1899." ' He glanced up sharply at that fact. 'This man's damn near as old as I am!' Deane thought for a moment, then went back to the paper. ' "Apprenticed at BSA Ordnance works; A.I.Mech.E., Coventry Technical School, 1922. Left BSA's 1924, working around in South Africa and Australia before returning to Europe in 1932. Employed in Norway on road-building projects and, later, in Finland on hydro-electrical schemes. Volunteer service with Finnish Army during Winter War, rising to First-Sergeant of Engineers and gaining Mannerheim Cross"—whatever that means exactly. "Returned to UK late 1940. Volunteered for Special Duties from Royal Engineers. Parachute training and school"—in order. "Languages—Norwegian, Finnish, some Russian..." ' Deane took off the glasses again and began tiredly rubbing his eyes. 'Well, Morgan,' he asked without looking up, 'what do you make of that one?'

'Pretty self-evident I'd say, sir.'

'Right.' Morgan caught the tone and read it accurately. 'Actually, sir, I chose him because of the Norwegian bit. They tell me it's pretty much the same as Danish, it'll do at a pinch, and he is a demolitions man—quite good at it, they say.'

'Dammit all, I'm looking for a leader not a ruddy mechanic!' Deane was getting shorter in temper the more he put off the decision. But Morgan was being dense today, and cautious. He could see no feasible way of getting a man to take that job within the next few hours if none of these men suited Deane. He shrugged politely.

'What of his age, Morgan?'

'Well, I suppose that if you let it tell against Erikssen, then it must mark down Shepherd.'

'Correct.' Deane closed the file with a thump. 'I'm willing to agree that these are the best we now have to offer—God save us all—and that every man is a skilled technician with just about enough background colouring to pass muster in Denmark, at least for a few days. But does any one of them have that extra? That extra quality I was at great pains to mention earlier on?' He didn't wait for Morgan's answer, if he had one. 'I think it highly unlikely.'

The problem seemed to be Morgan's once again. He took time

46

off to think by reaming out his pipe with a penknife, slowly knocking the dottle into Deane's ashtray. He looked up. 'So now we have the original team of democratic saboteurs, sir, three equals voting their way into the factory.' He didn't trouble to hide his opinion of this, or of its chances.

Deane kept surprisingly silent by making a big job of putting the glasses back in his breast-pocket, coldly arriving at a very painful solution to his problems with this operation. It was, at best, only an answer of sorts, a second-rate thing to do. He coughed. 'Not quite, Harry.' He stopped short, reweighing his words with great care, as he had done all morning. 'Not quite, there remains one last alternative for me to take. One last alternative to admitting that Knightsbridge can't be done, and sending in my papers.'

'I can't see it, sir.'

'You wouldn't, Harry.' Deane almost smiled. 'You're sitting in the wrong chair; I'm sending you instead of Madsen.'

'Me?'

'You.'

'I see.' Morgan tried to look cool. 'I thought I belonged to the French section, not the Danish?'

'You did.'

'Of course, sir, I'm quite willing to go along.' He was starting to box cleverly. Yet there were grave, serious reservations in each word—he hoped they'd be noticed and judged for what they were. 'That's very nice to know.' Deane was feeling brutal. 'However, nobody asked if you weren't!' Morgan held his breath tight, noting at great distance, the tripping pulse in his throat; the fog of hot suffocation; the loosening of his lower bowel. He breathed out as quietly as he knew how. 'Why me? Why pick on me?'

'Because you're now the best man I have left for this type of raid, that's why!' This sounded uncomfortably like an Irishman's raise in the making; Deane bored in. 'That, and the fact you already have two successful raids behind you—not unlike this one in many ways. Moreover, you won't need briefing on the target—this should save me a good couple of days that would otherwise be spent getting someone else ready.' Morgan hadn't really heard the end of this last sentence; he wiped his face. 'I've made three descents in all. That is, attempted three targets...'

'I know.' Deane wasn't encouraging.

'My third was not a success.'

'I've been told that, too.' Morgan went on patiently explaining himself aloud. 'My last raid, on a softer factory target than this

47

Mercur promises to be, my last raid was not a success.' He paused. 'I failed.'

'D'you see me weeping, Morgan?' The Brigadier had crouched into the light. 'Don't waste my time reminding me of facts I already know damned well! I don't doubt for one moment that you're very unhappy about what happened!' Deane's mouth snapped shut.

'You've quite misunderstood me, sir!'

Deane hadn't. Morgan was frightened; Morgan was finished. He'd fought well and worked miracles in the earliest days of Special Operations, no one could ever take that away from him, but he'd fallen heavily and been taken off. Only a harsh and inflexible hand would get this man moving again and, once he was moving—Deane shrugged his shoulders—it was anyone's guess whether or not the operation's momentum would keep him running till it ended. There was an outside chance it might; he looked back at Morgan, chopping the next, still unspoken question. 'I don't want to hear it, you're going to pay attention to me, understand?

'What you have *not* done is of marginal interest to me, Morgan. I can only see the fact that you have managed two copybook raids of this kind—and at a time when we had little more than penknives to issue. This man, I've reminded myself, has guile and resource of the highest calibre. If anyone is going to destroy Mercur; if anyone I now have is to lead the team, then it will be this man!' Deane edged back in his seat, all tensed-up by the torment of this shock therapy. Morgan gradually came round as he'd hoped; he cocked his head on one side and made a wry smile. 'I *did* say that I'd go, and I meant it.' He paused a fraction. 'You don't have to butter me, I know the score.'

'Never said you didn't.' Deane was still discouraging. But Morgan had something else to add, his secret defence against this horrible order. He began to smile a little as he got it ready to fire. 'You've overlooked one thing, sir.'

'What's that?'

'I've been on the staff, here at Special Ops, for close on six months.'

'So?'

'It would be very inconvenient if I were taken by the enemy.' He stopped dead, fully realising what he was doing; he went on with his eyes open. 'I'm not proof against drugs like hyoscine, or Pentothal, or scopolamine, I should talk. I know too much about our organisation and planning—apart from the fact that the Paris Gestapo have quite a dossier on me ...'

48

'Very nicely put, Harry.' Deane had been expecting this one to come sooner or later. 'You've really learned a lot from us, haven't you?'

'That's just what I'm trying to say, sir.' Morgan was growing hopeful. 'I've learned too much to go back.'

'I wasn't referring to that, it doesn't bother me much one way or the other. No,' he paused calmly, 'what I admire is the neat line in blackmail you're polishing up.'

'You misunderstand me, sir!'

'Oh no, I don't, Harry, I've been here a long time. I've had a good chance to notice, and remark upon the strange things Special Ops can do to otherwise "decent" people. People who've always "played the game", as you have, very soon learn the true facts of life with us. You quickly learn to cheat and lie, blackmail and doublecross in this kind of war, don't you? There's no room for a hyper-developed sense of honour. There's no standing around waiting for the other fellow to get up again so that you may fight all fair and square, toe-to-toe!

'And you've learned your lesson well, Harry. With us you've learned the gouging thumb, the cod-crusher, the cheese-wire garrotte done from behind. You learned them well because, if you didn't, you knew you'd end your days pinioned to a wooden stake, a flourbag pulled over your head.' He paused for several seconds. 'And now I can see you've also learned how to twist the arm of a senior officer—in the nicest way possible, of course.' Deane smiled. 'I'm proud of you, Harry.'

Morgan was badly rattled; he lashed out. 'It must seem so easy in your place!' He stared pointedly at the meagre row of ribbons on the other man's chest. 'It must be simple to pack off others to do your work!' He bitterly regretted what he'd said even as it came out.

'You're quite right, of course.' Deane nodded sadly. 'It must seem very easy to be me—and perhaps it is.' The Brigadier went quiet and thought it over. 'It must seem easy, especially when one is a dusty relic with red tabs, eh? With no practical experience of this war; no decorations that count for much; just another Blimp who signs your requisition orders and keeps an eye on the shop while you're away. In a word, one more whisky-soda pukka sahib with a few years to run before they retire him to pig-breeding and running the local TA Association, eh?'

'I'm sorry, sir, that's not what I meant.' Morgan was heart-felt, he'd struck low and hurt the old man very badly, he tried to explain. 'It wasn't that, sir. It's just that I *know* the pale fear of a sudden knock on the door, or of a car backfiring in the street. I

49

know the times when you can't take off your clothes for a week at a stretch as they hunt you from village to village, wood to wood. I *know* the betrayal of friends, by friends. All this, sir, I *know*!'

'So do I, Harry. Not in this war of yours, of course, I'm too old. And not so much in the first one, either.' He paused, seeing other faces. 'I was gassed too soon after getting my Company. But I knew it in the years between them, the Peace Years, so-called.' Deane paused again, wondering what value, if any, reminiscence might have for Morgan. Maybe a little of it would help steady the man's shakes, give him a little confidence in himself. The Brigadier cleared his throat and frowned down at his wrinkled hands laid on the personnel dossiers.

'For fifteen of those quiet years I was seconded to the Political Department of the ICS—Indian Civil Service. I was extremely lucky to be in work—it was that or taking a bowler hat. The details are unimportant now, but I did learn my trade—*our* trade. I learned it among the peaks of the Hindu-kush; in the hovels of Kabul; along the silk caravan routes of Chinese Turkestan.' He paused softly. 'I *know* as well. I also know that a very high proportion of the few friends this occupation of ours permits us, a very high proportion haven't even got so far as this forgotten desk under London, Harry. Their shins were cracked open long ago and the marrow scoffed out by jackals.' His voice dropped. 'We had our losses on service, too, nearly all in the least pleasant ways. I know what you know, I might even know a little more.' Neither man spoke for some time. Morgan looked, and felt, uncomfortable. He looked up. 'I wasn't trying to cry off, sir.' Deane smiled, almost gently. 'Oh, yes you were, and all credit for trying, but I need you to lead this team. You alone can get them inside Mercur and get them away again.'

'What about, well, Rogers or Pierce?'

'No go. You're our factory specialist—much of what we're trying to teach, you wrote. You're the best man, in the time left, to do this job.'

'And that other thing I mentioned?' Morgan went back to it with slight hope of good news. Deane shook his head. 'It's a risk I've had to calculate these last few hours, and take. You do know a lot about us, I haven't forgotten that for one moment, but I don't think you'll be taken.'

'How can you be so sure of that?' Morgan sounded tiredly amused. 'According to the latest informed rumours, the SS and Gestapo types are getting really hot, and they were mustard the last time we met.'

'You won't be captured, Harry.' Deane looked down as he

50

spoke. 'I'm counting on you knowing exactly what to do if things get too difficult.'

'It's easy enough for me to promise, but I'm not too sure of the outcome, not now.'

'I'm taking out an insurance against cold feet if, against all the odds, things turn bitter.'

'What's that?'

'Your team will have specific instructions to help you first.' Deane shook his head at the cluttered desk-top. 'It's quite bad when we have to say these things, but I hope you're realist enough to accept life as it is, not as we'd like it to be.' He looked up at Morgan again. 'You *are* going to lead Knightsbridge; you *will* get them into Mercur and *you* will get them away, across the Sound and into Sweden, all together and in one piece. He paused. 'But if things should curdle . . .'

'My men will shoot me first.'

'Correct.' Morgan felt quite detached from this place and this man; it was some other person they were talking about. He unrolled his tobacco pouch and pulled out a few shreds, tamping them into the briar. He lit up without haste and looked back at Deane. 'I wonder if anyone else, apart from me, has ever had such an offer made?'

'I shouldn't waste too much time speculating about that; we all have it put to us sooner or later.' The Brigadier coughed uncomfortably. 'It's a variant on the Conservation of Effectives theory, only this time the chief must die to save the tribe. It's been written in the rule book somewhere; you're not the first to get it, or the last. Now,' he leaned forward, bringing his hand down flat on the buzzer, 'let's have a cup of hot tea before we agree to get on with the war.'

The Orderly Sergeant stamped in and saluted, his right arm quivering with the intense effort. Deane looked past Morgan. 'Ah, Sarn't, what about bringing us a pot of that extra special tea you brew from time to time?'

'Yessir.' He halted awkwardly. 'There is no fresh milk, sir. It will have to be tinned.' Deane smiled. 'That's just exactly the sort we want, Sarn't.'

'Yessir.' He paced backwards, saluted again and skated away on his studded boots. Morgan twisted at the waist and irritably watched them go. 'I wish to heaven he'd take to wearing ordinary shoes around the place!' He sounded pettish and bad-tempered.

'Most probably feel very uncomfortable in a pair, there's less ankle support,' Deane commented mildly, putting away some papers. He glanced up after a moment. 'The Sergeant's a twenty-

51

two-year man, most of them spent in the Far East.' Morgan privately wondered what the hell this had to do with the question of wearing shoes or boots on a concrete floor. Deane read the worry. He coughed gently and stretched his legs, making himself easy for the moment. 'It makes a great difference, you know.'

'It does?' Morgan, predictably, rose to his lure.

'Oh yes, there's a world of difference between service in the UK and service in Burma, or India, especially the India which the Sergeant and I remember.' Deane paused again, selecting the way ahead with great care. Few things irritated him more than garrulous nonsense about the Good Old Days—they so very rarely were. But patching up Morgan and getting him reasonably sorted out called for a diversion, to get the man's thoughts off the operations and out of this bunker with its filtered air and aquarium lighting. He smiled wryly and looked back at Morgan. 'Everything out there is on a different scale, you know. And it's not only the fact that a man's salary goes about twice the distance in rupees, something which allows him to develop a keen taste for things he'd never find in Camberley.' He smiled quietly at some private memory.

'For the sportsman, well, India has everything the heart can wish for—Bengal tiger, wild pig, the finest gamefish—and if any of these pall, one can always go ruin-spotting, or mountaineering, or what have you.' He stopped short and waited, Morgan was growing interested, getting ready to use a question. 'What did *you* do, sir?'

'Me?' Deane looked a mite put out by this. He coughed again. 'For most of the time I was in uniform service I was a damned hard-up Subaltern, paying to educate my sister's children and carrying round a dose of Flanders gas all the while I was doing so.' He went on after a moment's embarrassment. 'There was precious little time for frolics in those days, especially as I'd set my eyes on the Staff College at Quetta—something which you Officers and Temporary Gentlemen don't have to consider.' He paused, maybe the hint of malicious jealousy in his voice, Morgan wasn't sure.

'No, that's not the answer you wanted to hear, was it? Well, to be frank with you, I did try to make time for one mild vice—ornithology—bird-watching, that is.' He shrugged ruefully at the memory. 'At bottom, I suppose, I always secretly fancied I might stumble across something new in the Central Provinces where nature is still pretty raw. And there was the idea of leaving a name to posterity; seeing my engravings published in a quarterly journal; it all tickled my vanity, I suppose.'

'Doesn't it any longer?'

'What odds now? Who will give a ha'penny toss one way or the other inside fifty years? In any case, I had my own moment of glory when I recorded no less than eighteen Spotted Eagles—of the genus *Aquila Pomarina*—eighteen at the same time, and from the same place.'

'That's good, sir?'

'Quite exceptional!' For a short moment he relived the old exultation. 'I was exercising a troop of Mountain Artillery in the hills round Darjeeling; it was dawn. As I remember we'd made a very early start from bivouac; the sun was only just beginning to clear the peaks of the Himalayas, staining their high, permanent snowfields with impossible shades of crimson and gold while the world slept below us. I felt really well in every sense, for once. The thin air was gin clear, icy and pure in taste, easy to breathe. For a short time I knew no limitations; I felt Olympian!' He stopped short.

'Anyhow, to get on with the story, we were pushing along an extremely narrow track to the crest of a steep ridge when, quite without warning, I saw the first of those superb eagles soar up in the air-currents, slowly wheeling towards the sky, pinion feathers absolutely motionless.' He paused, spreading his fingers, lifting one hand above the desk. He shrugged tiredly. 'I could have stopped and watched them for the rest of the day.'

'Did you?'

'At that time in history, Morgan?' Deane sneered viciously. 'At that time—not that you'd remember it, of course—better officers than I shall ever be were casually axed by the politicians; furtive little men with furtive little minds, looking and scheming for ways to run an army on the cheap! Speak out of turn but once and I'd have been given all the time in creation to go bird-watching!' He glanced up sharply at a point behind Morgan. 'Ah, thank you, Sarn't, bring it over here please.'

Morgan quite enjoyed the over-sugared, pale brown tea, even though it did look and taste more like a health food than a drink. Deane quietly glanced at the clock—just coming up to ten—he'd given this man a long break from the war. It was the best he could do.

He drained his cup, spooning out the undissolved condensed milk and sugar. 'Now, Harry,' he began to adjust the noose with a friendly smile. 'I want you to get your men together and bring them up to concert pitch as quickly as possible.' Morgan nodded intently; Deane had trapped his man. 'Get them over the obstacles, stressing the urgency but without mentioning anything of the last ones to go, of course.'

'Of course, sir.' Morgan began packing away his pipe.

'And, Harry, as from now I've relieved you of all Admin problems—I'll see you're cleared. I shall also see to it that you get everything you want, when you want it. The PM's said he'll countersign anything we indent for' (this wasn't quite true, but so what?). 'You'll be getting all the backing humanly possible. Moreover, the Air Force has been co-opted to provide whatever we demand—so you'll be on firm ground there, for a change.'

'Thank you, sir, it's good news to hear.' Morgan sounded a lot more relaxed as powerful allies swung over to his side. Deane concluded without dramatics. 'Ask, Harry, and it's yours. Go and get them moving; go in and do it.' He paused for effect. 'I'm asking Air House to have a Stirling on readiness every night after tomorrow. Remember the time, and remember the season.'

'We shall, sir.' Morgan got to his feet and saluted, still badly hung-over from Deane's thumbscrewing. He'd been tricked into doing another operation with all its familiar taste of green pennies on his tongue and in his throat.

54

CHAPTER FIVE

MORGAN tiredly shrugged into his Crombie and went out, absent-mindedly returning the Commando sentry's salute as he hurried down to the pavement. He bent left, collar pulled high, hands swinging against the cold. At the next crossing he bore left again, down a quiet side street only a couple of minutes away from SOE.

House 21 was a morbid enigma for Morgan, as it would be for many other operators who were to funnel through it during the years of war. Like them, it had no past, and it had no future.

He walked through its high, wooden gates and went up the short drive to the screened door. He stabbed one of several bell contacts set on a smudged brass plaque. The door opened and a slight, dark-suited man faced Morgan with a look of polite enquiry; an encyclopaedia seller would have had as much cheer on this doorstep. Morgan had his Special Services ID card ready. The man turned, studying it under the violet light before giving it back. 'Come this way, sir.'

Morgan followed him along a softly carpeted passage to a small office where an elderly man worked among a clutter of papers and manuals. 'Good morning, Doctor!'

'Good morning, Colonel.' The office door behind Morgan discreetly closed its eyes as the doctor stiffly got up to shake hands. 'Please be seated.' Morgan gratefully accepted, stripping off his coat to sit down opposite the man. 'Would you care for something to drink? Tea? Coffee, perhaps?' The doctor was kindly, but very distant.

'Not for me, thanks.' Morgan quickly raised a hand to stop him ringing. 'I've just had tea with Deane.'

'Good.' The older man relaxed a little and did an on-the-spot analysis of Morgan, thoughtfully noting the skin texture and fingernails. 'How are you keeping nowadays?' There was an unspoken question hidden under the polite phrase. 'Me?' Morgan tried to bluff. 'I've never felt better!'

'No migraine or other troubles now?'

'Not that I know of.'

'How are you sleeping?'

'Alone, generally.'

55

'Uh huh,' the doctor tapped his own chest. 'No discomfort here now?'

'Not a bit of it. I tell you, I'm feeling supremely fit and well!'

'Glad to hear you say it,' he paused a moment, 'but you should take more care not to overdo things for quite some time yet. You must try and get away from London for a few days; you'll feel much better if you do.' He let the words register. 'Now, what can I do for the war?'

'I'd like your verdict on the two men brought in last night or early this morning,' Morgan asked, unconsciously rubbing his eyes. The doctor didn't miss a trick; he quietly memoed himself to mention the matter to Deane. He looked back to Morgan. 'You have three of them now; the one called Erikssen, I think, has just been signed in.'

'Well, thank God for that at least!' Morgan sat back in his chair, obviously a lot easier about something. The doctor went on. 'You'll understand I haven't had time to look at him yet?' Morgan nodded impatiently. 'What of the first two?'

The doctor glanced down at some pencilled notes, then back at Morgan's creased face. 'They're both pretty average, I'd say, for the time of year. I had them put in their rooms at differing times so I could get a good view while they went through the maze—finding the missing door-key, fixing the electric light, you know,' he added, 'all the amenities which make a stay at our guest-house so unforgettable.' Morgan was smiling now. He could still remember the irritating series of accidents which often showed up the character defects, or virtues, which had to be known if a person were being put under the stress of a particular operation. He glanced at the doctor. 'They're all right, then?'

'Yes, they're quite all right for your kind of work.'

'I'm very happy to hear that,' Morgan sounded it, 'very happy indeed.' He hesitated a fraction, then went on. 'Would it be possible to look at them now?' The doctor pulled out his fob-watch and read the time. 'They've been given their breakfasts. It may be a good moment to look in on them—while they're unoccupied and uncertain of what's going to happen next.'

Morgan followed him through another door and up a short flight of deadened stairs to a narrow observation chamber. From here, by a simple system of lenses and prisms hidden in the walls, Morgan was able to scan any one of half a dozen rooms. It was a useful relic of other days when the place had been a kind of hotel. 'Numbers One, Three and Six are yours, Colonel.' Morgan quickly adjusted the first set of eyepieces and peered inside. 'Who's this?'

56

'Meyer...' A stocky, powerfully built man was sitting edge on to Morgan, muscular arms resting along the back of a plain chair by his bed, restlessly dragging at a cigarette, staring out at nothing in particular. Morgan frowned, watching him burn it down to his lips, flicking away the stub and immediately lighting up another. 'Likes his smoke, doesn't he?'

'The fact is significant to us.'

'Damned few things aren't,' Morgan commented laconically, shifting along to the next eyepiece. 'Who's this?'

'Shepherd.' Morgan focused the lens, intently searching round the small room. This man had stacked his bedding in a neat blanket–sheet–blanket pack and was now stretching out, using it as a pillow while he skimmed through a soft-backed Western. 'He, at least, seems to be contented enough with life.'

'What's he doing now?' The doctor had an interest.

'Made his bed just as they taught him at recruit camp. Now he's waiting for the squad to move off—in the meantime he's getting in a bit of serious reading.'

'I wouldn't make the mistake of underpricing Shepherd,' the doctor commented gently, following Morgan along to the third spy system, 'there's a great deal held in reserve.'

'This must be Erikssen?'

'Yes.' Morgan looked away from the newly arrived Dane, fast asleep and already little more than a thinning shock of tow-coloured hair in a drift of crumpled bedding. 'Can you get him processed for us by this afternoon, Doctor?' The man pursed his lips cautiously. 'Oh, I should think so. Yes, it can be done in time.'

'I'd be very glad if you would hurry it up,' Morgan added, following him out of the chamber and back to his office. He dragged on his coat and muffler, then turned and shook hands. 'I'll phone over the moment we're ready to use them.'

Morgan left House 21 and walked away with a little more hope. He spent what remained of the morning organising another series of briefings, writing lecture notes and bullying specialist departments into holding themselves ready for the afternoon session. It wasn't too hard since he'd been over this ground once before; the only difference was that, this time, he'd be going the whole route too. His temper suffered.

57

CHAPTER SIX

MORGAN phoned across to House 21 after a bolted sandwich lunch at his desk, and hurried out with Deane to a small annexe of SOE—the inner secret where most of the team co-ordinations were held. It was getting badly overcrowded as Sections and their work multiplied with each month of war; there was a strict list of priorities for the annexe, which had to be booked ahead now. Sudden panics like this Knightsbridge were apt to ruffle a lot of sensitive people as they found their close timetables being ruthlessly knived to make room for the newcomer. Deane hated the arrangement, but until they'd found him a new headquarters building it would have to do, and the hell with all sensitive people.

They flashed their passes and went in to see the department head—a thin, nervously precise man who had spent most of his adult life directing Hittite excavations in Asia Minor. He was working with two other men on the scale model of a large, three-span viaduct or railway bridge as Deane and Morgan pushed into his untidy, overflowing rooms. He straightened up and bustled over to shake hands with them. 'When do I get more space to work, Deane?' The Brigadier looked loud and long at the archaeologist's three shoulder pips and the '14–'18 Mutt and Jeff ribbons. He coughed. 'Very soon, I hope.'

'So, indeed, do I!' He turned and did a spot check of the viaduct's lines before trotting ahead to another door in the far wall. They followed him through as he palmed down the overhead lighting switches. 'I've had it all set out exactly as you asked, Morgan. But you caught me just in the nick of time; we were about to break up the models and use them in something else.'

'Thanks for sparing me that, at least,' Morgan commented aridly, moving round the room to see that everything was in place and ready to use—models and diagrams shrouded from curious eyes till he'd judged otherwise. 'Good,' he turned back, 'we could be finished by this evening.' The man pulled a long face and reluctantly let himself out of the room. Morgan sighed, more at himself than at Deane. 'That one gets more crabby each time we meet!'

58

'He has his problems too,' the Brigadier answered mildly, peeking under one of the dustsheets for a moment. 'He also happens to be the best person I've yet found for this thankless task.' Deane straightened up. 'For being that I'll forgive him many things.' He coughed and pulled out his watch, glancing at the time. 'Your people should be on their way by now, Morgan.'

'Yes, sir.'

'Well, I wish they'd get a move on!'

There was a discreet rap on another door, the one which led directly into the annexe's small courtyard. Morgan went across, opened it and let in one of the dark-suited men from House 21; he signed a receipt and handed it back. 'Bring them in please.' The man went out to a plain, unmarked ambulance with opaque windows and unlocked the end doors. 'All out.'

Erikssen, Meyer and Shepherd clambered down into the sudden daylight and followed him into the building—a building they would never be able to accurately identify, or describe, no matter the torture they were put to. The staff man hurried them into the briefing room; Morgan dismissed him and barred both doors of the sound trap.

'Meyer? Erikssen? Shepherd?' He politely shook hands in turn. 'My name's Morgan—we're going to get to know each other much better.' He smiled disarmingly, winning them over to his side. Very soon they would be in a place where rank, as such, could be a liability. 'I realise this must be the first time you chaps have met, too, but we'll have plenty of time to put that right. Now,' he turned away, 'let's go over and meet the boss.'

He took his awkward group between the model tables to a short row of old chairs set in a semi-circle round a lecture stand.

Deane got to his feet and returned Morgan's brief salute. 'Be seated, gentlemen.

'At one time or another you've all volunteered, and passed, Special Services training—small arms, combat, tactics and so on —before returning to unit for assignment. You all volunteered, a decision made of your own free will, and made by you alone. But in the meantime you may have changed your minds—perhaps you don't want to go operational after all.' He paused, studying their blank faces. 'If any one of you does feel this way, now's the time to speak out. This will be the last opportunity you will ever have to leave.' Deane paused again and looked them over, testing the effect. 'You already know a lot about Special Services and its work, but I intend to remind you of some unpleasant facts—just to refresh your memories.

'Firstly, there'll be no uniforms. As such you'll be completely

59

outside the Geneva Code, for what it's worth, from the moment you land wherever you're going. You will be treated as spies if you're taken by the Gestapo or SS, and as spies you'll be executed. You will have no friends, for nobody in their right mind will want to be found anywhere near you. You'll be hunted without rest once your cover is compromised, and you'll be hunted by men who will do everything and anything to get at you. They must. They know that a saboteur, even though he's hiding and alone, can still destroy. And while he lives they have good reason to fear him; you are a mortal sickness to them.

'Against this I have nothing to offer. Failure will mean oblivion—and success is never given much more. I repeat, gentlemen, now is the time to leave.' Deane had judged well and shrewdly. He knew the rare kind of man who chooses this kind of work, and the even rarer kind of person who survives the combing out and rejection procedures. Though they didn't look it to the eye, these men were the *élite* of the *élite*, they were the best. He'd said nothing positive to discourage them; they sat still and waited for him to go on.

'Very well, now that we clearly understand our positions in this affair I shall hand you back to your leader—Lieutenant-Colonel Morgan, a very experienced and successful officer—something which you would do well to keep in mind at all times.' Deane stepped away from the table and beckoned Morgan to come over and take his place. 'Thank you, sir.'

He turned and faced his team, falling back on his schoolmastering days to see him through the first moments. 'I intend to tell you a short story—a story which loses nothing by being entirely true.' He paused, it wasn't much of an opening.

'During the past two and a half or three months the war in Europe has reached the point where defeat, for the Allies, is all but certain.' He held their attention now, absolute and undivided. He wasn't gift-wrapping his words; it was an astute move. 'I don't enjoy saying this, but it won't go away even if we tried to ignore the matter. I say again, defeat is not very far away. I don't doubt that you've all read in the newspapers how things are a bit sticky just now, but that's not half the truth. The plain fact is that things are bloody awful, and getting worse as the weeks go by. Everywhere the enemy' (he nearly said Germans, but remembered Meyer in time) 'is on top and apparently winning. Their U-boat sinkings have now touched a new high with over half a million tons going to the bottom of the Atlantic every month. North Africa is a shambles; the Russians are only just hanging on to the perimeter round Moscow, and it's not yet winter; the RAF's bombers take a heavier beating on every raid they fly.' He paused sombrely.

'These, then, are just a few of the highlights. Taken separately they are very bad, very bad indeed. But put them together and they become disastrous! You see,' he went on patiently, 'the Allies are rather like an arch—knock away any section and the rest will surely fall. And if we fall, then the world as we know it will sink into a new age of devilry.' He paused again, wobbling himself a drink from the water carafe, only spilling a little round the glass.

'Now, underlying everything I've mentioned is one constant factor—supplies and munitions; fuel and raw materials. For our part we shall be beaten if the American convoys dwindle any further. And the enemy will most certainly lose if, comes the spring, they haven't assembled matériel enough to put Russia out of this war. The alternatives for both sides are quite plain.' He glanced across at the Brigadier for confirmation; Deane nodded. Morgan paused and took another sip of water before going on, carefully laying the groundwork for his master briefing. He was still civilian enough to believe that it wasn't enough just to tell men what to do, especially in a situation where they could easily find themselves cut off and alone. To do their work, and do it intelligently, they must be told the why as well as the when and where. It made him seem a little long-winded.

'Now, while the enemy is gambling heavily on his U-boats to choke off our supplies, we've put our faith in the Navy's blockade —and the bombers. The bombers *must* continue to get through. The bombers must continue to blast the Ruhr's arsenals; their steel mills and coking plants are everything this winter. Remember that every extra ton of equipment which they can forge and move eastwards now will be worth at least a thousand in the spring when their offensive opens.

'Bomber Command knows this and they're throwing in every machine they have, wherever possible and regardless of the cost. But, and this is the whole point of my story, there comes a time when losses more than equal total replacements—from our own factories and from America. The actual figure, for your information, isn't nearly as high as many would like to think.

'Bomber Command's been edging towards this point for several months—the graph going up a couple of points, dropping one, going up another two. There hasn't been much help for it, despite all that Counter-Intelligence have dreamed up.' Morgan shrugged tiredly. 'For a long time it was thought to be the result of better and more accurate flak prediction; bigger and more

61

guns with bigger and more searchlights backing them up. But after a while it began to seem differently. True, their flak *was* thickening all the time, but not in the same ratio as our bomber losses. Intelligence had to go back to square one, begin again and look elsewhere. For quite a time they were right out of luck.

'Then, one day someone in Holland managed to take some photos of an enemy aircraft which had overshot its runway and piled into a tree—don't ask me how they made the film, it's full of Germans on guard, but they did. Anyhow, a courier brought out the negatives through Spain and Gibraltar for the Air Ministry's interpreters to haggle over. They, in their turn, have identified the machine as being a Ju. 88 variant which the GAF has been trying to fake into a night-fighter—apparently without much joy.' Morgan was warming to his subject; the awkwardness was fading. He hitched up one leg and half sat on the table corner, foot swinging.

'This particular Junkers was believed to be in the Stone Age so far as fighter development was concerned—we thought. But under a staggering enlargement the Boffins were able to take a good look at the aircraft's equipment, and they found a nasty surprise waiting inside.' He smiled oddly. 'It seems that this mark of Junkers has been entirely redesigned and stuffed with all the latest and most sophisticated tricks known—the cause of our ever-increasing bomber losses. Now, at this point in the story I'd like you to hear a lot more detailed information than I can possibly give you.' He looked across at Deane, now sitting with the others, harsh and barren as the plot developed. 'May I call in Finlay, sir?'

Deane nodded after a moment's thought and Morgan crossed over to the inner door, coming back a few moments later with a youngish, slackly built man in well-tailored tweeds. His badly knotted tie wasn't central, a small part of Deane's mind noted down unconsciously. 'How far have you proceeded, Morgan?' Finlay was being very incisive and Edinburgh this afternoon. Morgan tapped a schedule of notes lying out of sight on the table by Deane's cap and cane. 'I've got so far as the new Junkers; perhaps you would carry on from there?' Finlay glanced up from the notes and looked around at his audience, carefully choosing his words.

'To begin very simply—something which is none too easy with this particular science—the Junkers 88 is now operationally equipped with a surprisingly advanced form of airborne radar called the "Flensburg Array", presumably after the Luftwaffe research station of that name on the Danish border.' Deane began fidgeting noticeably, but Finlay chose to ignore it.

'This fact has surprised and worried us because, until very recently, I maintained we held a more than comfortable lead in radar development. However, that's all water over the dam now.' Finlay was coolly laconic, glancing at the scattered Corps flashes on the three pairs of shoulders. He sighed quietly, maybe the Royal Signals knew what he was talking about, maybe not.

'Can I suppose you'll know what I'm referring to when I speak of airborne radar ... ?' He paused, hoping for an answer. 'Very well, imagine it as a gadget which "sees" far ahead of its aircraft and picks out any solid object, no matter how dark the night. I'll let you picture for yourselves what the result can be once cloud and darkness are no longer hiding-places for our bombers.

'To our cost we know just how accurate this Flensburg is nowadays. However, thanks to a fine piece of work by someone in Holland we've been able to unravel this equipment and find out how it functions, pretty much as if we actually had the display in front of us. I, myself, was immediately struck by the great similarity to our own 200 m/cs set—which is still under development.' He noticed Deane begin fidgeting again. 'So with this fact in mind it was only a short step to stripping down the entire device—in imagination, of course—thus discovering what had turned the clockwork primitive Flensburg of a few months ago into the blinding headache it's now become.' Finlay paused. 'But again I was very lucky, it was really quite simple once I'd isolated the set's TR cell—a gas-filled module which screens the Mixer Unit from instant burn-out once its Impulse Magnetron moves into high power.' He tried looking modest for what was, in all fairness, a remarkable piece of sleuthing. The only pity was that none of his listeners could appreciate the effort. He was quite alone with his triumph.

Deane had developed a hacking cough. Morgan quickly interpreted and turned to Finlay. 'Perhaps you could explain that last bit for us? It is very significant, I think ...'

'Of course, of course.' Finlay, for all his minor vanities, was working hard to help these unknown men in any way possible. 'Well, the Flensburg is really quite routine except for this one thing—a sub-assembly no larger than a quart beer bottle, in effect. But with it they can force up the kilowattage to previously impossible levels once they have the set airborne and out hunting bombers. This cell means that the Luftwaffe is able to multiply its radar range *and* achieve hairline prediction during interception sorties. Naturally enough, we're all groping towards the

63

same objective—so I can appreciate only too well what a lethal weapon this Junkers has become now it can aim its cannon, fire, and hit—all without ever seeing its target.' Finlay stood and absently chewed his lip. 'Frankly we're worried. We are worried, and we're going to have a lot more reason to worry unless someone goes in—and goes in very soon—to pull the plug on this Flensburg thing.

'Now, everything would be fine if we could destroy, let's say, all the equipment, or all the aircraft. But that's plainly impossible since it's under construction in a hundred or more sub-contracting factories hidden across Occupied Europe. It's out of the question for us to locate and hit each one, simultaneously. So, to coin a phrase, we've had to look for the weakest link; the delicate pivot around which all the rest revolves. D'you follow me?' Finlay stopped and looked at the soldiers, hoping that he wasn't outstripping them, or getting too windy. He couldn't help the way he spoke any more than he could help having freckles; both things made him rather sad and touchy at times. He went on.

'Fortunately for us this TR cell I mentioned fulfils this requirement exactly. No TR cell means no Flensburg; no Flensburg and the Junkers is blind. You see, it's really an elementary problem, looked at in this light. Another piece of luck—the cell must have a terrific rate of wastage. The unit can't last for ever; they must have a very frequent replacement programme in the normal course of events. So, destroy their source of production and, very soon, even those Junkers which are in service will be grounded until someone brilliant can dream up an antidote.' He made time to smile at a private thought.

'But, you'll think, the technicians will simply pack up the blueprints and shift their tents to a quieter place, only to start all over again. What would have been gained? A few days? A few weeks at most? Well, gentlemen, even if that were the case this would be a supremely justifiable attempt; Air Ministry could use a break just now, so could Bomber Command. But,' Finlay's laconic posing evaporated, he caught fire, 'but there remains one tiny, vital factor in our calculations—the gas! The gas with which they must fill the cell; the correctly balanced, inert gas which provides the screen's resistance. They must use helium. Helium, gentlemen, is one of the rarest of the inert gases—it cost well over £700 a cubic foot not so many years ago. True, it doesn't cost that much now, but it does have one other distressing characteristic for the Luftwaffe. Helium in usable quantities is only found in the United States—and the strategic embargo has cut Germany off from her only possible source. If the small

64

quantity of helium which they do hold in stock is destroyed, then the Flensburg programme as we know it will stop, and stay stopped.' Finlay ran to a halt and looked across at Morgan. 'I think that's all you wanted to hear, isn't it?'

'Yes, thank you, that's covered everything we need to know at the moment.' Morgan got up and quietly escorted him from the room. After a couple of minutes he came back, carefully locking the doors behind him. He stepped behind the table and picked up where Finlay had left off. 'Well, you're probably getting a clearer picture of what's been going on recently. However, not to worry if you can't add up all the details at the moment.' He looked round reassuringly.

'So, we'd got so far as the identification of our quarry, but we were still a long way from bagging it—or so we thought. But the photo-enlargements had already been shipped over to the Economic Intelligence bodies for some inspired guesswork. They took this TR thing's serial number—plainly stencilled on the outer casing, very careless of someone—and put it through their patent brain squeezer till they'd settled its company of origin almost beyond any shadow of doubt. Then real luck came our way,' Morgan glanced at Erikssen, 'when the Danish Underground Forces smuggled out photostats of some letters and invoices— routine bits of office bumf—but they pinpointed the TR's home in one wing of a commandeered factory just a bit to the south of central Copenhagen.' He paused to sip water. 'This factory, gentlemen, will be destroyed.' Morgan glanced along at Deane. 'Would you like to add anything at this point, sir?'

'No, you carry on.'

'Thank you, sir.' He turned and went across to the largest of the shrouded models, twitched aside its sheeting and snapped on the bank of top lights. 'Come over here.

'This represents the Copenhagen subsidiary of a well-known Scandinavian company, Mercur A/S. Mercur usually makes quality electric light fittings and radio valves, but since the German Occupation some people from a jawbreaking outfit calling itself Deutscherundfunkgerät—DRG for short—have moved in. They are now happily and securely assembling the TR cell before packing it off, under very strong escort, to the Luftwaffe's place in Flensburg.'

Morgan had picked up the broken-off tip of a billiard cue and was gently passing it through the air over the model, a brick-for-brick copy thirty inches high and about six feet down each pair of sides. Someone had hurriedly but accurately traced in the factory's new defences from the latest set of prints, glueing minia-

65

ture posts, wire and guards in their proper places. Morgan was trying hard not to notice these yet.

'You'll see from this mock-up that the factory forms an open-ended figure; two double-storeyed wings joined by a cross member and bounded on three of its four sides by quiet, suburban streets. Namely, Holmgade—here.' He tapped his pointer on the strip of black paint and sawdust ruled in front of the miniature factory. 'Strandvej—here.' He shifted round a left-hand corner and tapped the street lying at right angles to Holmgade. 'And Prags Boulevard leading into Vermlandsgade—here.' The pointer's tip moved round to the last strip, running parallel to the back of the building. Morgan looked across at his team. 'You will remember those names, and their positioning.' He took a long breather, steadying himself.

'Now, the fourth side is a miscellaneous jumble of small workshops—converted garages most of them—the largest of which seems to be a galvanising plant. Remember that, too. But,' he continued, 'the only part of this factory which concerns us at the moment is in this wing, here.' Morgan pointed out the block which lay along Strandvej. 'This is the one which has been taken over by the DRG specialists and very largely sealed-off from the rest of the factory, here and here.' He tapped briefly.

'The bottom floor of the third hall—our hall—used to be the production control unit, but now it's running under the name of Low Pressure Physics Area. The Germans have completely restaffed it with top personnel evacuated from DRG's main plant in Hanover. Mercur was a logical choice for them, I suppose, since Copenhagen still lies north of the bomb line. Anyway, the box of toys is under the control of one Professor Doktor Ingenieur Hoertl, a somewhat fancy title for a shadowy little man—probably with a toothbrush moustache and bifocals.' Morgan caught Meyer's hard look and realised that the tradition of Herr Professor still lived in Germany.

'In any case it keeps itself very much to itself. Only a few Danes have been allowed inside the place since it was taken over. One who did, however, managed to send us a fairly detailed drawing of the actual layout.' He paused. 'This, too, you'll know by heart. If I move this section wall,' he delicately lifted away a piece of the model's card and balsa sides, 'you'll be able to see something of the assembly. Both from Strandvej on the outside, and the loading bay on the inside...' The three men gathered round and quietly nodded in agreement as he pointed out their target in detail. Morgan stepped back a half pace to get a better perspective and nearly collided with Deane who'd been watching

66

over his shoulder; they swapped looks and Morgan slowly turned back to the model.

'From this you can see that there are just five ways of getting inside. One—by breaching the wall into Strandvej. Two—by coming in through this short passage here, which leads from a door by the courtyard boiler house. Three—by breaking into the assembly area from the main hall. Four—by coming in from the roof and then through the second floor, somehow. Five—by tunnelling.' The last choice was offered by way of light relief—not that Morgan hadn't seriously considered it during the last few hours. But nobody laughed.

'Now, just for the moment, let's take a look at the factory's defences.' He paused, gesturing casually at the puny strands of cotton which the model maker had used to show wire. He breathed out and continued in the same unconcerned voice. 'Here you'll see the enemy has been particularly unpleasant to us. They really don't want us to visit them, and they're going to great lengths to stop anyone like us who might have unfriendly intentions. So much so, they've left just two official ways in. This one which opens into the clocking hall and admin block; and this one at the back which appears to be the goods entrance. Both are barred by hefty looking gates and, at the last count, they were enfiladed by a couple of heavy machine-guns apiece behind these sandbag parapets. There are also these four pill-boxes which might house more machine weapons, and a largish squad of soldiery. You see,' he paused lightly, 'they're serious about the place too.

'Of incidental importance to us are the AA defences which they seem to be moving into the factory area—here.' He tapped the model's railway siding and single-gauge tracks which curved round from behind the factory, running dead straight at the beach about five hundred yards over Strandvej. 'And here.' He nodded briefly to a large patch of wasteland roughly to the south. 'At the moment they seem to be largely concerned with 20-mm automatics—the celebrated Quadruple-Twenty of theirs—which they've mounted on flat-bed railway wagons and then drawn in a long arc along this flank. From our point of view they have only one real importance—reinforcements. The factory's guards could whistle up more help if they needed it, so we'd better not give them any reason to do so.' He paused, going back to the wire; he fought hard to sound relaxed now that he must mention it in detail.

'The only really unpleasant time will be when we pass over, or through, or under this messy nonsense. Most probably we'll have

67

to choose a point of entry other than at the two gates—something which might grow a trifle tricky unless we go very carefully.' This was a pathetic little lie; it would be murder. It would be murder all the way. The heavy, three-centimetre barbed wire was going to snare the flesh from their ribs, tangling them like moths in the flaring searchlights while invisible machine-gunners zeroed their aim. Morgan could already feel the slap-whunk of striking bullets.

After a while he picked up again, casual and jaunty. 'Now, chaps, I've prepared three outlines for the attack—though I shall leave the final choice until I'm able to reconnoitre the area myself, you understand.' He glanced round briefly. 'Our first route could be from here,' Morgan tapped the model, 'starting in the galvanising yard where the fence runs along the wire for a good thirty yards. This could provide us with reasonable cover while we cut a way through.' He paused, analysing the idea in detail.

'The second possible route could be through the conduit which brings in power and telephone lines to the factory. Its inspection cover is almost certainly over here, round the corner from Holmgade and out of sight of the picquet based on the front guard-hut.' He smiled wryly. 'I hope that none of you chaps are frightened by spiders—it may be a long crawl in.

'Or else route number three. We could attempt to force one or another of the entrances, relying on surprise and firepower to batter a way in. Frankly, I don't like this one very much and I shan't seriously propose it unless we can find a lot of support among local Resistance workers.

'Of the three, I favour the first.' Morgan looked at his team over the model's roof and ran his sweaty hands along the billiard cue, quietening them by bracing their fingers against the wood's stiffness.

'So that's your first glimpse of our target's exterior; you'll have plenty of opportunity later to make a detailed study. Now,' he turned away, 'come over here.' Morgan led the way to another model table, dragged off the dustsheet and lit up a fairly accurate guess at the factory's internal structure.

'This is the whole reason for going,' he said, reverently setting the cue's tip on a small wooden block. 'It's supposed to represent a concrete and brick vault, proof against all but a direct hit by heavy AP bombs, which has been built round the helium storage flasks, their valving and the pipelines which meter it into the factory. By all accounts it's as snug as the Bank of England, from any angle, with an armour plate manhole cover clamped down by a massive padlock and hasp—they don't appear to trust

68

anyone nowadays. However,' he went on, ignoring Krupp steel and ferro-concrete, 'there'll be plenty of chance to go over that, too, later on. But you can all take heart from the fact that, when we do stick a charge under the helium storage, there'll be the sweetest little bang ever heard in those parts.' He smiled oddly. 'They tell me it's being kept at about six thousand atmospheres of pressure, with a large quantity of liquid oxygen and other gases stored alongside. It'll make a satisfying noise.' Morgan straightened up and went back to the lecture table with Deane to pick up the sheaf of notes, leaving the others still grouped round the model. 'Well done, Harry.' Deane kept his voice low. 'I believed you as well.'

'Thank you, sir.' Morgan tiredly stacked the pages together. 'How long have I, at the most?'

'For training them on the solids?'

'Yes.'

'Don't count on having more than a full day; two will be stretching things.'

'So really I can say just tomorrow?'

'Yes.'

'It's not nearly enough time.'

'I know.'

'I shall need three days at least for accurate training, and four would be that much better.'

'No.' Deane turned a fraction and fussily took up his cap and cane. He didn't look at Morgan as he went on. 'I want you to get them over to the training school immediately; exercise them on the solids as much as possible and try making time for a question and answer session; cut the rest if you have to.'

'I don't like it at all, sir.'

'That's a great pity,' Deane commented dryly. He softened a little, going on in the same low voice as they walked across to the inner door. 'Take them over the course and do what you can with them. I shall do my best to win you a reprieve from the Cabinet Office,' he paused tiredly, 'but don't bank on too much happening.'

69

CHAPTER SEVEN

KIERZNER was still resting after a light lunch when his communications officer rang up from the SS Signals Bureau. He reached across from his couch. 'Ja? Kierzner am Apparat.'

'Urgent and personal telex from Berlin, Herr Oberst!'

'Bring it up.'

'Jawohl!'

He spent some time carefully analysing the terse message ordering his immediate recall to SS Reichsführer Headquarters. He didn't like it, he didn't like it at all. Kierzner had good reason to worry as he browsed round the signature cypher with particular care—Strasser, SS General-Major, Himmler's office boy and Chief of Staff.

He'd been far too long in the provinces—Austria, Poland, now Denmark; the restless power structure of the SS could forget a person very quickly; a good, clean record was not always sufficient; corrosive lies and half-truths could etch away a man's life; it paid to be on the alert. Kierzner gnawed a fingernail while he tried his luck as a fortune teller; the short ride to total oblivion could be so swift and sudden. He sat up, abruptly tossed the telex at a wicker tray and rang for his own Chief of Staff.

Twenty-five minutes later and he'd finished handing over all routine work to Bethmann. He dismissed him to arrange a Luftwaffe transport from Kastrup and went across to the phone again.

'Give me an outside line; Kongens Hotel; extension 145.' He sat on the edge of the desk and made a big job of selecting a Turkish cigarette while he waited for the line to clear.

'Kongens Hotel...'

'Put me through to Frau Therese Kierzner immediately.'

'Jawohl, Herr Oberst!'

'Frau Kierzner speaking...'

'Hello, darling,' he drew on the cigarette and nervously wiped his forehead. 'I shan't be home for dinner tonight.'

'Berlin?'

'Yes.'

'I understand.'

'You remember what to do?'

'Yes, darling.'

'Don't forget,' he drew smoke, 'and take care of yourself.' He paused again. 'Goodbye.'

Kierzner rang off and strode over to his own, very personal armoured safe—thirty inches of concrete, Wolfram alloy and copper. He cranked the door and hurriedly stowed three sealed envelopes of photostats in a padlocked briefcase lined with thick steel mesh; the original letters, memoranda and keyhole snapshots of certain people stayed out of reach in the Züricher Handelsbank.

Bethmann jerked to attention on the headquarters steps and threw up a salute. He was still smiling between the rigid sentries as the Mercedes whirled Kierzner into the grey afternoon. Promising. *Very* promising. The way fortune's wheel turned nowadays this could well be the last he'd ever see of the man. Gently warmed by a happy thought, Bethmann pivoted and clipped back to his office.

SS Feldwebel Dorfer wound the heavy staff-car into the airfield access road, gunning it through the dispersal areas festooned with mottled netting, stuffed to capacity with the machines of a Heinkel bomber group being rotated east, to Russia. He braked hard alongside a Ju. 52, its three motors warmed up, idly turning over, waiting. Dorfer sprang out and strapped the Oberst's single travelling grip in the hold, jumping clear as Kierzner hurried up the aluminium ladder and ducked inside. A crewman leaned out, deftly swinging the hatch shut; the Junkers advanced to taxiing power and began fishtailing away.

Kierzner flew into Tempelhof well after dark. It had been a foul journey with headwinds and severe turbulence all the way down from Copenhagen. An SS staff-car was waiting for him by the darkened airport buildings; it nosed out from the shadows as the Junkers braked and shut off power.

'Herr Oberstleutnant Kierzner?' He stepped away from the ladder and squinted through the windy night at the silhouette, ears straining to catch any useful news hidden in the clipped, impersonal voice. 'Yes?'

'Leutnant Ott! ADC to the General-Major Strasser!' The outline saluted briefly. 'I trust that the Oberstleutnant enjoyed a pleasant journey!' A slight pause. 'A car has been placed at his disposal!'

Like much else in an aide's busy life this was formula flower talk; but news seeps very quickly through headquarters office strata. If there was a short rope with Kierzner's name tagged, the

71

chances were good this Ott already knew he was Gravedigger's Mate for the night.

The utility Opel saloon drove through the city as quickly as it could, cautiously chasing its own dimmed headlights down a secondary street, obediently following a chain of dull red kerosene flares marking the diversion round a recently hit building. 'Bombing?' Kierzner sounded easy, take it or leave it. Ott, a Berliner himself, chewed his tongue and scowled with safety in the darkness. After a moment he was ready with a bright reply. 'It sometimes happens that the English terror flyers penetrate our airspace and even drop a few, random bombs, Herr Oberst!'

'Only a few? That's good to hear.' Kierzner was a little out of touch with recent events in the capital.

They accelerated past the Column of Winged Victory, along the Eichen and wheeled right at the Brandenburg Gate towards the SS Reichsführer's new, five-storey headquarters at Prinz Albrechtstrasse, 8. A guard's handlamp scattered light as Kierzner brushed ahead of Ott, marching into the crowded building with a synthetic confidence he found hard to make. They rode the lift to Strasser's suite, Ott gratefully fading astern as Kierzner went in alone.

The SS General-Major Strasser was waiting, contentedly toasting himself in front of a gigantic, open wood fire. This, and the thick-weave blackout curtaining, forced up the temperature and humidity. Not that Strasser cared very much either way. He'd been dressed for the evening in full uniform, tightly buttoned at the throat, with breeches and black, glass-bright knee boots casing the other end. Someone with a malicious sense of fun had once told him this rig would lend an elegant line to his massive, all-in wrestler's body. He turned around as the double-width mahogany doors opened inwards, letting out a gasp of spent air.

'Lieber, Maxi!' Strasser crossed over to meet this man exactly halfway, always an omen that something was up, and folded his own paw round Kierzner's. 'Your punctuality is a byword in our Service; a standard for us all to attempt, but never achieve!' He began steering Kierzner nearer the fire. 'You must be cold after your flight; you must get warm again!' Strasser smiled. 'Quite like old times, Maxi, quite like old times!' Kierzner ran with sweat; he started to edge away. 'You must have a drink.' Strasser played the genial host even if the effort killed him. 'The only question is, what d'you want?' He didn't wait for the man to get out an answer. Instead, he turned and aimed his mouth at a far door. 'OTT!' The aide's name exploded a few inches from Kierzner's left eardrum.

72

'Herr General!'

'DRINKS!'

'HERR GENERAL!' The ADC sprinted for cover. Strasser glanced down at Kierzner again. 'I've got something that'll tickle you, Maxi, I'm absolutely sure of it!' He chuckled moistly. 'Picked it up in Paris only last weekend. Say what you like about the Frenchies,' he went on, dropping his voice confidentially, 'they *really* know how to live. Of course, they're complete turds as soldiers—one Upper Saxon can eat ten of 'em for supper and not know it—but they really know how to *live*.'

His attempts at sparkling, light conversation if they went on much longer were going to make Kierzner—an Oldenburger—choke. He was saved from that by the arrival of Ott pushing a very large, golden perambulator or street stall made of painted tin and shiny, anodised wire rods. A saucy red-and-white awning was stretched over a parade of wine and spirit bottles, jostling together shoulder-to-shoulder as Ott solemnly trundled it through the deep carpeting.

'There!' He waited for spontaneous applause. 'What d'you think of that, eh, Maxi?' Kierzner smiled dryly. 'I doubt if anyone else in Berlin has one like it.'

'Exactly so!' He strode over, lifted the awning and turned to his guest. 'You name it, Maxi, and you'll find that I already have it! Go on, just you name it!' But Kierzner was being dumb this evening, saying nothing. Strasser had to go on alone. 'I've Slivo-vitz from Jugoslavia—good powerful stuff with a real jolt. Chianti from Italy—red, vampire's pee to my taste, but some like it. Something from Greece that's like pine essence—but explodes in the belly. There's a bottle from every big wine-growing area in France, they tell me. I've even Scotch whisky liberated from the English at Dunkirk!' He paused for effect. 'What d'you think of *that*, eh?'

'Pretty impressive.'

'I knew you'd start thinking that way, Maxi, so what'll you have *now*?'

'A Dortmunder.' Some of the light went out in Strasser's eyes, but Ott was able to find a bottle of beer in the staff mess—ready chilled—and rush it up to the suite.

'Auf Ihr Ganz Spezielles Wohl!' Strasser mechanically raised his tumbler of Jugoslav plum brandy to eye level before starting on it.

'Danke.' Kierzner damped his lips on the cool glass rim. Strasser was treating his drink like a fizzy lemonade; he wiped his lips along the back of his hand and grinned. 'Probably wondering what's brought you to Berlin so suddenly, eh?'

'Mm?'

'Things are beginning to happen in Copenhagen, big things...'

'I'd prefer to think they were not.'

'Of course, Maxi, but there's no denying you have just had troubles with parachutists.'

'Troubles?'

'That business of the Mercur factory—and it's been awarded a Schwarzwald security rating, too.' Strasser paused. 'But you will have ample opportunity to explain yourself in a few minutes.'

'Explain myself?'

'That's right, Maxi. Explain yourself to the Reichsführer; he wants to see you,' Strasser turned and looked at the heavy gilt clock over the fire, 'just about now. But first, give me that pistol and your briefcase...'

'What the devil for!'

'Orders.'

'This is dishonourable! My case contains Reich Confidential material of the greatest delicacy, details of our counter-espionage services in Denmark and Norway!'

'They will be taken care of—believe me. Now,' Strasser hardened, 'stop defending your virtue and hand them over!'

Kierzner marched down a short corridor; buttocks clenched; neck muscles corded; head erect, mouth down-curving as Strasser went ahead through a pair of very tall, white-panelled doors. He came back. 'The Reichsführer is ready to see you now.'

Kierzner stepped through and sensed the latch flick shut behind him. Arms swinging like pistons he marched down the gleaming parquet to a brass rail screwed just six feet from Himmler's desk. He halted at the line, crashing his heels together, throwing out an immaculate salute, fingers taut. 'Kierzner; Director, Reich Security Intelligence; Copenhagen. At your orders, my Leader!' The arm plunged and locked itself tight by his side.

Himmler blinked behind his rimless lenses, frowning across his paper-free, emperor-size desk. There was a long pause. 'I have received a disturbing series of reports about your activities in Copenhagen, Kierzner.' The voice, like the man, was thin and unfortunate. 'Activities at a certain Mercur factory; activities in which English terrorists attempted to sabotage the Reich; activities in which they seemed near success!' He paused again. 'What do you say?'

'They are being punished!'

74

'I am glad, but I never expected to hear less!' Himmler went quiet for a moment. 'The question is, should I let the punishment stop there, you understand me?' He understood. Himmler went on reflectively. 'Why should they alone be punished for their crime? Why not punish *all*?' Kierzner's pants were sour with moisture. Himmler suddenly shot off at a mental tangent. 'I've consulted expert opinion about the direction of Schwarzwald sites, Kierzner, particularly Mercur. I had your horoscope cast, and this precaution saved me from making another tragic mistake.' He paused on a sudden thought. 'You *were* born in Westerstede-Oldenburg on April the 18th, weren't you? At seven thirty-one in the evening?'

'My Leader!'

'Then you are an Arian subject, exactly like our Führer—but under the influence of Venus, the bright evening star, *and* Mars, the red bringer of war, of destruction, of action!' He seemed to fall into another reverie for quite a time. 'Aries, Venus, Mars. Aries the ram—dynamic, fearless, ruthless, dedicated, ardent! You will live to serve the Reich in the very highest capacities, Kierzner! The Reich will need your life!' Kierzner dumbly sensed that a dynamic comment of some kind was expected from him, and soon. 'My life is the Führer's!'

'And He knows it, He knows,' Himmler dived his voice to the level of confidential anecdote. 'He told me so only this afternoon while we were still discussing your report on the attempted sabotage. Our Great Leader knows!'

'I honour His trust!' Himmler nodded approvingly. 'It makes me happy to hear you say that. It is for this matter, so that you will recognise your duty to the Fatherland, it is for this matter you have been recalled. Now,' he went on briskly, 'tell me what you know of the Mercur installation. Tell me frankly, don't be afraid, I am here to help you.'

'In Reich·Security Order A/7—Schwarzwald—binding orders were given for the maximum defence of the designated area!' Kierzner instinctively kept himself on safe ground; he couldn't be faulted if he quoted the original draft verbatim. 'Essential War Material is being manufactured, the production of which is vital to the Reich's continued war effort!'

'Yes, yes, yes, but I can see you haven't grasped the full importance of your task. Essential War Material, Kierzner, is a category which blankets almost everything now in production— from toilet paper and trouser buttons to the 2000-kg torpedo, it is not unique.' His voice began to rise steadily. 'Schwarzwald sites, however, are!

75

'I shall explain myself, confide something known only to the All Highest.' He paused, opening and closing his eyes. 'Schwarzwald is a new conception in the history of human warfare,' the voice climbed. 'Our Führer's master plan is almost ready for execution, Kierzner! Weapons are coming which will make all else known to man obsolete and useless; weapons of a frightening nature undreamed of!' His pupils glittered as the words scattered across the room.

'With the complete annihilation of the Bolshevik conspiracy this spring, we shall once again turn our gaze to west and order elimination of the English Incident. Beyond that lies the neutralisation of America. And beyond America, Kierzner, the world!

'Cosmic weapons of a horror unimaginable—but there must be no interference in their production, none at all!' His voice flattened abruptly. 'Sadly, though, there are still occasions when English gangster aircraft pierce even the Luftwaffe's mighty sky shield and so strike at the Reich—THIS MUST CEASE!

'No English bombing aircraft must be permitted to live in the skies above the Reich, none! But Schwarzwald, and the Mercur site in particular, will provide us with the complete answer to this irritating problem. Mercur *must* be held secure against the English!

'It is to this end, Kierzner, that the Führer himself today ordered its elevation to the honoured status of a Fortress Area; the special Führer Orders governing the conduct of all Fortress Areas will now apply to Copenhagen! Never forget that a Fortress must be held against the enemy on pain of death for the Commander, his entire staff of officers and every tenth survivor of the garrison force! Copenhagen is now an armed Fortress— Festung Wotan! So named after the great father of our Nordic gods—Wotan the ruler of the world; king of heaven and earth; the all powerful! Be equal to that most hallowed of names and it could be yours in history!'

'My Leader!'

'Because you are now the first commander of Festung Wotan.' Himmler brushed aside what could only be stumbling words of gratitude and devotion, plunging on with his monologue. 'You will be invested with all the power and authority of a Fortress Commander, to enforce total security in your area of operations. You will be given the highest priorities. You have now joined the elect, the front-line fighters of the Reich!' He stopped, his voice awash with the weight of emotion it carried. 'Tell me, what positive steps have you taken to improve security arrangements at Mercur?' Kierzner seemed to come back from a very great dis-

76

tance to sketch his existing operational orders. Himmler nodded as he finished. 'Good, of course, but not good enough for a Fortress Area.' He leaned forward, lenses catching the light. 'What forces *do* you need for the effective defence of Wotan?'

Kierzner thought fast. Whatever he asked for, and got, would be under his command entirely. Any more than five hundred and he could expect to go up another grade to full Oberst; but too many troops, especially Deathshead SS, billeted in the city and he'd create problems with the Danish authorities. He didn't want any Incidents. 'My Leader, I shall require three combat companies of SS Assault Infantry,' that gave him 630 troops, his silver oak-leaves and made him quite independent of the Army.

'A machine-gun company; headquarters and supply personnel; transport details; Luftwaffe liaison for improved flak defence and fighter cover; Kriegsmarine liaison for additional naval patrols on the Sound; overriding authority to call on all Wehrmacht establishments for whatever troops I may require to make Wotan utterly secure!' Kierzner was stunned by the incredible toughness of his nervous system. In one long breath he'd promoted himself to be a kind of miniature C-in-C Northern Europe, not bad going for a Lieutenant-Colonel with only a few months seniority.

'It will be done.' Himmler immediately rubber-stamped the idea and sat forward again, carefully weighing something in his mind. 'This is going to prove a heavy responsibility—even for the first of eighty-three names graduating from our Staff College.' He smiled thinly. 'Or even the husband of the charming and cultured Therese von Arnim—a symbolic coupling of our new, virile Germany with the old, aristocratic one which pleased the Führer, Kierzner. A wise choice.' Himmler paused again. 'I consider that General-Major Kierzner sounds far more authoritative than just plain Oberst, don't you?'

'Mein Führer!'

'I thought so too. Go and rest well, General, your orders and commission will be prepared immediately. You will receive them before you leave for Copenhagen tomorrow morning.'

The new General-Major let himself out into the corridor, pulled the doors shut and collapsed against the wall. Strasser gently tapped him on one shoulder and led the way back to his rooms. 'I imagine you could use something more bracing than a Dortmunder now, Maxi,' he commented dryly.

'I'll try the Scotch.'

'Another wise choice.'

Some time later, Strasser's own Mercedes drove Kierzner to the Hotel Adlon where a suite had been hurriedly emptied for him.

77

He slumped on the edge of the bed and rang for an external line to Copenhagen. 'Put me through to Frau Kierzner. Very well, waken her if you must!' A short pause. 'Hello, darling, Max here.'

'Anything new?'

'I shall be coming home tomorrow, after all, there's no need to do anything.'

'Everything's all right, then?'

'Quite all right.' He paused tiredly. 'I'm even promoted General-Major.'

'What's that? I'm sorry, darling, I didn't hear you right.'

'Forget it, I'll tell you when I get back.' He rubbed his eyes. 'G'night, liebchen.' Kierzner cut the line, wearily kicked off his boots and dragged the eiderdown over his tiredness. It kept him sleeping right through an air-raid alert, and the not so distant krump of bombs bracketing the Oranienburg oil refineries.

The Ju. 52 bucketed back to Copenhagen through weather that seemed to be growing worse by the hour. Kierzner tried to quieten his nervous stomach by taking over the controls from the Flieger Leutnant for most of the flight north; steering an accurate compass course through driving cloud and mist; circuiting low over the city; lining up for a smooth wheeler landing.

If Bethmann felt any disappointment at Kierzner's sudden reappearance, then he kept it well out of sight as he stepped into his chief's office and rammed his heels together. 'Congratulations, Herr General!' Kierzner glanced up and biliously waved him at a chair while he went on playing with a glass of Seltzer water. 'Everything in order while I was away?'

'Nothing to report, Herr General!'

'No Incidents?'

'No Incidents.'

'No parachute reports?'

'No parachute reports.'

'That's something at least.' Kierzner fell silent while Bethmann quietly tested the air for hostile vibrations. 'Tell me, Bethmann, what exactly would you do to become an Oberstleutnant?' The golden question swooped down without warning. 'An Oberstleutnant?'

'Yes—blast you!—an Oberstleutnant.' Kierzner sounded out of stomach. 'It should look very decorative after the war, when you get back your old police job. You'd be an ex-SS Lieutenant-Colonel. Such a thing might swing you a Chief-Inspector's hat; there's even an outside chance it'd make a someone of you!'

'Oh, I shall do my best, Herr General! You may count on me

78

to do my very best!' The man's obvious excitement made Kierzner squirm; he got ready to let Bethmann have it right between the legs. 'Very well, my heartiest congratulations!' He paused acidly. 'I'm promoting you Oberstleutnant, acting unpaid, with effect from now. I'm also appointing you Chief of Staff to the GOC Festung Wotan; my congratulations once again!'

'Permit me, Herr General, where *is* Festung Wotan?'

'At the moment it's contained within the four walls of this office.' Kierzner paused for another slug of the Seltzer water. He glanced up. 'That—unfortunately for us both—is no joking matter!' Bethmann's timid smile died the death. 'Because DRG has that Schwarzwald rating, Copenhagen—and particularly the Mercur factory—has been declared a Fortress Area, with all the trimmings. Failure to defend it against the enemy will mean decimation for the garrison survivors and death for every member of the staff! *Every* member.

'Let one saboteur within viewing distance of that factory and we shall *both* get a night call—so kindly shelve those ambitious dreams you've been hugging. From this moment, Bethmann, we shall work together or we shall hang together.' He paused without a trace of humour, got to his feet and went over to a huge wall map. He jerked down the light toggle. 'Come here!

'By tomorrow noon at latest I shall have three full companies of Deathshead Assault Troops drafted up from Kiel; prepare suitable billeting for them in this area, here!' He dragged his index finger in a rough circle round the Mercur factory. 'Institute a twenty-four-hour watch rota; messing; telecommunications; Luftwaffe liaison!

'Order VI Korps pioneers to erect another wire perimeter, immediately and in greater depth—use the Führer Prinzep if Pannenburg has anything to say.' Kierzner paused for breath. 'Prepare for the immediate rescreening of all Danish personnel working in or around the factory area; issue new passes; cancel all old ones; intensify physical search both in and out.' Bethmann rocked under the bombardment of commands.

'Order—no!—*request* the fullest co-operation by Professor Doktor Hoertl and all senior members of his staff—remind them of my Führer Authority if they show signs of growing restive.' Kierzner's mouth snapped shut. He evaluated the other man. 'You *do* understand your orders, Oberstleutnant?'

'Herr General!'

'Then why are you standing there, wasting time! Go to work!'

CHAPTER EIGHT

SHEPHERD ducked in from the pelting rain, kicking their billet door shut. He nodded at the other two men and went over to the iron-bellied stove on its concrete plinth in the middle of the hut. Erikssen abruptly stopped working on his Sten and folded from the bunk. 'Where did that come from?' He was hard, nervy and suspicious tonight.

'Out there.'

'I didn't see any.'

'I'm not surprised,' Shepherd dumped the ripped planking in an empty coke tub and started shredding a security notice on the wall, 'it's locked and guarded.' He finished what he was doing, looked round and beat Erikssen to the next question. 'Got a match?'

'Got a match, what!'

'Got a match—friend.'

'Got a match, *sir*!'

'All right, have it your own way.' Shepherd fussed with the tinder and searched his own pockets. 'Only remember I'm more likely to help a friend than a "sir"—so take your pick.' He glanced up very sharply. 'And unless you want to stay cold and wet, start passing me those bits of wood!'

'Where've they come from, Sapper!'

'Stop it f'Chrissake!' the little man shouted back at Erikssen's knees. 'From the bloody lavatory, where else!'

The Warrant-Officer was tired and worried; his normally very astute judgement gave way. 'On—your—feet! I'm having you for this! I'll have you for so many things you'll still wonder what hit you when you're wheeled out!'

'Balls.'

'Wilful Destruction of Army Property *and* Gross Insubordination! Quite a Janker Sheet, Sapper!'

'Balls.' Shepherd looked up without feeling. 'Who's worried about five bobsworth of thunderbox in a war costing three million quid a day?' He began feeding bits of wood down the stove's throat. '*I'm* not. The Army's not. And if you've any sense, neither will you!'

80

'Quite a good point.' Both Erikssen and Shepherd turned round abruptly at the third voice, dark and cool. Meyer finished pinching out his cigarette stub, then swung down from the top bunk. 'I agree with you, nobody will notice or even care.'

'Oh, they won't, won't they?' Erikssen stacked his shoulders. 'And what do we mean by that, Corporal?' He waited a second. '*I've* this hut on charge. *I'm* the one who carries the bucket. *I'm* not signing for any of *your* breakages!'

'You worry yourself far too much,' Meyer observed, steadying one end of a stolen telephone flex for Shepherd to knot over the stove. He glanced back at the angry, and baffled, Dane. 'Very soon we'll all be gone away from here—and after that it won't matter, will it?'

Erikssen—outnumbered and speaking another language which couldn't scare this couple—did the unexpected. He shrugged a hand through his skimpy yellow hair. 'Oh well, what the hell! You could be right, you could be wrong.' He knocked the stove open and looked in at the flaring wood. 'We'd better fix some coke, and quick about it.'

'Something else we should've been issued with today,' Shepherd grunted, strangling his socks with the flex. He scowled. '*You're* supposed to be in charge, you say?' Erikssen gently picked his teeth and watched grey smoke eddy round the stove lid. He glanced up after a long moment. 'NCO's get screwed for what isn't—not what is. Lesson number one after seventeen goddam years in this goddam army.'

'Naturally,' Meyer cut in, 'but it doesn't solve our problem.' He turned to Shepherd. 'The fuel compound is guarded?'

'Aye.'

'So we must look elsewhere.' He lit another cigarette with a spill from the stove. 'Fortunately, while you both waited for our Mr Morgan to finish his breakfast in the Officers' Mess—speaking of which,' he turned to Erikssen, 'why are *you* eating and sleeping with the so-called Other Ranks?'

Erikssen shook his head in a wet sneeze. 'To keep you company. To try making something gel round here. To find some team spirit someplace.' He flagged a handkerchief. 'God alone knows there's little enough just now.'

'Morgan told you?'

'Officers like that,' he blew and tiredly patted his nose, 'can't tell me anything about my job.' Erikssen looked up, tired and worn. 'This *is* my job, Corporal. I'm Joe Doakes who guides unwilling soldiers through blood, crud and corruption without too many mishaps.'

81

'You get paid for doing it.'

'Thank you, Sapper.'

'Don't mention it.'

'Of course,' Meyer cut in again, 'but as I was telling you only a moment ago, *I* went for a walk. I found at least six tons of good coal behind a fence near the officers' kitchen.' He puffed smoke and dug through the leg pocket on his tan parachute overalls. 'Fortunately I kept my wire-cutters,' he palmed them like a conjurer, 'so we should be able to carry a sack apiece.' Meyer coughed discreetly, tugged on his groundsheet and led the way out.

They managed about one and a half hundredweight between them and humped it back to the billet, one of a small jerry-built hutment kept well away from the school's main block. Shepherd took some time rinsing off the coal dust with cold water, before coming in from the ablutions shed.

Meyer and Erikssen had stoked up the Caliban stove and strung most of their damp clothing along the flex. They'd squatted down on upturned fire-buckets, quietly nursing cigarettes. Erikssen pulled his alight and glanced sideways at the troll-like German. 'Don't you *ever* run out of smokes?'

'No.'

'What's the secret? My ration won't last more than a couple of days at the outside.'

'These are wages.' Meyer drooped his eyelids. 'I earn them.'

'Wages? What for?'

'Entertaining.'

'I don't get you.'

'It's really very simple, my dear Erikssen.' He swallowed smoke. 'You see, whenever the officer corps wants an inexpensive laugh—which is quite often—they send out for Doctor Meyer And His Piano. They're quite willing to pay for the privilege with cigarettes, or butter, or something useful.' He shrugged. 'I've found one can live without pride—but not without tobacco.'

'That was your act in vaudeville?' Erikssen was interested.

'Please?'

'I said, that was your act? Your turn in the theatre? That Doctor bit?'

'Yes.'

Erikssen stood up and rescued his trousers from scorching on the stove-pipe as Shepherd came over and stripped off, hanging the itchy woollen shirt to air with his socks and battledress. 'Want one?' Meyer offered up a packet of twenty Gold Flake from his last public performance.

'Nuh-huh.' Instead, Shepherd sat on his heels and started unwrapping something in an old brown paper. They watched him brush bits of fluff from a link of beef sausages, a cube of margarine, some cut bread and a jar of piccalilli. He leaned across and began scrubbing the fire-shovel fairly clean with the screw of paper. 'Another present; the kitchen ventilator was left open; care to join me for supper?'

Erikssen enjoyed the gritty hamburger—in spite of himself. He chewed away and tried sizing up the other two men. Meyer—ugly, cold, calculating. Shepherd—whispy, cruel, rat-fast. Neither reminded him of anyone else he'd ever seen in the Army, Canadian or British; he tiredly puzzled how he could've fallen among these bandits in the first place. Shepherd was still frying the odd seventh sausage for himself as Erikssen licked his fingers clean and started finding out. 'What's your trade in Civvy Street, Shep?' The little man glanced up. 'What do you do for a living, outside?'

'Engineering.' His Midland twang bent the middle syllable.

'Uh-huh.' Erikssen nodded. 'Married? Got any kids?'

'Not now.'

He shrugged the tone away and carried on, trying very hard to pull these unlikely people together. He nodded up at their battledresses, a pair of fraying Airborne wings stitched over each left breast-pocket. 'How come you're in this lot?'

'If I'd the mind to, I could ask you the same question.'

'True,' the Dane grinned affably, 'but I got there first for once.'

'All right.' Shepherd flipped the sausage to see what was happening underneath. He looked up. 'I wanted to.'

'This isn't the first time you've been in uniform, is it?' Erikssen looked shrewd. 'I watched you go over that obstacle course. Nobody taught you in just two months' recruit camp, or up at that place in Scotland, did they?' Shepherd speared the sausage with his claspknife and lopped the crispy end with uneven teeth. Erikssen sighed. 'Was it the First War?'

'No.'

'Well where the hell *did* you learn? And where did you pick up that trick shooting?' Shepherd chewed and slowly emptied his mouth. 'That BEM must've taken some getting.' He looked at the ribbon under Erikssen's wings. 'Been in the Army a long time?' He took the hint.

'Since 1925.' He sucked his teeth and thought of other things. 'I imagined it'd be better than starving to death on a farm, knee deep in corn nobody could buy.' He thought some more. 'But

83

what the hell, anyway. How about you?' He turned to Meyer. 'What brings *you* here?' Meyer went on smoking.

'Jezuz O'God—not another wit!' He stood and tiredly felt how his socks were coming along. He looked down after a moment. 'What shall we talk about, then?' Meyer jetted smoke at the stove. 'Try the war, and the next couple of weeks, it concerns us all.' He drew on the cigarette. 'And Morgan. Particularly Morgan.'

'Why?'

'He's nervous.' Meyer talked with the stove. 'He's tense. He's worried. He's also supposed to be our leader.'

'You noticed?'

'Of course. He deliberately ignored at least four points in the Question and Answer session. Very odd.'

'Could be you're right.'

'Could be I am.'

'And he loves that goddam cable conduit ...'

'You don't?'

'I didn't say that!' Erikssen abruptly splayed his palm in the air between them. 'I'll go along just so far. It's as good as any other way he's found—and any amount better than blowing the wire belt.' He paused, thinking. 'That conduit's all right.'

'Even though nobody's sure where the bloody thing goes to?' Shepherd chipped in, flat and terse. Erikssen turned irritably. 'He's going to find that out; you heard him!'

'I heard.'

'OK, so why didn't you speak up if you're so smart? You had a chance just like the rest of us!'

Shepherd finished the sausage, wiped the knife-blade on his left boot and carefully worked the fat into its wrinkles. He looked up. 'I haven't any better ideas, if you must know, but that doesn't mean I have to *like* what's being done to us. I don't like *any* of it.' He snapped the knife shut. 'But let me tell you one thing—I do know when there's a cock-up happening to me!' He turned to Meyer. 'What about you?'

'Me?' He stretched to his feet and had a good scratch. 'I'm going to brush my teeth, read my prayers, get my head down. If, once that's happened, anything disturbs my sleep, I shall get up and reluctantly see to it.'

'Attaboy, Tarzan.'

'Please don't make the easy mistake of thinking I wouldn't,' Meyer continued in his precise, academic English—carefully grinding out the cigarette and storing its tiny stub in a cough

84

lozenge tin. He looked back at Shepherd. 'However, I'm sure you've more sense.' He paused again, waited for a comment, then turned and went across for his toilet kit—hanging with the Sten and rain-stiff webbing behind his bunk.

CHAPTER NINE

DEANE phoned up from London well before breakfast. He sounded troubled and more than usually irritable. 'Harry?'

'Sir?'

'How's your team coming along now?' Morgan switched the receiver to his other hand, picked up the towel again and continued dabbing his face dry. 'I'd say we were progressing, little by little.'

'Oh?' The Brigadier sounded as if he'd lived through a restless night, too. He coughed down the line.

'How's the training going, Harry?' Morgan frowned at the tone; Deane was setting a spring-mine for him. 'After only one day of training,' he laid the stress as thick as it would spread, 'they can all go over the assault models without confusing their feet, or getting lost.'

'I'm very glad to hear you say that.' Deane stopped awkwardly. 'I'm glad, because that's all the training they're going to have.'

'What?'

'You've had all the time there is now.'

'Come off it!'

'I'm sorry you feel that way about things, Morgan!'

'I'll bet you bloody well are! We can't go—just like that—with only ONE DAY'S TRAINING! You *must* be wrong!'

'Control yourself!' Deane's voice was thin and distorted by a bad Scrambler connection. 'I've done everything in my power to get you extra time—but the Cabinet Office isn't listening any more.' He paused. 'They won't see yours as an isolated attack; they deliberately confuse it with the first attempt. Someone's added the two periods together and made weeks, he won't wait any longer for results. You're on, even if you don't know all your lines.' Morgan shrugged tiredly at the telephone. 'When do they expect us to go?'

'Eight Group are sending a Stirling down to Tempsford. Weather permitting, you'll go tonight.'

'And the Reception Committee? Or hasn't anyone had time to arrange that, just yet?'

'The Danes know you're coming soon. We'll get the BBC to

86

slip in your rendezvous group at the end of their nine o'clock bulletin.'

'That's very kind of everyone.' Deane knew this voice; he tried smooth talk as an antidote. 'I'm really sorry things have turned out like this, Harry, I wouldn't have wished this on anyone, believe me.' Morgan abruptly clamped down the receiver, blinked and hurried back to the bathroom. The sour flush of nausea left him quite quickly. He straightened up, carelessly spooned fruit salts in a tooth glass, topped it under the cold tap and gulped it empty. The telephone shrilled again, but for a long time he continued to sit on the edge of the bath, studying the unravelled end of his pyjama cord with quiet fascination.

They took Erikssen, Meyer and Shepherd to the fenced-in Equipment Section where a Staff-Sergeant was waiting under a porch. 'Are you the Knightsbridge types?' Erikssen nodded curtly. 'Right, follow me.'

He led them inside the building, along a brown linoleum corridor spotted with fire-buckets and reeking of mothballs. 'In there.' He pushed a door and let them through. Two other men, in unmarked uniform, were impatiently marking time. 'Are these the men, Sarn't?' one of them asked tersely.

'Yessir.'

'Good, and about time too.' He glanced down at his clipboard to check something. 'Right, now pay attention to me! Strip off everything—clothes, watches, rings, ID tags, the lot. Stack them on that table.'

In less than an hour they were dressed again, only this time in used, dark worsted suits; flannel shirts and plain ties; shapeless tweed caps and thick-soled walking shoes—all issued from stock with the right stitching, buttons and continental name patches sewn inside. The tailor took a moment longer, chalking alterations over their soiled raincoats, chanting out the fittings to an assistant. He spoke through a mouthful of pins. 'Note the large pockets, gentlemen,' he said, beckoning Meyer over to the light. 'Our clients like them extra roomy, we find. You'll see I've stitched in elastic loops here, and here, to stop the grenades fouling—and to hold down the arming lever if you like to carry them de-pinned. I've also, bend your elbow a bit more, sir.' Meyer did as he was told. 'I've also cut the left arm nice and comfortable— the issue shoulder holster is really too big in my opinion.' He clicked his fingers at Meyer. 'You can turn round now, sir, thank you. Anyhow, you're the best judges of that, but I think I've overcome the problem by simply letting out a pair of back seams . . .'

87

The photographers were just as quick, deftly blurring time with cosmetics to match the dates on their passes and ration cards. Shepherd was a problem, but in the end a hair-piece, rouge, skill and a lining brush took him back to thirty-five again for one document.

More taciturn and anonymous people were waiting for them in the next building, a small warehouse divided down the middle by a long, smooth-topped bench of the kind used by parachute packers. Yellow crayon lines had been drawn, dividing part of it into three boxes—they were each told to stand facing a box.

'Class One equipment, first!' an elderly man called out to his staff. He began reading off a list of articles from his clipboard, pausing as they hurried them over from the shelves and dropped them in their first present—a cheap, well-used fibre suitcase. It turned into a mad, unbalanced birthday party where Danish soap and German razors, cigarette lighters and spring-blade knives, ox-hide shoulder rigs and new Colt .380 automatics were awarded as the prizes in this deadly charade. '...L capsules.'

One of the assistants brought over a shallow wooden tray of silver signet rings in various sizes and styles; she flipped up one of the seals and dropped out a small, rubber-coated tablet. 'The Lethal Capsule; potassium cyanide; effective in five to ten seconds once it's crushed between the teeth.' She looked at the three complete strangers. 'Would you care to try one for size, gentlemen?' They hesitated; she went on softly and persuasively. 'We're told they can be a very great help, at certain times.' Meyer nodded and slowly reached out for one, then Erikssen, then Shepherd.

'Hurry up and get your cases packed. Quickly now!' The stores officer handed out the receipts for them to sign. They did as they were told and followed him into the Technical Equipment Section. They hurried Erikssen through without stopping, but Meyer and Shepherd were each shown into separate cubicles where their specialist kits were stacked on tables, waiting for them to check and initial out.

Meyer sat astride a chair and scrupulously circuit-tested his Mk. III transmitter/receiver—the airborne model built in the bottom of a commercial traveller's case. He demanded, and got, another set of valve spares, a gutta-percha flask of sulphuric acid for the second accumulator and another specific-gravity measure —three things which didn't like parachuting either.

They put Shepherd in the next cubicle but one. He was more tight-lipped and dour by the time he'd started to unsnap the four satchels of RDX, proving that each of the soft, marzipan slabs of

88

explosive was properly wrapped and sealed in waxed paper. 'Get me the detonators and primacord spools,' he ordered, without looking up.

'All of it?'

'Aye, you bloody nitwit!'

The assistant hurried back with the fuzing packets and spools of slug-white cord. Shepherd took an impossibly long time over this—fingering every inch, looking for breaks and chafing, completely ignoring the other man's aching impatience, gently repacking the delicate timers and lead azide initiators to his own, very personal satisfaction.

'Ready now?' Shepherd nodded and scrawled a chit for the stuff before going into a fair-sized room where Meyer and Erikssen were waiting around with Morgan.

'Right, chaps, sit down and listen to me.' Morgan moved to face them, still in uniform, hands tightly knotted behind his back. 'The waiting's over. Our performance yesterday, plus the fact that this operation can't be delayed much longer, has decided the matter for us—weather permitting we go tonight.

'Now,' he went on, a shade too briskly, 'you've all been issued with your things, it's all in order?' He turned to Meyer. 'There's nothing wrong with yours, I hope?'

'Not yet there isn't, but this is too sudden for me and it'll seem that way to the Receiving Station as well.' He looked annoyed. 'I've a brand-new Mk. III; it will take hours to put it exactly so; the RS still has to note my key on this particular set.'

'That's unfortunate. I can appreciate your problem, of course, but there are some things which we shan't be able to do according to the book. This is one of them. Anyhow, the chances are good we won't even need a radio link.' He waited for Meyer to look satisfied. 'Well? What else is bothering you now?'

'When do I get to work on the call signs and frequency changes? They can't be left undecided.'

'I realise that too, you know. I shall see to it that you're given some time later on today.' Morgan grew stern. 'I also realise that we should all like more time to familiarise ourselves with the target and with our equipment, but it just can't be done. So,' he went on talking, 'let's decide to make the most of what we do have which, incidentally, is plenty. And you can all take heart from the fact that this is scheduled to be a lightning raid. There'll be no hanging around once we reach the other side. Half our usual precautions and checks won't ever be put to the test.' He made another brittle smile and picked up a sheaf of foolscap.

89

'This is your programme for the rest of the day, so pay attention. In a few minutes you'll be given your new identities, the papers and a full biography—this *must* be learnt by heart. After that you'll be examined till you are word perfect, which takes us through to mid-afternoon. Transport will then come and pick us up for the journey out to the holding area where we'll have our final briefing, tea and—if we've a bit of time left over—rest.' He glanced at his notes again. 'Then we'll be taken to the airfield and readied for take-off at 22.00 hours.' He looked round at his team. 'Any questions so far?

'Good, then come this way.' Morgan led them into the raw air and over to a large hut standing apart from the others. He ushered them inside and showed each man a plain, harshly lit room out of sight, and nearly out of sound of the others on either side. Erikssen sat down at the smudged deal table and waited for something to happen. After a short while Morgan came back with a staff major carrying a canvas security bag locked to one wrist.

'Erikssen?' Morgan nodded for him. 'You're in luck. We've been able to use your existing name and many of the particulars without much alteration.' He started to lay packets of papers on the table. 'Identity and ration cards; social security and state pension.' He tapped each one in turn. 'I've given you a full driving licence—motor-cycle as well as car—you might find it handy. This is your Electricians' Union card—fully paid up to the end of the quarter. Wallet, money and exam sheet.' He laid the last thing in front of Erikssen. 'Memorise the facts and be ready for the first questioning in an hour's time. Now,' he concluded, 'check your money and sign here please.'

Erikssen unzipped the black, silk money-belt and riffled through sudden wealth—five thousand Danish Crowns, some small change and ten pounds in gold sovereigns. 'I'd keep that back for unexpected bribes,' the Major commented, taking the signed receipt book. Morgan led the man along to the next room and left Erikssen in peace.

He carefully recounted the money and pushed most of it back in the belt, leaving only the small change to drop in his pocket and a couple of hundred kroner, in tens, for his wallet. He flicked it open and stopped short, a slow grin moving across his wind-burnt face. Under a celluloid window, opposite his ID card, the unseen experts had slipped in a startlingly frank print of a very attractive, sunlit girl—half lying, half sitting in long grass. 'I shall remember you always—Kirsten,' he read, in Danish, across one corner. The grin changed, became deeper as he realised what

90

she was there for—if ever his papers were checked by the Militia or Police, her knowing smile could drift a lot of attention off the forgeries opposite. Very neat, he thought, this world of cheats and liars, thieves and murderers, was being directed by people with brain power. It made him feel much better.

The Major had been right, the life story was easy for him. They'd changed his place of birth, of course, since he'd be now operating in Copenhagen; this way there would be a natural delay in getting the facts if ever the police rounded him up. The English had known his mother was originally from Aalborg—it must have been on his enlistment forms—so they'd made out all his papers for the Aalborg commune, too. They'd also made him into an Electrical Fitter's Mate—he knew enough about simple electricity to fob that one off. All in all they'd done a fine job on the rebuilt Erikssen. Only one thing kept him thoughtful—his language. Close on twenty years in Canada, with only one or two months' holiday in Denmark, had dulled his hearing. He knew it; he worried.

The new biography wasn't so easy for Shepherd. He was now a Norwegian engine mechanic looking for work in Copenhagen with special permission from the German labour organisation in Central Norway. He also carried a useful pin-up in an old wallet stuffed with bills from shops in Bergen; a creased Oslo tram ticket, three months out of date; a few letters and some blurred family snapshots to colour up his new life. The whole pack was held together by a thick rubber band cut from a motor inner-tube. He had to work hard on the question sheet.

Meyer had the toughest part to learn. He was now a radio technician with a conveniently blitzed address in Dortmund that should clog official enquiries for days. He was also in transit to a secret defence site in the tundra of Arctic Norway—something else which should bug accurate questioning. His papers laid a special stress on an impeccable Party record, and he had some important-looking cards and a gilt lapel badge to prove their truth. The English had done their best, he realised, but Meyer was sceptical. A bead of sweat teetered down the tip of his nose, hesitated and then abruptly splashed off. It raised a bump on his exam sheet. He knew what to expect. The SS, or Gestapo, or Kripo would reserve him for special interrogation. Berlin had a complete dossier, fingerprints, photos, the lot. He'd still be dying long after the others had been broken up, carried away and shot. Nobody would be nearly so merciful with Solomon Meyer.

Morgan had been right, they weren't finished with their biographies till well into the afternoon. With the short exception of

91

a ten-minute break for tea and bloater-paste sandwiches, they'd been questioned, screamed at and all but thrashed by a fierce team of skilled interrogators in Gestapo-style plain clothes. They'd screwed up the pressure till the right answers whipped back without thought or hesitation; three men in leather topcoats and black Homburgs who really knew their business; three men working against time like everyone else in the school to get Knightsbridge ready and away.

Morgan had finally chosen to be a French agricultural buyer visiting Denmark to study fat-stock production—something so vague it barely threw a shadow. He was far from happy with the way things were being rushed through. It stank. The whole plan stank from beginning to end. He chewed the inside of his mouth and unconsciously began to pray. He prayed that they might find the factory; break the wire; do their stuff, and get over to Sweden without any delay. If they did that; if they were quick enough and lucky enough; if. Another acid flush started up his gullet; he spun and barged into the open, all but running down the school's Commandant and Deane.

'Everything under control, Morgan?' Deane sounded harsh. He couldn't miss the slumped shoulders and sagging face. 'Well?' Morgan turned away from the question, abruptly folded in the middle and convulsively threw up a grey chyme of tea and bloater paste.

The two men held a shoulder apiece and steadied him. The Commandant had a clean handkerchief waiting as he slowly recovered. 'Here, use this. There's some on your nose, and under your chin. That's better.'

'Thanks.' Morgan carelessly wiped himself clean. 'Thanks.'

'You look peaked.' Deane coughed. 'What's happening in there?' Morgan cleared his mouth and spat. 'That to you and the shiny-arsed bastards above you!'

'Colonel!'

'Listen to me for once!' Morgan's voice wobbled under control. 'Listen to me very carefully because this may well be the last time you'll hear from me, or any of us!' He shook. 'It's now three in the afternoon, three in the afternoon, understand? We leave in five hours' time AND MY MEN ARE STILL LEARNING THEIR PARTS.' His voice started to climb sharply. 'Still learning their parts; what sort of murder is this? Dear Jesus Christ, what are you doing to us?' He giggled shrilly. 'A target among the most impossible on this planet!' Morgan stalled on the point of hysteria, waving from side to side, tears streaming down his face, hands limp as Deane pounced, viciously crossing with his right. Morgan

92

jerked over the cinder path, his face splashing water as it hit a puddle. No-one else had seen it happen.

The Commandant knocked Deane aside and gave Morgan an arm to climb up. They didn't speak till he was standing, face the colour of dough except for the gritty mud and a mauve welt on the side of his jaw.

'Get to the sick bay and have that dressed!' Deane hadn't softened one iota. 'And look smart about it!' Morgan stared as if he would gut Deane, then suddenly turned and marched away.

'Was that really necessary, Deane?' the Commandant was coldly furious. 'The man's not fit to be sent operational.'

'I know.' Deane slowly kneaded his right fingers.

'I sincerely hope you do!'

'I know.'

CHAPTER TEN

TIME later a blacked-out ambulance turned off the Huntingdon road and cruised up a deserted track between misty beet and potato fields. Erikssen, Meyer and Shepherd were flaked out on the stretchers, using their suitcases for pillows in the vehicle's one-bulb darkness; Morgan sat up front with the driver, bitter and still in a horrible mood. He fingered the tight swelling under his face and looked sideways at the driving mirror, coldly watching Deane's Humber coming up astern. The Brigadier, it seemed, was making sure no-one defected; no pierhead jumps from the good ship Knightsbridge. Morgan went back to the road ahead, judging from memory how much of it remained before they had to turn off.

A scant hundred yards past a melancholy spinney of dead bracken and young oaks, the driver wheeled hard right into a big woodland where the War Department had put up a stand of Nissen huts on the far side of a small RAF field.

The reception committee wrapped round the new consignment and hurried it from the ambulance to one of the dozen or so tightly shuttered buildings which made up the maximum security area. Morgan stopped at the door and set down his case while Deane almost caught up with him. They turned and walked into the place. Meyer and the others had already begun snooping round a stuffy, overheated room which some humorist had papered with Cook's continental travel posters from a time before the war.

'Sit down and pay attention!' Morgan was curt, unrolling a large-scale, prepared diagram on a chipboard screen. 'This will be our dropping zone tonight—code name Hector. Remember that since it will also be our countersign with the Resistance at the other end. Now, look at these.' He turned sharply and rapped his fist on the diagram. 'They're two lakes. The larger of the pair is called Furesø and it's only a few miles north of Copenhagen proper. However, fortunately for everyone concerned, Hector is separated from the nearest housing, here, by this fairly extensive wood or tree plantation at Ravnsholt, here!' He thumped the diagram again.

'We shall go out at minimum altitude, landing at 03.30 hours,

94

calculated on a maximum delay of just thirty minutes. In other words, we mustn't land any later than 04.00 hours. It's quite a narrow field, grassy and apparently used for cattle pasturage which means a good, sprain-free landing for once. And, for once, there aren't any fencing stakes or high-tension cables. Now, bearing in mind that it is narrow, once you've cleared the bomber get your descent trimmed to miss the lake on one hand, and the wood on the other—both should be quite visible against the ground mass. There won't be any spare time, so get it done quickly, and get it done well.' He damped his lips.

'We're taking in a full load of arms and other stuff for the King Frederik Group—our hosts—which should help pay the rent for the time we're staying with them. It's been packed in five cylinders, with our own gear in the one lit by a green marker. Remember, ours will be green—the rest will have red markers!' Morgan unconsciously reached into his groin to ease his underpants.

'We shall all zero on the marker while you, Meyer, get the radio out ready to move off with the rest of us to Lyngby station, here.' He pointed out a plainly drawn rail track which ran from the woods and slanted past Hector. 'Note the bearing, 130 degrees, in case you should be separated in the darkness and so have to make your own way there. No matter,' he went on tersely, 'you won't go far wrong if you face the lake and then bear left to the small path, here, then bear right again. The station is just over two miles from the DZ. Come what may,' Morgan pitched his voice a shade too high, 'we must be on the first workman's train into the city when it leaves Lyngby at 04.45. Stick close to your guide and let him do all the talking. While you're on the train, do not smoke, do not speak, do not even think!' He paused. 'Pretend to be asleep and stay that way till your guide tells you otherwise, understand? Any questions so far?' Shepherd pushed up to his feet. 'Yes?'

'Shall I move the demo-bags the same time as Meyer's getting his stuff?'

'No. They're obviously far too bulky—even if the plastic didn't stink to high heaven. You'll have to collect them later, when we're ready. The Resistance is going to cache everything, which reminds me,' he turned to Erikssen, 'you get over to the cylinder as fast as possible and be ready to cover up for Meyer. Remember he can't speak Danish; there could be an unpleasant accident unless someone's there to explain him.' Erikssen nodded.

'All right? Anything else? You're clear on your frequencies and procedure now, Meyer?' The man made an abrupt move-

95

ment which could have been a nod. Morgan slowly faced Deane, standing a little to one side, fingers knotted round his malacca cane. 'Is there anything you would like to add,' he paused a measurable time, 'sir?'

'Yes, there is, and I'll make it short.' He stepped up and cleared his throat. 'It's no exaggeration to say that success is vital this time—there can be no repeat performance. It *must* be rammed home, successfully and with the maximum effort because, now, no price is too high to pay for the destruction of this target. Remember that, whatever you may be called upon to do.' He paused, softening his voice a fraction.

'I shan't insult you by minimising the risk. In this sort of work risk is the norm—you knew that in the beginning. But, you know, nothing is really proof against determined men—no matter what the enemy may think. And you are lucky that, in Colonel Morgan, you have a most skilled and experienced leader. A leader with more knowledge of this target, and of this kind of target, than any other man I know. Between you I cannot imagine any obstacle yet built remaining an obstacle for very long.' He stopped and glanced sideways at Morgan.

'But there is one last thing I have to mention before I leave you.' He coughed harshly. 'One last thing. Colonel Morgan also knows a great deal about other matters; matters that would be of the greatest value if ever they were known by the enemy; they must never be found out. As a result you will all have a duty— and in this *I* am the one giving the orders—you will all have a duty to help Colonel Morgan first in the event of capture by the enemy. The precise nature of that help I shall leave to your discretion. Only remember one thing, he must never be interrogated by them. Now,' he rounded off, 'it only remains for me to wish you all a safe and successful return, good luck and Godspeed.' He turned and left the room rather abruptly.

Morgan took his place. 'So that's it,' he sneered. 'Nice to know who's helping who, isn't it?' He rolled the diagram and put it away. 'On your feet! Let's go and get your parachutes and overalls sorted out!'

None of this took very long, maybe half an hour at most. Even the meal—ham with two eggs, chipped potatoes and processed peas for Morgan, Erikssen and Shepherd; a large cheese omelette for Meyer—even the meal passed in a quick, nervous silence. Each man sat alone in his most private thoughts. Now and again someone grunted or spoke half a sentence as he reached out for salt or more bread. They ate well by civilian ration standards,

96

but no-one would ever remember what it looked like, or how it tasted.

One of the permanent staff came into their small canteen and discreetly marched up to Morgan. 'Squadron-Leader Dewar to see you now, sir.' Morgan slowly looked up from his plate where he'd been cutting squiggly patterns in the congealed fat with his fork. 'Thank you.' He nodded after a moment and pushed away from the table. He stood undecided, then looked down at the others. 'There's still a good couple of hours in hand. Take it easy, but don't go outside the hut area, that's bad form in this place. What you don't see you won't know.' He turned and followed the staff man along to another blank-eyed room and shook hands with a young RAAF pilot. 'Well? What's the final verdict?'

'Touch and go. It's flyable only if the clag doesn't get any nearer the ground.'

'I see.' Morgan sounded all balled-up inside. 'What's the future in Copenhagen?'

'Murky,' the Australian grunted. 'Our Met jokers promise stratus from a thousand feet up most of the way, with rain and squalls across the North Sea. Hopeful to the last they say it could ease over the Danish islands by dawn.'

'Nothing else?'

'No.'

'What about the wind?'

'Light; 140; veering south. Glory hallelujah it's nowhere near your fifteen-knot limit.' Morgan nodded and tiredly wiped his face. 'All right, put us down for some tickets—we'll travel with you tonight.'

'A very good idea, if I may say so. We're now the oldest company operating the line.' They shook hands again before the staff man escorted Dewar away from the area.

Morgan was alone now. He breathed out quite slowly and spread his fingers wide, watching their tremor with a detached fascination. His head split across the eyes and a lunatic cinema projectionist had taken root behind his left temple, whirring chewed up scraps of memory against the white walls of his skull. The tremor intensified and worked back along his wrists. He let them fall away and tiredly walked out into the rainy darkness to find himself a dry tree he could prop up.

The three others finished their meal in silence and drifted away from the table one by one. Erikssen dourly plumped a pillow from his smock and parachute pack before cautiously stretching out on one of the bare iron bed frames. For a short while he tried to get away through a two-year-old *Picture Post*

97

someone had forgotten to put out for salvage. He lost interest in a half-remembered world, humped over and faced the wall. Within seconds he'd drifted asleep.

Shepherd pushed into the room with a mug of tea, set it down on the table and looked round for something. He found Erikssen's *Picture Post* and opened it flat under the single light bulb while he sat down at the table and took a long pull at the tea. He leafed through the old weekly for a few moments, lost interest and reached into his clothes for the new Colt .380.

Factory new; nicely balanced and nicely finished; a real Yank job of work with no rough edges anywhere; that looted Mauser in Finland hadn't been a patch on this.

Shepherd drained the mug dry, pushed it away and began to strip down the Colt, methodically laying its pieces across the front cover of *Picture Post*, holding each one to the light, testing its fit before wiping off the packing grease with a stray rag.

Too much of this and she'll clog with fluff and dirt. There won't be a second chance with a misfire. The first one out and shooting wins the big box of chocolates. Morgan ran into a doorpost by the look of his face—who did that, and why?

This whole effort stinks of slapdash organisation. That Brigadier and his pep-talk were real rays of sunshine. How much of that vital success talk was bullshit? *Taurus omnia vincit*—a good motto for Morgan and his sort. Success is vital this time, so success was vital last time, too. Who else twigged it? Not Erikssen. When Morgan orders him, he'll obediently hop on the shovel. Nor Meyer. That one's fast enough for ten others—but English isn't his first language.

Shepherd concentrated on hooking the fat brass shells from his Colt's magazines—standing them on end in two rows, seven a line. He began polishing each one as Meyer came in, moodily kicking the door shut.

For a moment he wandered around like a restless thunderhead looking for a church spire, then drifted across to the table and twiddled round one of the chairs; sitting down, arms along the back, watching Shepherd work. He fumbled inside his pocket for a cigarette, one of the rough-tasting German Alphas now that he couldn't use British brands any more, and thoughtfully lit up.

Shepherd had gone back to his pistol, thumbing the gleaming shells against its hard springs. He palmed the heavy magazine into the Colt's grip and slapped it shut. 'What are you doing?' Shepherd looked up. 'What's it look like to you?'

'You handled that as if you're accustomed to such things,'

98

Meyer went on being blandly conversational. Shepherd was quite equal to that tone. 'Happen I might be.'

'I thought so—I can generally tell an expert hand when I see one at work.' Shepherd didn't reply at once. Instead, he used Meyer's discarded matchstick to clean out the ridged grips on the cocking slide. He looked up for a moment. 'That must be pleasant.'

'So so.' He drew smoke and narrowed his puffy eyelids. 'I would say that you've either used one of those a lot, or otherwise been with them.' Shepherd locked the Colt's safety and deftly holstered it in his armpit. He looked at Meyer again. 'What about you?'

'Me?' He thought a moment. 'I regret to say that I've never mastered the knack. To be quite crude, I couldn't hit an elephant even if I jammed the pistol up its backside.'

'Then why have one?' Meyer shrugged. 'I sometimes wonder that myself. I think maybe it gives me a sense of comfort.' He coughed and wearily ground out the cigarette on the table-top. 'These are truly terrible! It's the Roumanian tobacco, you know, an acquired taste.' He looked back at Shepherd. 'You don't smoke, do you?'

'No.'

'You are fortunate, I wish I could leave them alone,' he commented, taking out another Alpha and delicately sniffing at both ends. He glanced up. 'This *is* awful tobacco—it never used to be so bad.' He paused, shrewdly watching Shepherd come to a calculated decision. The faded little man slowly looked him over. 'You're from Germany, aren't you?'

'Yes.' Meyer hoped this wasn't going to upset his plans for Shepherd. 'Does that worry you?'

'No—why should it?'

'We are fighting them at the moment . . .'

'Aye, they tell me it's in all the papers. What part are you from exactly?'

'Heilbronn.'

'That's in Würtemburg, just a bit to the north of Stuttgart, isn't it?'

'Correct, it is in Würtemburg!' Meyer was staggered. 'How did you know?'

'A firm I worked for, in Australia, used to get its larger diameter drill bits from there.' Meyer nodded wistfully. 'That must be a great country to live in, Australia.'

'It can be cold in winter unless you're up North.' He paused.

99

'For most of the time I was mining down in Tasmania. What about you? You're a musician, aren't you?'

'Yes.' Shepherd eyed him, sizing up the heavy shoulders and hairy wrists. He shrugged. 'I took you for a worker at first.' Meyer went for that. 'Just *you* try exercising eight hours a day, seven days a week and see what it feels like! A pianist *works!*' Shepherd nodded, happy to score off Meyer. The other man sensed it and began smiling benignly. 'But what matter? One can inherit a certain build and shape, can't one?'

'Your father was that way?' Meyer made time to think by slowly lighting the cigarette he'd been rolling between his stubby fingers, carefully estimating how much he might need this man in the next few days. 'My father, you said?' He let the smoke gush. 'I can't be certain; he died of fever when I was about six or seven; he was the pharmacist of an Army field hospital somewhere in Mesopotamia.' Meyer drew smoke and wondered if he'd given enough to justify bigger confidences in return. 'Not very dramatic is it? Now, what of yourself?'

'Like how?' Shepherd wasn't taken in by this or any other man. Meyer seemed casual. 'Like, for example, taking after someone—resembling someone, your father or mother, mm?'

'Maybe,' Shepherd was tightly controlled, 'or maybe not. I don't know the answer to that myself—and neither did the nuns who gave me this funny name.' Meyer had a large share of natural tact, he coughed and changed direction. 'How about Australia, then? Will you ever go back there?'

'I doubt it.'

'Where will you go?'

'I haven't decided yet.' Shepherd wasn't being helpful, and he knew it. After a moment's thought he finished off the sentence. 'I don't know, and I don't think I care very much now. In the end I'll probably follow my nose and track upwind to the money; there must be good pickings in South America, still. The Bolivian tin mines perhaps.'

'It's a bad, very rough place to find oneself—a bad climate and worse, much worse.'

'It sounds better—you know it?'

'Only Argentina and Paraguay; I had to come back to Spain.'

'Spain.' Shepherd thought for a moment. 'The war?'

'Yes.'

'Red? Or the other side?'

'Would it make any difference?'

'Could do.' Shepherd was more than usually terse. Meyer drew on his Alpha. 'Let's say I was a little younger, more idealistic perhaps, a Progressive Anarcho-Syndicalist.'

'Red.'

Meyer decided it was time to change the direction of this conversation again; he selected a theme at random. 'You've been around a lot, haven't you? At any time have you ever been *really* happy?'

'Happy?' Shepherd saw this as a trick question. Meyer nodded. 'Yes, happy. That's what most people are seeking, isn't it?'

'I'm not most people. And it sounds like heavy thinking for men in our place, doing what we're doing.'

'Even so, it *is* a perfectly valid question!' Meyer loved to argue. Shepherd sucked his teeth for a moment and looked down at a smudge of dirt on the table. He shrugged. 'Okay, to match up with you—since we intend playing at Intellectuals—I'll answer something like "No man is to be called happy until he's dead"—or whatever it was.' He looked up. 'Rich food for thought while you're waiting to jump over a target.' Meyer was rapidly learning not to be surprised by anything this odd little man said. He was delighted. 'Then you *approve* of Aristotle's view on happiness?'

'Maybe. But take my word for it, much of the rest they claim he said I won't even pretend to understand—so don't try me.' He thought about something else for a short while. 'But if you want a real answer, that makes real sense, then I suppose I came nearest to being happy the time I found a pair of brand-new boots on a Russian officer—bobby-dazzlers made from thick, oak-grained hide; soft and pliant with natural grease.' He grinned slyly at Meyer.

'This Colonel must have pulled them on just especially to come out and meet us. That was very thoughtful of him since we'd been slopping around in foot cloths—bits of sacking and birch bark knotted at the ankles—for well over a couple of months. It was getting to be winter, the air was nippy, my feet were cold. I showed Ivan he could walk just as well in stocking tops as ever I could.' He paused. 'Now, what about you?'

'Me?' Meyer was guarded now that the questions were coming the other way. 'What do you want to know?'

'Anything you care to tell me—I'm not fussy.' Shepherd felt around in his jacket pocket while Meyer thought it over. 'Shall I say that real happiness, for me, is music? And that music, for me, is real happiness? Does that surprise you?'

'Not particularly, it's your work. I've a tin ear myself, but if you like music, then it's quite all right by me.' Shepherd had pulled out his spring-blade knife and started carefully cleaning his nails. He looked up after a moment. 'That's the happiness settled. What about the country?' Meyer smiled distantly at that. 'Which one do you think I should choose?'

'Not Germany.' Meyer nodded. 'Correct, do you give up?'

'Uh huh.'

'Palestine . . .' He waited for some reaction. Shepherd looked up from his knife-point. 'That makes sense, all things considered.' He folded the blade. 'Been there yet?'

'No.' He paused delicately. 'I had to get off at Cyprus for a few months.'

'Illegal immigrant?' Nothing, it seemed, could shake this little Englishman. Meyer nodded again. 'And yet you're now serving with us,' Shepherd studied his nails, 'in this jovial troupe of comedians too.' He smiled oddly. 'Happen I could know of some-one who's learning the practical sort of partisan warfare? While getting paid by the British?'

'You're right—of course.' Meyer gestured casually at their parachutes and stacked equipment. 'All that could be of use, sometime in the future somewhere else.'

'You'll make some country a good citizen.' Meyer coughed and looked round the room. 'There's a board and chessmen on the window-ledge behind you—can you play?'

'I think I'd better,' Shepherd replied dryly. 'This kind of talk could bugger up a potentially great friendship.'

They set out the pieces and drew for first move. Meyer won. He casually turned one of his pawns loose on the enemy; Shepherd countered with an orthodox Sicilian. Meyer slowly nodded to himself and reflexed with a shade more energy. Six moves sprang in near silence before he caught Shepherd's eye. 'You play very well indeed!' That, from Meyer, was praise. 'Would you mind telling me where you learnt?'

Shepherd sat back, rolling a captured bishop between his palms. 'A lot of the trickery came with those boots I was talking about a moment ago.' Meyer nodded, almost as if he'd expected this. 'Ivan and me used to play by the hour at one time. It didn't seem fair, of course, since he now wore my foot cloths—and I his boots, but,' he shrugged, scanning Meyer's lines of battle, 'that's the way the world turns.'

'I suppose so, I suppose so.' Meyer dodged his surviving bishop out of trouble and glanced back across the board. 'And yet he still played with you?' Shepherd grinned a little. 'You heard me wrong—I played with Ivan. *I* played with *him*. There's a lot of difference.'

102

'Oh?'

'Oh yes.' Shepherd scratched his nose for a moment. 'If he didn't beat me at chess, and so teach me all he knew, he didn't get fed. At first he got half a regular prisoner's allowance, but towards the end of our time together he was gaunt.' He paused to review his game's strategy. After a moment he went on just as affably. 'He knew what it was like to be *really* hungry—it made him fight like a lunatic for every move. I learned a lot, and he put a bit of spice in an otherwise dull game.' Meyer had to change the direction of this conversation once again, and quickly. 'Where—how can I say?—where did you meet the Russians?'

'In Karelia mostly.'

'What opinion did you form of the Red Army—from a soldier's point of view that is?' He advanced a knight and looked up again. Shepherd was almost smiling at some private joke. 'Fortunately for us they had a greater number of potato heads than we generally carried along,' he studied the board with interest, 'even so, I wouldn't be in the Germans' frosty mittens for all I could see, not near Moscow at any rate.'

'Why is that?' Meyer said, making his next move. Shepherd abruptly leaned back, mouth sour. 'Because it's now the Russians' turn to fight at home. They might not be too fast in the brain at times. The Red Army's commissars disapprove of original thinking, and they've some pretty vivid ways of showing it, too. But,' he stared at Meyer, 'although Ivan attacking was fun, just like potting a swarm of rabbits, in defence he's superb. We beat the shit out him in Finland, our land. He's going to do the same to the Wehrmacht in Russia, his land.'

'We?' Meyer spoke with a neutral, studied lack of concern. 'You make yourself sound like a Finn.'

'So I was. So I was while I had a home, and a wife, and children.' He glanced down at the board, pointedly killing any other questions. 'And it's your move again.'

The door slapped open a quarter of an hour later and Morgan stamped in. He scowled at the stuffy, poorly lit room. 'Get your things together!' Shepherd went over and shook Erikssen awake. 'Come on, soldier, the war's waiting for you outside.' The Dane grumbled upright, chasing an itch across his scalp, deftly zipping himself in the rot-and-mud-coloured jumping suit before dragging on his loose, canvas overboots. Meyer was the first to finish. He knelt and carefully laced a dull-bladed fighting knife round his right calf muscle, low and ready to hand. No-one spoke till Morgan picked up his padded helmet, the suitcase in its special

103

valise and swung the D-chute across his shoulders. He was still in a savage mood. 'Ready yet, you lot?'

Two staff men went ahead of them into the night where a fifteen-hundredweight Bedford stood waiting, headlights dipped, engine hunting. The four men heaved their packs over the tail-gate and scrambled aboard, instinctively sitting two-a-side on the hard benches. One of the staff jumped up after them and linked together the safety chains; he rapped his knuckles on the drive cab and they moved off down a service road between wet, unseen trees.

It was not a long ride. The Bedford ran out of the woods, across the perimeter track and up to their Stirling's dense silhou-ette, braking gently under the bomber's high, slanting nose. 'Are these the customers for Copenhagen?' the despatcher called up, moving away from the undercarriage leg. The staff man jumped off. 'Five para-cylinders plus four bodies, all told.'

'Right, I'll take them, sport.' The despatcher turned and looked into the truck. 'Come on down, fellahs, we shan't eat you.' The four shapes bumped on the tarmac and off-loaded their kit. 'D'you all understand English?' He paused. 'OK, now listen very carefully, because there won't be any chance to explain once we get moving.'

'I'll be sending you out through the floor. It'll be draughty, but try and get nice and comfortable round the hole; sit with your legs clear and valises ready, get it? Mind your chins on the rim as you go out, but that's all you have to worry about—the rest's up to me. Just you relax and take it easy.' He stopped the slow, reassuring drawl and looked round at their shapes in the gusty darkness. 'All clear?'

The Stirling's tail and mid-upper gunners came down and helped them clamber into the aircraft's belly, barely lit by feeble blue bulbs spaced along the raw metal walls. Their despatcher fussed around, showing them where to find the Elsan, shaking out an old mattress apiece for what was going to be a long and tiring flight.

Dewar and the rest of his crew had already come aboard and gone up for'ard. 'This is some night for aviating, Skipper,' the navigator peeved, settling in with his maps and instruments under the Astrohatch. 'They really want these ones to go.'

'Then it's tough tit on us all,' Dewar grunted acidly, climbing up to the Captain's pedestal seat to the left of his second pilot. It was lighter here, thank God, under the perspex glasshouse. A nervous spray of rain drummed its fingers overhead; it was some night to be dicing with storm and headwind.

104

Dewar dragged the Sutton harness tight and felt around for the intercom jackplug. He hooked up, listening to the static mushing his earphones while he latched the micro-oxygen mask. 'Skipper to crew—come in.' The measured ritual of take-off followed with the cold certainty of eventual death, each man testing and reporting on his station in the bomber. Dewar smoothed on his silk inner-gloves and looked over to the second pilot. 'Ready?'

'Ready to start. Battery accumulator and current on,' he checked from the card. 'Motors primed; extinguishers positioned.'

'Contact port-outer.'

'Contact port-outer.' The Hercules' starter whined; labouring its heavy propeller through a full arc; sucking mixture to each of fourteen cylinders; exploding blue flames and oil smoke astern.

'Oil pressure?'

'Steady at seventy pounds.'

'Oil temperature?'

'Plus forty.'

'Fuel pressure?'

'Steady at five pounds.' Dewar thumbed to transmit. 'P-Peter to Control...'

'P-Peter, you are cleared to taxi. Runway zero-nine; wind one-zero...' Dewar turned his bomber loose; cautiously trundling round the peri-track; braking and turning seventy-thousand pounds deadweight on throttle to spot up zero-nine.

'Mixture?'

'Rich. Friction nuts—locked, tight.'

'Boost?'

'Plus three.'

'Flap, fifteen degrees.'

'Flap, fifteen degrees.' Control cleared Dewar for take-off. He nodded to the second pilot and slipped the brakes.

Morgan and the others dozed uneasily in the vibrating, freezing darkness; stunned by the motors' clamouring drone; sensing the airframe flex as they bored through rain squalls.

All normal time froze still and silently waited outside for them.

Much later, well after midnight, their despatcher came aft, shaking them awake with one hand while the other balanced a Thermos of tomato soup and two rolls of plain biscuit spread with processed cheese.

Dewar gently wristed the Stirling on to his last heading but one, tucking the lights of neutral Sweden under one wing; darkened,

105

occupied Denmark under the other. A few startled sparks of light flak bubbled up from a German destroyer moored in the Sound—but Dewar had passed, lost in the trailing skirts of cloud.

'Steer two-one-zero.'

'Roger.' Dewar cut the coast a scant dozen miles north of Copenhagen, uneasily shying away from the fighters scrambling aloft over Kastrup. 'Dee-Zed in five minutes from—now.'

'Roger.'

A warning bulb started blinking above the men huddled round the exit.

'Bomb doors—open. Release circuits—on.'

'Roger.'

'Left a bit, Skipper. Left. Left. Left again. Railway and lakes dead ahead!'

'Signals?'

'No!'

Dewar charged his bomber across the loom of dark woodland, the backwash of six thousand horsepower blasting the district awake.

'Gunner to Skipper—lights astern!' The Stirling's port wing dipped at the ground, slewing heavily, aiming back at the pewter bright lakes where three feeble lamps winked hysterically in a rough triangle. The despatcher tensed for his cue and punched the container release. 'Go—ONE! TWO! THREE! FOUR!'

The humped men lurched away, bundling down the roaring slipstream, trailing dark silk, braking fast. Swinging free, sinking under gently humming shrouds. The dew wet ground reached up, somersaulting them into collapsing canopies. 'Hector! Hector!'

'Yes—hurry!' Panting men ran up through the sodden grass, dragging their parachutes together. 'Quickly! Get those things off!' The overalls were screwed into lumps and stuffed into the gaping cylinder with their harness. 'Radio?'

'Yes!'

'Where's Colonel Morgan?'

'Seen him, Shepherd?'

'No!'

'Christ!' Erikssen grabbed at one of the shapes running past. 'One short!'

'How many?'

'Should be four, we're three!'

'Oluf!' Another man dashed up, cradling a Sten. 'Yes?'

'One fallen wide.'

106

'Right. Get the cargo drowned. You, you and you, the guides are waiting.'

'But we're still one short!'

'Yes, I know,' Oluf was controlled, 'we'll find him in a minute. This sometimes happens. You must be moving off.'

'He can't even understand Danish!' Oluf, no longer so controlled, said nothing for a moment. 'That's brilliant!' He twisted his head away from Erikssen. 'We'll throw out a search once we've got the landing ground cleared—now, follow me!'

They set off in Indian file, suitcases tucked under one arm. A shaded torch winked through the murk. They bent towards it. 'All in order?'

'No, it bloody well isn't—one's lost himself.'

'Right. First three away. Anders, you stay here with me!'

The small group stumbled off down an uneven track between overhanging thorn bushes—one of the guides probing ahead with his Sten, the rest trailing ten paces behind. Twice a dog started to howl, jerking and snapping at the chain as night strangers hurried past. Then a soft, cold rain began to fall.

'Lyngby station,' the Sten-gunner breathed in Erikssen's ear. 'Keep your men hidden behind the cycle sheds. Wait while I get your tickets.' Erikssen nodded and the man trod from cover, the machine carbine hitched up under his long coat.

More early shift workers began walking or cycling into the forecourt. A gas mantle popped yellow light inside the station buffet; a fresh batch of substitute coffee and saccharin pastries were ready for breakfast. A semaphore clanked up the track; five minutes to the first train.

Their guide drifted over, passing round their cheap, workers' return tickets. 'First pair now.' He stepped to one side to let Shepherd edge past, strolling out to get a place in the growing queue.

The train shuffled in, sooting the night with bits of brown coal dust. The waiting men were nudged into different, dimmed out carriages. A whistle shrilled along the platform, the locomotive moaned back and crept off for Copenhagen.

Meyer lounged on the bench opposite his guide, a dumpy, middle-aged women in a faded blue coat who ignored him completely. Instead, she'd already pulled out some wool from her handbag and placidly carried on knitting a baby's romper suit. His eyelids drooped, he seemed to doze while his mind restlessly tested the atmosphere, guessing which of the other twenty or thirty people sharing the compartment had noticed him, the stranger with two heavy cases and muddy shoes. But no-one

107

spoke. Some tiredly pulled at cigarettes or pipes of herb tobacco, others yearned or tried to read in the feeble light. But no-one spoke.

They pulled into Copenhagen Central well before dawn. Meyer followed his guide along the echoing platform. He rested his cases at the ticket barrier before shoving past with a muttered apology to keep trailing the blue coat. It led him down two flights of steps and out into the dark, wet streets. She slowed a little to let him nearly catch up before leading off to the left along Vesterbrogade.

It was still far too quiet after curfew as the woman hurried into a covered doorway beside a grocer's shop. A latch shot open, letting them through a sour-smelling vestibule and into the yard where someone had already let down the fire-escape. The woman led him up its padded treads to the top of the building where she had to sit, breathing hard before tapping at the skylight.

It blinked open. 'Come in! Come in quickly!' The woman touched Meyer's shoulder, then set off down the escape as he scrambled into the attic. He turned, pulling in his cases as the skylight shut tight. A bulb pinked light overhead. Erikssen and Shepherd had already landed and stood waiting while a tall, nervously thin man stuck out one hand and briefly shook it with Meyer. He turned to Erikssen. 'Where's your other one?'

'He'll be along soon.'

'Oh dear.' The man bit his lip with vexation. 'What's going to happen if he comes once it's light outside?' Erikssen shrugged that one. Their host stopped frowning by degrees and slowly turned to them again. 'I am Doctor Borg,' he said in carefully rehearsed English, 'you are welcome.' There was no surplus warmth in the greeting. He went on, pitching his voice very low. 'You are now at my clinic. Keep absolutely quiet and come this way...'

Borg led them from the attic down to a small, over-furnished living-room which doubled as an office for his clinic. Someone had laid out several plates of cold meat, tongue, sausage, rye-bread and thin toast. A globe of real coffee chuckled to itself over a spirit burner. 'Sit down please,' he flicked a hand at the food, 'please eat if you want to.'

Erikssen started layering butter on his first square of rugbrød in years, then hesitated and looked up awkwardly at Borg. 'It's all right, please, just help yourself.' His eyes fluttered weakly as he shifted his weight from one foot to the other. 'There's lots more where that came from.' Erikssen looked surprised, at the same time happily gouging his knife-tip through the yellow kilo pat. 'Rationing can't be as bad as they say?'

108

'It's average, I suppose.' Borg twitched slightly. 'All this I take as part payment for my treatments.'

'What *is* he talking about?' Meyer cut in suspiciously. Erikssen half turned, impatient at the interruption. 'He says we can eat up; this stuff's off ration; he says his patients give it to him.'

'Please!' Borg shushed in unfamiliar English, finger over mouth. 'Not so loud! I have three Germans in private wards.' Everyone stopped eating at the same moment, mouths shut tight.

'Three Germans?'

'Yes!' Borg licked his lips and retreated into Danish again. 'They're sedated, but one can never be sure, not with the sort of drugs we get nowadays.'

'Where did you get them? The Germans?'

'Their officers are good patients.'

'What the hell sort of place is this!' Borg drew himself up with shabby dignity. 'This is my clinic, where I treat the sick.'

'I'll bet! What about your Deutschers?' Borg didn't like Erikssen's face either. 'They pay well, because if they didn't, and if their own MO's knew what they'd contracted on active service,' he sniggered, 'they'd be shot—or sent to the Eastern Front. Anyhow,' he paused caustically, 'don't *you* look so moral and good. Remember that *your* safety depends on it now. *You're* only safe while the Germans don't think of looking here for you.'

'What *is* he saying!' Meyer jumped into the meaningless river of words again. Erikssen turned on him. 'This is a clap shop, patching up Teutonic supermen who don't want to go to Russia. Because of it he thinks we're safe!'

'Some hopes.'

'Shut up, Shepherd!'

'Please!'

'What do you think?'

'Maybe he's right. With his background he'd be one of the last persons they'd ever think of looking over.'

'You really think so?' Meyer crumbled a square of bread, rolling small pellets between his fingers. 'I wish I didn't know my own people so well.' He came to a decision. 'All right. Ask him what he intends doing now.' Erikssen turned to Borg. 'What do you intend doing now?'

'I'll put you all in a private ward—I have five, you know.' The doctor seemed a mite hesitant. 'My nurses were all chosen for their absolute discretion, but I have already prepared charts and case-papers for you should anyone else want to know.' Erikssen played it back for the others.

109

Meyer thought a moment, then looked at Shepherd. 'Do you agree that we take his word?' The little man heaped another slice of bread with beef and mustard pickle. He looked up. 'Only within reason, and only because we've precious little choice till Morgan comes in.'

Borg showed them the way to their ward. Within ten minutes they were stretched out between grey linen, fully-clothed except for their coats and shoes, listening to the rising mumble of traffic as day broke. One by one they edged under a light, watchful sleep.

CHAPTER ELEVEN

'MORE coffee, dear?'

'Please.' Kierzner's left hand came round the newspaper after a moment and carefully measured in the cream. 'Thanks.' It hurried back to the centre spread of *Das Schwarze Korps*.

'Anything interesting in there today?' his wife asked with affectionate irony. There was a longish pause. 'Not much. Ehrlich's been seconded to Norway; he should knock a bit of sense into the Vikings; taken a step up, too; he's a fast worker,' Kierzner summarised, sipping the coffee. 'There's a call for increased contributions to the Winterhilfe comforts fund. I suppose that means we'll be circulating another hundred-mark subscription list. Still, that's better than actually taking a trip to enjoy the brandy and chocolates in a foxhole near Minsk.'

'Could they do that to you?'

'Oh yes—especially if something went wrong here.' Kierzner paused to fork up a fragment of Bismarck herring from his plate. 'They could do quite easily, too easily in fact. However, liebchen, here's something more your style—reduced holiday travel for SS staff-grades.'

'Oh? Where to?'

'Innsbrück. Small skiing parties, I think.'

'It'd be nice if *we* could get on one this year...'

'Mm?'

'Oh, Max, I do wish you'd pay attention!' She paused, changing her tactics. 'I said it'd be nice if we could get away for a change, we don't have much time together, do we?' It didn't work. 'And Mareka writes of heavy, early snow in the mountains...'

'There's no reason why we shouldn't,' Kierzner commented through the paper. 'I've still three weeks' leave oustanding—and another due at Christmas—I can run them together and make a full month of it.'

'Could we?' She brightened. 'Then we *could* visit Mareka and Jurgen for a few days.'

'Vanity, thy name is woman.' Kierzner abruptly dropped the paper on his lap. 'You'll only be happy when you've shown off the new General-Major to your sister and her husband.'

'After the way they treated you last time, I'm not surprised!'

'Neither am I,' he commented dryly. 'However, time is a great leveller of the haughty, my love. And we've only just started to *really* move.'

'What do you mean?'

'I didn't tell you the half of it, what the Reichsführer and I were talking about.' He smiled with his mouth. 'Oh no, my dear, we're *really* going places now. Did you know that, as a General-Major, I'm entitled to a resettlement estate in Eastern Poland? Twenty-five thousand hectares all told. I've put in for one on the Pripet Marshes.'

'Why in heaven choose that dreary place, Max?'

'For the duck shooting—what else? And there's some wonderfully flat agricultural land, too. It'll be a good place to retire, my love.'

'In winter?' Kierzner chuckled patiently. 'Hardly. Even I can see that. No, I'm thinking of a villa on the Wannsee; it's time we moved a little nearer the centre of things in Berlin.'

'And Denmark?' she asked with uncomfortable accuracy. 'Will the Reichsführer SS release you that easily?'

'I could wish he would—it's not all movie stars and champagne. Still,' he went on, 'I'll outgrow it soon enough.'

'And the English?' Therese Kierzner could be a discouraging realist in many ways. Her husband chewed his lip for a moment. 'I've not forgotten them, for one moment, but they won't be trying any more of that parachute-soldier business.'

'Oh?'

'Not after their last blunder. Mark you, I do expect they'll try again—they must—but only after they've had time to digest their failure and learn some new tricks. I've studied history, my love, I know that in the end the English always fall back on something traditional—like a seaborne commando raid—and I've taken active steps to nip *that* in the bud. Or a massive bombing assault —and that's been taken care of, as well. You see,' he drained his cup, 'Festung Wotan is already a *reality*; I didn't lose any time seeing to that!' He grinned at the memory of hard work and effort. His wife didn't smile. 'Don't be over-confident, Max. Remember, I saw you when the Luftwaffe rang through last night...'

'Puf! An Intruder Alarm—probably the same one that Northern Air Command is squabbling over.' Kierzner folded the newspaper neatly down the middle. 'They're not impressed at a swap of two night-fighters for the one Tommy—and I can't say I blame them, either.'

112

'And the troops?'

'My dearest Therese, that was routine staff work. The Wehrmacht is rummaging around out there more as a shake-down exercise of Wotan's defence ring than, well, because I take an aeroplane noise seriously.' He paused, tossing the paper at a side table and getting to his feet. 'It's nearly ten; time for the office. However, I'll let you——' The Command telephone jangled. He frowned, marched over and pulled the green handset from its hook. 'Ja!'

'Hier spricht Oberstleutnant Bethmann, Herr General!'

'What the devil do you want *now*?'

'Herr General, I regret I must report an English parachutist!'

'What!'

'An English parachutist, Herr General. A patrol found him still hanging in a tree; the cords had snared his neck.'

'Dead?'

'Yes, Herr General!'

'Damn! Where was he found?'

'In a plantation near Ravnsholt.'

'Then concentrate the Immediate Search Procedure on that area!'

'It is already being done, Herr General!'

'For your own good be sure it is!' Kierzner thought fast. 'Where is he now?'

'They're bringing him to the police mortuary, Herr General!'

'Be there!'

'Jawohl!' Kierzner slammed the line shut, turned and bellowed for one of his servants. 'Herr General?'

'My tunic!'

'Herr General!' He punched both arms down the outstretched black sleeves.

He was still buckling on his pistol belt as he started down the hotel's long, marble staircase, face set hard, boot irons pinging on every second tread, civilian staff and SS slamming to attention where they stood.

A squad of troopers had sprung into position along the wet pavement twenty paces either side of the hotel doors, automatic rifles crossed, holding back the pedestrians till the covered Mercedes had stormed away.

Kierzner's brain had plenty of time to plot this bad news during the short ride to police headquarters. Dorfer braked hard, flung open the door and stiffened to attention as the General hurried past. Inside, Kierzner curtly noted Bethmann's glossy salute and

113

stepped into the lift cage. An SS Gefreiter threw the gates shut and they rode down to the basement area.

Bethmann tailed Kierzner up a fairly steep concrete ramp, through a pair of self-closing swing doors into the police mortuary; chilly, brightly lit and normally very quiet. A small group of SS and plain-clothes Gestapo were chatting affably round one of the zinc-topped benches. They went silent and instinctively moved back as Kierzner clinked over the floor tiles.

'Is this the parachutist?' Bethmann nodded obediently. 'Let us take a closer look, then.' After a few moments' interest he let the pink rubber sheeting fall back while he glanced along the faces across the bench. 'Herr Doktor Sieben—it is indeed a great pleasure to see you back in Copenhagen so soon. How did you find your detachment to the Serum Institute?'

'Notable research work is being followed there, Herr General!'

'I am glad.' Kierzner looked down at the cadaver again. 'Herr Doktor, will you be so good as to start this examination for me?' The SS doctor stepped forward, briskly working on a pair of latex gloves before directing the autopsy.

The Englishman's tangled parachute and torn overalls were peeled off and carefully laid on an unoccupied bench for laboratory testing after Sieben had anatomised and radiographed the body. He was methodical and expert, uncovering layer by layer while two assistants double listed everything taken from the pockets and valise.

'Really quite thorough, aren't they?' Kierzner drawled to Bethmann as he finished glancing through the parachutist's identity papers. 'Though I must confess that I *am* puzzled by their choice of a French agriculturist: it is very curious and very strange.' Bethmann looked dutifully blank. Kierzner flipped the wallet shut and tossed it over to the mounting stack of articles. 'I ask you, would it be logical to send, let us say, a Hottentot to London if we intended planning a raid on Buckingham Palace?'

'I suppose not, Herr General.'

'You're not very sure of yourself today, Bethmann. You really ought to cultivate more self-confidence; you'd be surprised at the change.'

'Herr General, is it safe to assume this was a reconnaissance agent for another sabotage attempt on the fortress?'

'What on earth can you mean, Bethmann? What dazzling forked lightning is about to dart from that mouth of yours?'

'I meant that, well, maybe he's unrelated to any such attempt, really.' Bethmann found the courage to put his dearest hope into words. Kierzner gently shook his head over Bethmann's simple-

114

mindedness. 'Perhaps he was sent all the way from England just to report on the present quality of butter and cheese in Denmark?'

Someone across the table thought this was the signal for a General's joke and hurriedly began to lead the tittering. It was badly timed and he had to dive for cover under a shock of embarrassed coughing. Bethmann pluckily defended his dream to the last. 'I didn't mean that, Herr General, but there are other strategic targets in the Protectorate, aren't there?'

'Enjoying the same priorities as Wotan?' Kierzner lost interest in the argument and glanced back at the naked body again. 'So now we have one dead V-Mann, but without either equipment or radio. Tell me, Oberstleutnant, what does that suggest to you?'

'That they are missing, as he was, Herr General?'

'You're beginning to think: I must be careful, mustn't I?'

'Herr General?'

'That's better. Have you checked the Intensive Search yet?'

'As you ordered!'

'Then let's go and see what progress they've made so far.'

The Mercedes ran out through Copenhagen's misty suburbs and raced north along the open highway to Helsingør, tyres singing on the smooth asphalt. Minutes later an MP's curt hand signals shot the staff-car up a line to the left, under a railway bridge and through about four hundred yards of woodland to the edge of a lake where military vehicles were already parked nose to tail. The Mercedes bit mud behind a half-track troop carrier as Kierzner jumped out, returning a Wehrmacht Major's icy salute. 'Well?'

'A thorough search plan has been drawn up, as instructed,' the elderly Reservist answered, unfolding his map board. 'There are signs that people were in this field, here, last night.'

'How many?'

'That's hard to say: I estimate the number at between twelve and fourteen.'

'Waiting for this man to be parachuted?'

'It seems possible.' Kierzner thoughtfully gnawed his underlip and craned his neck to follow a Storch artillery spotter as it flew low overhead. After a moment he looked down again. 'Anything else?'

'My men are combing the grass and undergrowth with mine detectors in case something was dropped by accident.'

'Good thinking.'

'I've also ordered a search of the lake area.' Kierzner nodded and set off towards the water, the Major and Bethmann trailing

115

close behind. They left the narrow lane and scrambled up a low embankment which overlooked both the landing ground on one side, and a mirror-flat lake on the other.

A few hundred yards offshore two small launches and a rubber bridging float were slowly dragging grapnels through the water. A skein of mallard suddenly exploded away from some reedbeds, beating into the grey air, setting course for quieter parts.

'How long have they been at that?' The Major pulled back his glove and read the time. 'One hour and twenty-six minutes.'

'It is not a large lake.'

'They cannot be hurried.'

'Well, tell me how much of it remains to be searched.' The Major sighted with a field compass on some distant mark, carried the figure back to his map and then looked at Kierzner. 'Seventeen comma four hectares, or exactly eighty-three prozent of the available area.'

'At this rate we could be here till midnight.' The SS General-Major pursed his mouth, mentally calculating the chances of a parachute falling wide and sinking without trace in the lake. They didn't seem very bright. He was about to expand this line of reasoning when the rubber float abruptly fired off a yellow cartridge, tossing away a smoky flare. 'What's that!' Kierzner pulled the binoculars from the Major's eyes and focussed them to his own.

The two launches had already put up their helms and swung round to help the float crew winch in several heavy things. It was too far off to see them clearly, but Kierzner was radiant as he slowly handed back the glasses. 'Results—and so soon!'

They moved down to the water's edge as the small flotilla chugged back to land. Somewhere to the right an NCO yelped and eight soldiers splashed out through the shallows, man-handling the boats nearer before off-loading the find and wading it ashore. Kierzner was still smiling to himself as they dumped five brown-painted cylinders on the bank.

A garrison photographer struggled through the watching troops and began shooting his Leica at an armaments officer who'd knelt on a groundsheet delicately checking each cylinder for booby traps. He pulled off his stethoscope, nodded and stood clear while a couple of pioneers with hammers struck open the watertight locking clips.

The first four emptied were like a page torn from Death's mail order catalogue. Nearly two hundredweight of plastic blasting compound; ten dozen spools of primacord; time pencils; packets of detonators; Sten-gun kits; sealed tins of cartridges, medical

116

supplies; iron rations, cartons of grenades; a PIAT with six cases of anti-tank bombs; three snipers' rifles and their telescopes; twenty Enfield revolvers.

Kierzner's eyebrows collided as the fifth cylinder gave up a tangle of parachutes and overalls. 'GET THOSE OUT!' The pioneers jumped to obey, hurriedly separating the three overalls, spreading them on the grass.

He straightened like an old man, paused, then beckoned the Wehrmacht Major and Bethmann to one side where they couldn't be overheard. 'Oberstleutnant, this is your big chance to show me your true worth.'

'Herr General!'

'Run over to the Signals Section.' He pointed out the knot of trailers moored round a temporary aerial mast. 'Start the full plan.'

'Jawohl!'

'Major?' He turned wearily, forcing himself to think ahead. 'Call off the search and return to barracks; be prepared to take up new dispositions immediately.'

Kierzner rode into his city like a black whirlwind. The Mercedes was quick, but not so quick that it missed the first convoys of steel-helmeted troops rumbling out to their map co-ordinates. Brilliant staff work by VI Korps was using manpower to completely seal off the Mercur factory for several miles in all directions.

Crash-proof barriers of old oil drums filled with bricks and cement were being thrown across main street junctions, screening all civilian traffic. Bridges, canals, railway stations, bus and tram depots were all woven into the master strategy of a tightening garrotte. And by early afternoon the Danes knew it as the first batches of suspects were herded together in synchronised police raids and driven away for intensive questioning. The house-to-house searchers moved in. Disguised monitor vans started prowling the empty streets, patiently waiting for the hidden transmitter to break silence.

117

CHAPTER TWELVE

KIERZNER pulled himself together and immediately convened a tactical planning conference at Shell House to review the first phase of their progress before adjourning to a working lunch with his senior officers, Army as well as SS.

After that he was free to ride out to the factory and see for himself what was being done. But he had no need to worry. The armoured barricades across Strandvej, Prags Boulevard and Holmgade were at full strength and active—nothing was getting inside the area without a triple pass check. The private houses standing inside the perimeter had, of course, been evacuated and turned into Deathshead SS billets with light machine-guns mounted on three of the roofs to fill in blank arcs of fire. Around the factory building itself, VI Korps had doubled the amount of chain fencing—adding, for good measure, corkscrew stakes which held up fronds of thick wire festooned with several hundred fragmentation grenades. These had been fuzed to burst on contact if anyone ever crawled under, through or over them.

The drab Mercedes rolled to a halt by Mercur's rear gate. Kierzner took his time in climbing down and returning an SS Hauptmann's confident, unhurried salute. 'Alles in Ordnung?'

'Ja! Alles ist in Ordnung, Mein General!' Kierzner nodded thoughtfully at the man's tone and glanced round at his organised bustle. 'Very well, you can show me what you've done.' He turned abruptly and led the way into the guard-hut's own sub-perimeter of sandbags, ruthlessly putting its defences under the microscope of his temper.

'That!' He pointed at one of the Spandaus, cartridge-belt threaded, ready to fire. 'Traverse!' The gunners ran to obey while Kierzner crouched, sighting over their shoulders, calculating the field of fire. 'But what of that!' He stabbed a finger at a low, plain garden wall over by one of the evacuated homes, maybe fifty yards away. 'Herr General?'

'It masks your left sector; have it demolished!'

'Jawohl!' A detail of pioneers with sledgehammers and shovels doubled away on the order.

Slowly, meticulously, he uncovered every remaining weakness in the entire defence system—enjoying the keen, sensual pleasure of directing a perfectly constructed plan, seeing it run by acknowledged experts. A small, obedient tail of officers followed him as he strode out into the weeds and rubbish of the wasteland which covered one flank of the factory. The Luftwaffe Flak Regiment had set up another sixteen Quadruple-Twenties on railway wagons, deploying them along the old sidings, filling in the fire patterns of an outer curtain of 88-mm pieces and searchlight clusters. The Air Liaison officer was handy, waiting his chance.

'The Herr General will observe the improved light flak which now consists of some one hundred and sixty 20-mm barrels regulated at six hundred rounds delivery. This consumes ninety-six thousand shells a minute with a barrage weight of twelve thousand kilograms.' He paused for breath. 'If the Herr General would care to inspect the Predictor bunker I will explain the heavy flak pattern...'

Kierzner decided not to walk out that far. Instead, he used one of the wagons as a lookout to survey his fortress. He liked what he saw, he liked it a lot. Now his base was secure he could screw down hard on the civilians and squeeze out the three saboteurs. Much of his careful diplomacy with the Protectorate Government was going to be soured by claims for damages from grumbling Danes; they weren't going to like his decrees ordering death by public shooting for anyone found helping the English either. He nodded at some private thought and tiredly jumped down.

Kierzner reached the Mercedes and abruptly hesitated, one foot on the running-board, ready to step in and go. The tail of officers stood by, obediently waiting to wag farewell. He thought a moment longer before turning and slowly crunching across the road towards the first of two narrow gates through the wire.

Four SS troopers in field equipment and mottled rain capes guarded the corridor cut between concertinas and hedgehog obstacles—exploded stars welded up from steel girders. Kierzner paused, sighting along the dense thickets of barbed stakes and wiring sandwiched between double fences and lights. He nodded, almost reluctantly admitting this to be a perfect defence, incapable of improvement.

He trod into the courtyard, glancing round with cool curiosity; Kierzner had not yet taken time off to see the inside workings of this place. Another sentry dragged open a small door near the boiler house and let the officers tramp past, down a short, whitewashed corridor. 'To the left, Herr General!' Bethmann hurriedly shoved a thin steel-and-wood door to let Kierzner cruise into the Low Pressure Physics Area.

119

'Herr Professor.' Kierzner stuck out one hand towards the civilian director. Professor Doktor Hoertl rhythmically chewed a cigar in its amber mouthpiece. After a moment he took it out. 'Afternoon, Kierzner.' They shook hands. 'Everything in order?' the SS General-Major queried with polite concern, peering round the assembly hall with real interest.

'For me, yes.' Hoertl put the cigar back in his face and made smoke for a couple of seconds; he coughed. 'What of yourself?'

'Fine.' Kierzner smiled back at the civilian. 'Simply fine.'

'You've got enough troops out there now, haven't you?'

'Oh yes, quite enough.' He paused ironically. 'Two hundred changing guard every eight hours in twenty-four, leaving me four hundred in reserve, and those are just the *élite*, of course— Deathshead SS, every man a picked storm-trooper. Screening them, Professor, I have guns, lights and dogs; nearly five thousand soldiers of the Wehrmacht and supporting Panzer Lehr units. Above them, in the skies, the Luftwaffe. Beyond them, on the Sound, Kriegsmarine patrols.' He gently slapped his boots with the leather switch. 'Quite enough you would agree?'

'Then I can expect no further attempts at sabotage by the English, eh?'

'Correct.'

'I'm relieved to hear it.' Hoertl puffed his cigar alight and looked around. 'I could only wish my demands for a dozen cups and saucers received the same Reich Priority!' He glanced back at the SS General. 'D'you know that my staff has been reduced to drinking from the laboratory's fire-glass beakers?' Kierzner clicked his tongue in genuine surprise. 'I am sure this can be put right—through SS channels, of course.' He began pulling out a notebook and silver-mounted pencil from his tunic. He glanced up. 'Will one dozen be enough?'

'Better make it two, with matching saucers. And get some spoons, some decent spoons.' The Professor-Doktor blew smoke down his nostrils. 'And coffee, Viennese roast—Zigeuner or Donau brand.' Kierzner nodded sympathetically, jotting down the shopping list. 'Now,' he tucked the pencil inside his breast pocket, 'in return you can help me.'

'How's that?'

'Show me around; teach me something new.'

Hoertl frowned at the tip of his cigar for quite a long time before answering Kierzner. 'You know damn well it's against the strictest regulations to discuss this installation with anyone, *anyone* not held on the Gamma Register. Failure to observe this ruling is punishable under articles 491 and 492 of the Civil

120

Code.' He paused for a long moment. 'So I think you'd better put me down for two boxes of Upmann Perfectos as well.' Kierzner chuckled with real amusement. 'Natürlich, Herr Professor, natürlich!' The pencil jotted again. Kierzner was still chuckling. 'Believe me, it's always a pleasure to have dealings with a person who thinks along the same clear lines as myself! Now,' he looked up, 'what's it you're hiding in here?'

'How much do you understand of simple Physics—particularly electricity?'

'Not a thing, not a single thing. I can't even change a light fuze without scorching myself.'

'That's a bright start.' Hoertl paused and slowly picked a tooth with the end of his little finger.

'Look, just forget the technicalities for a moment—I'm sure they're very interesting and all that—but I just want to see what makes this place of yours so special. Why is Berlin cheerfully signing pay and ration vouchers for one hundred and forty thousand reichmarks—*a week*—just to garrison this immediate area?' Kierzner stopped to look round again. 'Believe me, Professor, we of the SS have never seen the like before!' Hoertl shrewdly wrinkled his nose. 'A hundred and forty grand, eh? Is that what's bothering you?'

'Herr Professor, nothing ever bothers me.' Kierzner spoke with severity. 'I am puzzled, that's all.'

'I'll believe you. However, at ten times the money, we'd still be a bargain. Come here and let me show you something.' He led the SS General-Major between two lines of droning, gasping machines in their own strictly balanced atmospheres; protected behind glass and aluminium enclosures; guarded by several dozen white-gowned specialist technicians. Kierzner lagged farther behind and pressed his nose to the four-centimetre armour glass which boxed one of the installations. 'Pretty impressive, I must admit.'

'Elementary mechanics—easy to replace within a couple of weeks,' Hoertl snapped, looking back over a pallet of equipment chassis. 'This, however, isn't. No matter how many milliard reichmarks you're willing to spend, this cannot be replaced—ever!' He paused and beckoned. 'Step over here!'

Kierzner walked round the chassis and faced a low, reinforced concrete hump—something like an U-boat in contour, he thought—about forty feet by ten. 'Is *this* it?' Kierzner gently stubbed his toe against the heavy steel manhole cover which sealed the only way inside, testing the thickness, listening to it ring solid. 'Is this the reason for all the shouting?' He was amused. So was Hoertl, but for different reasons. 'It's reason enough, Kierzner. Nothing you could ever do would replace this vault—nothing.' He made ready to light up another cigar.

'Under that carapace—one metre-fifty of iron, concrete and insulating asbestos—under that you will find the metering lines, valves and storage flasks of various essentials we use in our work. Liquid oxygen, nitrogen, argon, krypton—-and helium. Helium, Kierzner. For that alone Berlin would sign vouchers promising the moon—if they had it. Helium. Symbol: He. Atomic Number: 2. Atomic Weight: 4·003. That's helium. We know all about helium in this laboratory—and so, apparently, do the English!

'Ironically it was discovered by a Dane, working here in Copenhagen, did you know that?' Kierzner shook his head. Hoertl drew on his cigar, already seeing other things. 'Indeed, it *is* ironic that Janssen first observed it in the solar spectrum around the year 1868—hence the name, from Helios, Greek for sun. Helium the sun gas. Everywhere in Creation, and yet the only way in which I could synthesise it would be by the controlled decay of such extreme elements as uranium, or thorium, or pitchblende—of which I'd need tons before I even started.'

Kierzner had been strictly reared to believe in German technical miracles like the Haber–Bosch nitrogen fixation process; he couldn't follow this helium problem. 'But surely, my dear Professor, it can't be all that scarce? There must be other gases you could use in its place?' Hoertl slowly shook his head. ' "No" to both questions. By itself helium isn't all that rare—for the Americans. They extract it in concentrations of up to eight-prozent from their damned petroleum gas wells out in Utah.' He paused for a lungful of hot, numbing smoke. 'And no, there isn't any other substance nearly a quarter so effective for the units we are now developing. Did you know that the Luftwaffe must send back all the old cells for rebuilding? That's an indication of how scarce helium has now become for us.' Kierzner looked at the vault with a new respect. 'Quite the Ultimate Victory Weapon, eh?'

'What's that?' Hoertl had been thinking of other things.

'I said that it seems to be quite the Victory Weapon.'

'Victory Weapon?'

'Yes.'

'Let's stave off defeat first, my dear Kierzner.'

'Defeat?' The SS General-Major had almost forgotten the word existed in German, too. He viewed the civilian with a new, hard eye. 'You seriously think that military defeat is possible? For the Reich?'

'Yes.'

'Herr Professor, you *do* realise what you're saying? And to whom you are saying it?' He paused, waiting for an answer. 'Very well, while you're busy quoting the Civil Code at me—don't forget the articles which order death for *any* person spreading defeatist sentiments.' Hoertl slowly puffed his cigar to a red glow and solemnly winked at Kierzner. 'I don't frighten that easily—save it for the Hitler Jugend rallies.'

'So you think bullets will bounce from your chest? Because of some undiscovered scientific principle, perhaps?'

'Oh no, my dear Kierzner, I must die like the rest of mankind. Only I intend to do it my way—in bed. I'll be a *very* old man; a litre of Korn and a drum of Hansa Ceruts will be on the locker beside him; one will still be burning in his mouth while a gramophone softly plays Mozart's Requiem Mass and a couple of busty, blonde nurses wait on him hand and foot.'

'You sound very sure of yourself, what's the secret?'

'There is no secret—I'm a scientist. Nobody's going to shoot me, Kierzner, I'm too valuable.' Hoertl gently puffed smoke. 'Strictly between ourselves, I'm irreplaceable.

'In your case, of course, things must be different. I don't doubt that a pack of ambitious subordinates growl and snap round your ankles all the time. It must be tiring and very irksome, especially as every one of them has a pair of narrow shoulders that could support your epaulettes at a pinch.' Kierzner looked ill.

'Now, in my case, to shoot me would be a grave mistake. To get a suitable replacement you would have to find a somewhat precocious child, one endowed with great scientific curiosity too. Then you'd have to give him luck—lots of luck—and arrange for him to become a Doctor-cum-laude at twenty-seven; lecturer; and, finally, a full Professor at thirty-two.' Hoertl drew his cigar alight before carrying on in the same blandly confidential voice.

'Of course this is not unique, but it is a little unusual even though I do say it myself. Then you'd have to rewrite several textbooks on rather advanced subjects—books which have become the standard not only in Germany but in the world at large. Finally, to round off the picture, you'd have to wait fifty-three years to get the very thing which you already have—me.' Hoertl gently shook his head. 'By that time it will be almost the end of the century—the year 2000—and victory won't wait that long, my dear Kierzner.'

123

The SS General-Major still looked a bit pale. He coughed harshly. 'That may be so, Herr Professor, but now I hear you talking of Victory! A sudden change of heart perhaps?'

'Get your ears syringed, clear out the wax, life's hard enough for you already!' Hoertl toughened. 'I spoke of preventing defeat, you should pay more attention when I speak.' He turned abruptly. 'Come over here!'

Kierzner obediently followed him to the far end of the assembly hall. Hoertl stopped and faced him again. 'In this place I work on only two things—nothing else. One is the Reich's surest shield against bombing aircraft; the other is a dagger to stab our enemies to the heart. D'you see that?' He jabbed his cigar at an experimental bench and something which looked like an open-sided biscuit box filled with glass, wire and servo motors. The team working on it had fallen back to a respectful distance from the twin brilliance of Der Chef and the SS. Kierzner was bushed. 'What the hell is it?'

'Rheinfall's telemetry control system. Simple, cheap and vastly superior to anything else ever designed. Diplom-Ingenieur Scharne of our Peenemünde Establishment,' he waved the cigar at one of the men standing near by, 'produced this supremely beautiful device.'

'Rheinfall?'

'You *are* on the Schwarzwald security list?' Kierzner was glad of the chance to get one back. 'Naturally. Would it be otherwise since *I* am the General Officer Commanding this entire area?' He paused, lips down-curving.

Hoertl elegantly spat a flake of tobacco from the end of his cigar. 'I'll believe you, if you insist. Not that it matters very much since the entire world will soon enough learn of our work here.' Kierzner said nothing. Hoertl strolled over to the telemetry bench and shrewdly evaluated Scharne's progress. After a few moments he looked back at the SS General-Major. 'Come closer.

'The units which I make, and which you defend, are only steps One and Two in a planned progression of events, Kierzner. It is imperative the Reich's skies be kept clear of hostile aircraft—we are all agreed upon that. Step One is doing it most successfully. Safe under the Luftwaffe's umbrella, other, vastly superior developments are taking place.' Hoertl's diamond-sharp mind was ranging well beyond the normal limits of prudence.

'My Rheinfall is step Two.' He glanced lovingly at the telemetry device. 'With my Rheinfall to guide them, Dornberger's

124

rockets will soar beyond the stratosphere! Consider that for a moment—if you are capable of it!

'This little thing of mine can aim fourteen tons of roaring oxygen and alcohol at a point one hundred kilometres—yes, one hundred kilometres—above the earth's surface! The globe will have shifted whole seconds of arc about its axis by the time Rheinfall begins the re-entry, smashing its target at unheard-of speeds!' Hoertl ran to a halt, breathing heavily. Kierzner looked reverently at the experiment. 'So *that* is the Ultimate Victory Weapon.'

Hoertl snorted impatiently. 'If it were, then Schwarzwald would simply be another mare's-nest of bright ideas. No, *that* is not the weapon we seek. Not when we are already harnessing the very sun's energy, all twenty million degrees of it. Did you know that? No, of course you didn't, how could you comprehend such things. Twenty million degrees of heat in one explosion—and Rheinfall to carry it—*that* will be the moment when defeat becomes impossible!

'Rheinfall will carry the destructive force of the universe across the world. Cities like London and New York and Moscow will become mere ancestral memories, geographical expressions on old maps unless their governments cease making war on the Reich!' His voice dropped, suddenly became tight and guarded. 'I know you were in Norway earlier this year, at the Norsk Hydro, you know what I mean? The Satan Bomb?'

'Of course, SS Counter-Intelligence is responsible for Project Satan.'

'Careful,' Hoertl scowled at the man's lack of discretion, 'to us it must always remain Lake Konstanz. Nothing more.'

'I'm sorry.'

'It is to this end we labour night and day—to bring Schwarzwald to a successful conclusion before it is too late.'

'Too late?' Kierzner was beginning to smile again. 'I really don't understand you. Too late for what?'

'Too late to keep the Americans actually out of this war.' Hoertl had lost a lot of his bounce in the last few seconds. Kierzner went on smiling, hugely amused by this man's absurd fears. 'The Americans? My dear Professor, I cannot see what they have to do with our Victory.'

'You can't?'

'No. Even allowing that the English trick them into entering the war on their side—at this very moment, let us say—it won't make a scrap of difference! None at all. The actual fighting in the East will be over within six months—after the Spring Offen-

125

sive. Take it from me, I *know*. England will be mopped-up in just three months, which is nine months all told. Now, can you see the Ami's getting ready for war against us in nine months?

'No, of course not, they can't. They may be able to produce more electric ice-cream freezers, or automobiles, or toothbrushes, but they can't stop just like that!' His fingers snapped. 'They can't halt the production of such junk inside eighteen months, not and start the construction of Tiger Tanks, Stuka machines, field cannon more and better than ours!' He paused. 'I *know*.'

'So do I.' Hoertl's cigar had gone cold, not that he seemed to care. He was studying Kierzner with a peculiar smile. 'How long have you spent in the United States?'

'Not a single minute; not yet at least.'

'I thought so.' Hoertl sounded very sad and alone. 'I once spent two years and four months with Steinmetz at GEC's Schenectady plant in New York State, doing pure research. During that time I had the chance to form a somewhat different opinion of the Americans than you now hold. I, too, know something, Kierzner.

'I know that we must have the absolute power to destroy cities without trace if we are to keep them off our backs—an American expression which I commend to you, Kierzner. They also have another which I fear more as this war drags on.'

'Which other word frightens you?'

' "Know-how"—Fingerspitzengefühl to us—their national genius for making the technically impossible, absurdly easy!'

'Dollar power!'

'Oh yes, those as well! Money to them is not something to be hoarded up and kept under the mattress in an old sock! No, to them it is a precision tool—and by God they have so much of it!' Hoertl was shaking with emotion. 'At GEC's whenever I needed anything I simply had to initial a piece of paper. The company "picked up the tab" for me, and nobody seemed to mind if the article cost them five cents or a million dollars—just so long as it worked! In those days I didn't have to go crawling to the military for a dozen cups and saucers!

'Kierzner, you cannot even imagine how frightened I am of fighting America. You and your sort are incapable of imagining what real, technical might and power is. Of course it *is* money—limitless dollars—dollars with brain and "know-how" in quantities you will never begin to understand.'

They paced up the assembly hall, Kierzner glancing sideways as they passed the helium store. 'You *really* believe that stuff to

126

be worth a hundred and forty thousand a week?' Hoertl ditched his dead cigar stump in a fire-bucket and raised a sad smile. 'Less than the cost of three Messerschmitt fighters and it assures us our victory?' He paused. 'Oh yes, my dear Kierzner, it's worth every last pfennig we have.'

CHAPTER THIRTEEN

DOCTOR BORG ran into the ward. 'Go quickly!' Three men tumbled from the beds, dragging on their shoes and jackets, pistols cleared and cocked. 'No shooting—please!'

Meyer was flat against the wall over by the windows, sighting a course across the roofing leads. He spun. 'Ask him what's happening!' Erikssen caught and fired the question—but all he got was another urgent moan. He tried again with the same result, and his patience was spent. His open palm flapped the doctor's head from side to side. Borg started to cry, bitterly regretting the human weakness which let the King Frederik Group blackmail him into giving shelter to these Englishmen. 'Please, please, please go away!'

'Why?'

'The Germans know you're here!'

'Here?' Erikssen split Borg's nose. '*Here?*'

'In Denmark! Oh, please go away and leave me alone! They've found your fourth man, dead! Your weapons! Everything!' Erikssen translated and Borg rocked into a dead faint.

'You frightened him,' Meyer observed, hurrying across from the windows. Two blunt thumbs clamped Borg's ears, twisting him awake. The man wriggled hard; Meyer grinned. 'Ask him how he comes to know so much.'

'Please let me go! They're searching for you now; stopping everyone in the streets; questioning and opening things; it's terrible!' Borg's voice cracked. 'They're arresting suspects by the hundred—please go away from me!'

'He still hasn't answered.' Meyer sadly kneaded first one ear, then the other. 'How does he know?' Borg stopped drumming his fists on Meyer's solid chest and collapsed with pain.

'I have colleagues in the police who tell me when to be careful. Now they tell me the biggest hunt ever is being raised for the three English parachutists. I can see it for myself in the streets— soldiers, the Militia, the police, everyone is after you now!' He sobbed. 'I don't want you here; they'll shoot me.'

'Tell him I'll do the shooting myself if he doesn't shut his mouth, and quick!' Meyer's wrists easily supported the fainting man by the bits of ear gristle. 'Tell him we'll be glad to go—

128

when it pleases us. And tell him to remember whose side he's on now!'

'What do you plan doing?'

'What's that?' He turned on Shepherd, now mounting guard on the window. The little man looked back for a moment. 'What's in your mind?'

'This,' Meyer nearly tore an ear from the lolling head, 'knows who brought us here—he can get them to come and take us away again.' He looked back at Erikssen. 'Tell this thing we want someone from the Frederik Group—now.' Erikssen translated word for word.

'But that's impossible!'

'Really?'

'I have only a number! They'll be listening in to all the telephones now, monitoring them at the exchange!'

'Tell this creature I haven't even started to trouble him. Tell him that he will go to the telephone and dial this number of his. Tell him not to fail, for his own sake.'

'Very well. I'll do as you ask me. But the consequences will be on *your* heads!' Borg sobbed dry and tried to look defiant. Erikssen's lips spread. 'Thanks for the warning, Lover Boy.'

They fanned out and followed him back to his office. He fell on a chair and hesitantly dialled a city number. Erikssen pressed close to overhear every word both ways. 'Hello?' Borg tried hard to sound normal against all the odds. 'Oh, hello? I must speak with Jens immediately.' He scowled at the receiver. 'Of course this is important!' His voice started to climb. 'Tell him the seed potatoes are ready any time he cares to collect them from me!'

There was a short pause at the other end of the line while a man came to the phone. 'Doctor? I am so very disappointed to hear that you can't keep my potatoes in store any longer.' The tone was as flat and hard as a river-bed stone. 'I seriously think you ought to try with more effort. Keep them in the dark for just a few more days and prevent them from sprouting. You understand?'

'No!' He halted. 'That's quite impossible. They won't keep. They'll be rotten by morning.'

'Very well, that being the case I must have the seed-bed dug ready, mustn't I?' Borg didn't reply. Jens still sounded unconcerned by the news. 'Thank you, old friend, for all your help. I'm sending round one of my gardeners.'

'Please be quick about it!' But all Borg got for his pains was an abrupt dialling note. He hung up, turned to face the three men in their shapeless clothing and blinked back a tear.

129

No-one took any notice. Instead, both Erikssen and Shepherd waited for Meyer to carry on with the talking. He stood alone, thoughtfully scratching his nose before methodically rifling the huge cigarette-box on Borg's desk. 'Egyptian?' Borg nodded dumbly. Satisfied, Meyer lit up and hitched himself on the desk, both legs swinging free.

'Doesn't seem too hot, does it?' Shepherd prompted casually. Meyer nodded, slowly inhaling. 'I agree. To have lost our leader, or our cover, or our equipment, would have been very unfortunate indeed.' He suddenly wheezed and stared down at the guilty cigarette. After a moment he glanced across at Borg's tear-red face. 'You are easily fooled. These are pathetically indifferent Georgian, most probably from Tiflis or Shemakha. You have the most atrocious taste.'

He looked back at Shepherd. 'As I was saying, to have lost any one of those three would have been bad. Two would have been worse. Three...' He tiredly shrugged his shoulders. 'Under the circumstances I consider it best that we try and find a quiet place and arrange for a transmission to London, to find out what they want with things as they now are.'

'You'll be wasting your time,' Erikssen cut in quietly, 'you won't hear a thing.'

'How do you mean?'

'I mean we're for Sweden—this whole goddam operation's gone up in our faces.' Meyer rubbed his neck. 'You could be right.'

'You can bet I am—but there's still a good chance the Home Army can get us over the Sound, if we move.'

'How easy is that?' Erikssen thought a moment. 'When we were boys we could all but swim it in places. Things must be different now, of course.' Shepherd chopped in. 'How long is the other way, by boat?'

'Two, maybe three hours, I guess.' Erikssen conceded the point after a moment's thought. 'I guess three hours should see us over there, once the boat's been arranged.'

'All right, that's good to know.' Shepherd jerked a thumb at Borg, now sitting up with a little more life in his face. 'What about Tiger Tim?' Meyer heeled the cigarette through Borg's carpet. 'He sits right there—till we go.'

'My patients!' The Doctor evidently understood that much English. Meyer went on looking at him with calm interest. He coughed. 'What of them?'

'If I stay here for more than another five minutes, you'll be found out!' Borg jeered as his confidence went up sharply. 'In

130

five minutes from now my nurses will have the afternoon treatments prepared, ready for *me* to give. If *I* don't appear then, one of *them* will come to find me!' He'd found his paws as top dog. No one spoke, it was still Meyer's own problem. 'How many victims have you got?' Erikssen cuffed him, hard. 'Twenty-seven!'

'Then twenty-seven treatments are going to be delayed, aren't they?'

'Impossible!'

'Oh, what a bad judge of character you are, Doctor. Now, pick up that house-telephone and speak with your senior nurse. Tell her that you will be delayed for a short time. Tell her that she's to keep the customers happy, in the meantime you are not to be disturbed.'

'No!'

'No?' Meyer slid off the desk, cracking his finger joints. Borg grabbed at the telephone.

Shepherd went over to the window and peered round the yellowed lace curtains. A convoy of Wehrmacht lorries hummed past, going somewhere in a great hurry. 'Anything interesting out there?' He looked back across the room. 'Half the bloody German Army.'

'Leave them alone—let's get our cases in.' Meyer turned abruptly, carefully replacing the house-phone. 'That was incredibly careless of you, Doctor. It's put you about two seconds from leaving this life behind for ever: that's all the time I'll need to blow out your brains if that nurse heard anything, and informed on us. Understand?' Borg understood.

Meyer faced the other two. 'As I see it, we must be ready to move off. Let's get out what we can carry in our pockets—dump the rest.' Erikssen agreed by dragging on a second shirt and loading his raincoat with half-pound chocolate rations. Shepherd followed suit.

A short time later, the clinic's door-bell shrilled in the corridor outside Borg's office. The man smiled as someone, probably one of his nurses, went along to answer it. Meyer's Colt blocked one ear. There was a longish, muttering dialogue; some protesting, then the office door slapped open as Jens' man pushed in, hungrily thin and old in a dirty windbreaker. They were to leave immediately; there were three bicycles waiting for them in an opening a few yards along the street; there could be no luggage; they must shift.

'What about him?' Erikssen pointed at Borg.

'He knows what's healthy.'

'It'll be no trouble.'

131

'No—the police don't like it.'

'OK.'

'I said no luggage!' Erikssen translated for Meyer's sake. 'This goes wherever I go!'

'Radio?'

'Yes.'

'Right—but follow well behind us, see?'

They moved out of the clinic, losing speed as they neared street level. Their guide went ahead, neither sauntering nor hurrying, the others trying to imitate him. It was getting hard not to look furtive. The pavements were running empty now the security clamp was almost complete. It would have been hard to pick a worse time to break into the open.

The short grey afternoon was giving way to night and the curfew as they mounted up and set course through the city—making two long diversions round known road-blocks by wheeling their cycles over private vegetable allotments. Their luck held just long enough for them to pedal up a dingy street—unsuccessful workshops, empty corner stores and faded terrace-houses.

The guide hopped off his cycle and ran it into a small painter and decorator's yard, dumping it under a stack of scaffolding boards. He turned and hurried off between the deserted sheds to a broken fence, squeezed through and branched up a narrow alley, the Englishmen following close behind. Meyer was having difficulty with the radio case—but nobody volunteered as the Dane hustled them into an enclosed yard. 'Wait here.' He went on alone, returning after three or four minutes. 'Come.' They tailed him into an old house, facing a different street. The door rammed shut and someone flipped on the light.

They faced an elderly man and woman across a small, well-ordered scullery. 'I am so glad you've been able to visit my home,' he said in slow, impeccable English, moving forward to shake hands. 'My wife,' he made a short, courtly gesture, 'and I will be very happy to help you in whatever way possible.' Coming on top of Borg's recent performance, this man's welcome had an unreal quality. They nodded awkwardly, pushed off balance by the sudden change.

'Herre and Frue Sørensen.' Their guide coughed, moving away and getting ready to lose himself in the dusk. 'You'll stay with them a little while. Later—tonight perhaps—there'll be another visitor.' He shook hands and let Sørensen show him into the yard.

'You will be hungry,' Frue Sørensen spoke with more difficulty than her husband, 'please come.' Shepherd swapped looks with

132

Meyer and followed the woman into her living-room where the best linen and crockery had been spread with a thin assortment of food. No one said much as they ate—Shepherd carefully taking the minimum—finishing off with hoarded coffee and chasers of full-strength Aquavit.

'Follow me, gentlemen.' Sørensen quietly stood up and led the way out, across the yard to a tall, two-storeyed building slightly to one side of the house. He closed the door tight, putting them in total darkness. 'Don't think I'm being rude, or ungrateful, by offering you this place to sleep in tonight. But it's safer than my home, and there are more ways out if you have to leave in a hurry.' His voice chilled. 'I am an undertaker by profession, and this is my workshop.'

His hand fumbled with a light switch as he went on, up a steep flight of wooden steps to the loft where he stored his ready-to-wear coffins, urns and spare equipment. It was lit by a single naked bulb hooked from a roof beam. 'I think you'll be quite safe here since the buildings on either side are empty now and—for my work—the windows are always kept covered over.' He turned. 'Please use the blankets and straw bags to make yourselves comfortable. However, don't go outside on any account. Later on I shall come over and see how you are.' Sørensen nodded to each of his guests, turned and left.

Shepherd let his breath go in a thin, controlled hiss as he counted some blue pottery urns drawn up on parade along a shelf. 'Isn't it?' Meyer was dryly non-committal. Erikssen selected a couple of blankets and draped them like a shipwreck survivor, tiredly trying to remember this day in detail.

They were still mooning around an hour or so later when a door closed softly and two pairs of footsteps trod across the cobbles. Sørensen led the way into the loft, taking the background as the second man counted heads. 'You may call me Jens,' he began in faultless English. 'I believe you've already heard the news from Doctor Borg?'

'Yes.' Meyer came forward, weighing up this stoopy man. 'But I'd like to hear it again—from someone reliable.'

'I can understand your problem.' Jens smiled distantly. 'Put very simply, your friend's parachute failed to open properly. He was found by the Germans, dead, in a wood near the landing ground.' He paused. 'My reception committee wasn't able to find him in the darkness; I'm very sorry.

'However, since this morning the occupying forces have been acting like maniacs. They've now fully mobilised an entire Army Corps and alerted special SS troops brought up from Kiel—all to

133

look for you, gentlemen. If it is any consolation, you are now worth twenty thousand kroner alive, ten thousand dead.' No one felt like commenting. Jens went on in the same quiet voice. 'The enemy actually believe that you were sent to make another attempt on the Mercur factory.'

'Another?'

Jens looked puzzled. 'Why, of course.'

'It's already been attempted?'

'You didn't know?'

'I'm beginning to think I'm the only person left who doesn't!' Meyer controlled himself. 'How did the last one fail?'

'It was betrayed.' Jens no longer looked so cool. Neither did Meyer. 'By whom?'

'One of us.' He looked away from their three unshaven faces. 'A solution has been arranged; she won't trouble us again.'

'What happened?' But Jens brushed Meyer's question aside; it was of little importance. 'I feel dreadfully sorry for you all.'

'Why?'

'You've obviously been tricked into attempting the impossible.'

'How do you mean?' Jens faced Shepherd. 'How much do you know of the Mercur factory?'

'Where it is, what it contains.'

'And the defences? Especially now that they know you are here, in Copenhagen?' 'That was for the fourth man,' Meyer chipped in, 'the leader as it happened.' Jens smiled tiredly. 'Someone's made a mistake. Not you, someone in London.'

'Why so?'

'That factory has been officially declared a fortress area.' Jens paused delicately, searching for a word. 'Permit me. You *are* German?' Meyer's head tilted. 'Yes.'

'Then you will understand me when I say that Mercur, indeed Copenhagen, eine Festung ist? That there are guns, fences in great depth, lights and hundreds of picked troops holding the perimeter zone? They learned from your last failure. There will be no discredit, gentlemen. Your party never had a chance—and no party ever will.' Meyer glanced at the other two, then back to Jens. 'Now what's to happen?'

'Preparations are being made to get you over to Sweden as quickly as possible.'

'How quick is "quickly"?' Erikssen asked. Jens spread his hands. 'Maybe tomorrow night, maybe the night after. To be quite frank with you, gentlemen, we shall all breathe a lot easier once you're reported to be safe and well on the other side.'

134

'Tomorrow night or maybe the night after?' Jens nodded at Meyer's thoughtful question. 'Yes, that's right.'

'So there'll be at least another twenty-four hours before we leave?'

'Correct.'

'London is going to have a lot of questions to ask us, you know. And we're going to have a lot of answers to give in return.'

'I don't understand you.'

'It's going to be unfortunate if we arrive back completely empty-handed.'

'There will be no discredit in that, either.' Jens drew himself upright. 'You will be acting as our couriers. I shall give you microfilms which, among other things, explain the true situation to your leaders in London.' He smiled a little oddly at them. 'Your reputations will be taken care of.' Meyer knew the tone. 'Thank you. But it will go better with London if one of *us* sees this factory before we leave,' he paused delicately, 'to support your facts with our words.'

'There will be no need for that. Everything is taken care of.'

'Yet wouldn't it be an excellent idea if one of us saw this place, as well?'

'No, that is quite out of the question.'

'Surely, if you've been able to prepare and microfilm plans of this factory—then it can't be entirely out of the question, can it?' Meyer was being obstinately polite. Jens was getting through his slender stocks of patience, explaining the elementary facts of Occupation Life to this troublesome stranger. 'You are being very difficult, very difficult indeed!'

'Don't flatter me,' Meyer grated. He softened a fraction. 'There has to be at least one eye witness for London to interrogate—you must see that?'

'No I do not see that!' Jens had gone the limit with these men. 'This city, this entire country is full of troops and police—all hunting for you—and *you* want to walk right to the centre!'

'Oh no, I don't! I have even less reason to like them!' Meyer stopped short, lowering his voice a shade. 'But someone has to know what it is we came for! So,' he paused, 'do I get your help or do I try it myself?' Jens shook his sad, grey face at them. 'You must be all touched by the moon—you're insane. Worst luck, I cannot make a decision without consulting others who are involved. It is for our Liberation Council to decide what becomes of you.' He paused sourly. 'Personally, I shall press for you to be taken—unconscious if necessary—and thrown ashore in Sweden the moment we are ready!'

135

'When do I get an answer?'

'When I say so—not one moment before! Meantime,' he glanced round the coffin-stacked loft, 'I recommend you keep out of everyone's way.' Jens curtly shook hands and led the way out, Sørensen following close behind.

CHAPTER FOURTEEN

THEY were finishing off a breakfast of potato pancakes in nettle *purée* and breadcrumbs when Sørensen showed Jens into the scullery. Meyer looked up. 'What's the news?' Jens said nothing. Instead, he tiredly accepted a cup of skimmed milk and downed it in a few short gulps before going over to rinse it at the sink. 'Tusind tak, Frue Sørensen,' he bowed slightly and faced the Englishmen. 'I spoke with the Council.'

'What did they have to say?' Meyer asked, wiping his plate with a small piece of bread.

'They think one of you should see the factory; to report when you reach London.'

'You don't make it sound very good.'

'It isn't.' Jens was quietly furious. 'The only time I want to see you outside again is when you're bound for Sweden. The idea of arranging an excursion to see the sights is lunatic, irresponsible and very, very dangerous. Dangerous for us, the people who must stay behind when you leave.' Jens glanced at the Sørensens, then back at the three men across the table.

'Our contacts in the police tell us the first hundred hostages are already selected. If you aren't handed over, the shootings begin tomorrow morning—at nine o'clock—on the range at Kastellet. Twenty Danes will be shot for every day you remain free.' Meyer slowly took the bread from his mouth. 'I didn't think they'd start so quickly.'

'I don't suppose you did. How could you? To be blunt, you are all very bad bargains. The weapons you brought us are all lost, though you cannot be blamed directly. But you are now costing us lives, and for that you will be blamed. We prefer your room to your company.'

'We're in it too, you know.' Jens turned slightly and weighed up the one called Shepherd. 'I know. But whereas many other people will suffer with our deaths—I imagine it will be a lot more personal in your case.' Shepherd didn't answer. Jens looked back at the other two. 'Now I hope we understand our positions in this affair.'

'All you say is true,' Meyer began tactfully, 'but since we must

137

remain here for today at least—there won't be any delay if someone does go and see this factory, will there?'

'Your famous factory! You speak as if we were planning a trip to Tivoli! You make it all sound so nice, so easy, so agreeable! You idiots know nothing!' Jens leaned forward, knuckles doubled on the table-top. 'Do you know the route we must take to get to the Mercur? Do you know what your German friends have done now?

'Between us and Amager Island in the south lies the main harbour, continuously patrolled by launches. There are now just two bridges across—one filtering the traffic to Amager, the other filtering the traffic off—and there's a physical search of everyone and everything going in both directions. So you can tell me how you, or you,' he turned on Shepherd, 'are going to pass the checkpoints. Go on, tell me!' There was a long and uncomfortable silence.

'So that leaves me only one possible choice—you.' He looked down at Erikssen. 'Do you seriously think anything's to be gained by risking your life, and mine, and a lot of others', merely to see forests of wire and guns?'

'Don't get at me, friend,' Erikssen answered in flat, colourless Danish. 'All this one wants to do is to get across to Sweden just as quickly as possible—that's Gospel truth. I don't want to stay here a moment longer than's necessary. But I *do* know they'll have my cods on a plate if I get back to London without ever seeing that bloody factory; these English are not gentlemen.'

'Well?' Erikssen nodded. 'Be it on your own head!' Jens strode over to the scullery door. 'Come on man, hurry up!'

He took Erikssen along the alley and back to the decorator's workshop. Another man was waiting for them, sitting astride an empty paint drum, calmly smoking with his middle finger crooked round the pipe-stem, peacefully watching the doorway. 'This is the parachutist.' Jens introduced them curtly. 'He's one of us, though.' The waiting man slowly tapped out his pipe on the paint drum. Jens turned to Erikssen again. 'Put on those work-clothes.' He nodded at a distemper-splashed bib-and-brace snagged over a cupboard door. 'How do your papers describe you? Here! Let me look, I haven't all day to waste!' He held them into the light. ' "Electrician's Mate"—at least it's a start in the right direction!' Jens pushed the papers back and began changing into overalls himself.

'We'll be going in to do a bit of repair work on a house in Prags Boulevard, standing about two hundred metres from the factory building, we've made a watch-post up in the roof which

138

overlooks much of the defended area. It's the nearest you'll ever get to Mercur.

'Your excuse for coming with us will be to fix some electric wiring. I have receipts and work orders made out and stamped by the municipal engineer—they might fool the Militia just once more.' Jens paused to slip off his wedding ring. He went over to the cupboard and began rubbing a mixture of grease and dust under his fingernails, massaging the pallid skin, hiding the soft look of a lawyer's hands. Erikssen didn't need to try so hard. Jens continued to rub dirt into his neck and hairline as he rounded off.

'We'll cross the Lang bridge on our way in. I shall be going first; you second; Nils will be third, covering your back. If there's trouble—which pray God there isn't—scatter along Kalvebrod and get lost in the railway sidings and scrapyards.' Erikssen nodded, and Jens turned to the other man. 'Ready, Nils?'

They went out and uncovered their cycles. Jens swung aboard the first one which towed a box on wheels filled with paint cans and work-bags; Erikssen carried a short ladder and a few coils of electric cable; Nils was travelling light, he'd a Sten-gun rolled in his carpenter's tool kit.

Far too soon for comfort they'd begun pulling up the steep ramp which led on to the Lang bridge. A piercing grey wind slowly dragged itself off the Baltic, numbing a thin crowd obediently waiting to pass through the checkpoint.

The decorators dismounted and patiently joined the queue. Jens sniffed the sea damp. 'Looks like another early winter, Lars.' He playfully punched at Erikssen's ribs. 'You and the missus doing anything tonight? If you're not, we could all go round to Sigurd's after work. Pick up a few beers on the way back and spend the evening with them—it'll make a bit of fun. Anyhow, since your Knud and his Lisa are coming from Aalborg, I thought we'd...'

'Papers!' The Militia sergeant snapped his fingers. He scrambled the wallet and began spelling through the ID card. 'What's your name?'

'Lars Erikssen.'

'Y'full name, prickhead!'

'Lars Christian Erikssen.'

'What's your mother's name?'

'My mother's name?'

'Yes.' The sergeant looked up very slowly. 'Your mother's name.'

'Er, Amelie Schroeder.'

139

'That's better.' He went back to the ID card. 'What's your date of birth?'

'May 17th, 1903.'

'Place of registration?'

'Aalborg.'

'Why are you here in Copenhagen?'

'To work.'

'And very nice work too.' The sergeant was distracted by the photo opposite Erikssen's papers. 'Very nice.' He gloated for another couple of seconds before reluctantly handing back the wallet.

The three workmen veered left and pedalled up an unnaturally quiet street of houses. Towards the end, about a hundred yards short of the manned barrier, they stood their bikes against the kerb and began carrying the paints and ladder into one of the taller buildings. Jens led the way up to a small skylight overlooking the galvanising workshop and troop billets inside the factory perimeter. Erikssen blinked and hurriedly pulled back from the dusty glass.

They now shared the view with a pair of SS machine-gunners freezing up on the next roof, huddled together behind an LMG. 34 sighted across a few green sandbags. As he watched, one got up and stiffly crawled over to the chimney to wash his fingers in the warm flue gases.

'They've more gunners on another couple of roofs,' Jens explained, setting up the prismatic telescope and tripod he'd hidden in the loft a few days before, 'so keep well back from the window.' He wiped the eyepiece and objective lens with his handkerchief before stepping aside. 'Be my guest; go ahead; look at your factory as much as you like; I wish you luck of it.' He turned and went downstairs to talk with someone else.

Erikssen took over, focusing on the vernier screw as he started tracking round the defence system—counting the obstacles; soberly calculating the distances between the lights and their wire entanglements; estimating the number of troops on patrol; plotting the fire zones; the siting of each flak cannon and its shell dump; the SS billets and rest-areas. He remained cool and unmoved with the tight, habitual discipline of a professional soldier.

After a time he looked away and took a sheet of paper from his wallet, sat down on a packing case and started drawing a detailed map of the defences as he could see them. He noted everything on the dead ground which led right up to the wire in one part of

140

the galvaniser's yard. Half a lifetime of training went into the sketch; it was superb.

'Seen enough to be satisfied?' Jens had climbed back into the loft. Erikssen nodded. 'Very well, let's go down and get ready to move off. The picquet on the barrier is changed on the hour—it's the best time for us to go through.'

The decorators cycled back to the second bridge, dismounted and joined the queue. But this time the checkpoint was also manned by a squad from the crack 124th (Würtembergische) Regiment of the Alpenkorps—Erikssen carefully noted for London's interrogation team—probably on detachment from Norway. The actual donkey work, of course, was being done by the Militia. They were more than usually vindictive, piling up good marks with their protectors.

Jens was the first of the three to go through the screen, and he made it without too much trouble. Then it was Erikssen's turn. He stepped up, papers held ready for the Danish collaborator to check.

'Name?'

'Lars Christian Erikssen.'

'Commune Labour Permit?'

'Why, this is my Labour Permit.' Erikssen meekly touched one of the papers the Militiaman was holding. 'That, you obscenity, is franked for the Aalborg Commune!' He looked up, a knowing smirk growing in his face. 'You aren't even registered in Copenhagen, are you? You're dodging the labour draft, that's what you're doing. You're just another windy rat who fancies he can escape from taking a little trip to Germany by hiding in the great big city!' Two other grinning Militiamen started away from the wood brazier near their watch hut, one of them cheerfully loosening a pair of handcuffs on his belt. It was time to go.

Erikssen delicately twitched back his papers, swung the edge of his fist and death-chopped the Militiaman's larynx. He swerved the cycle, dropped his head and raced down the slope for Kalvebrod.

'HALT!' The Wehrmacht Feldwebel raised his arm. 'Sperrfeur —LOS!' A storm of automatic fire ripped over the barricade, gnawing up the road, swiping chunks of stone round the wobbling cyclists. The soldiers were too busy finding their aim to notice the shabby carpenter drop his bag, crouch and rev through a full clip. Nils ran, crabbing down the ramp, switching magazines, winning time for Jens and Erikssen. A dying Militiaman brought him down with a kneeling pistol shot in the spine.

Erikssen overtook Jens at the bottom of the ramp, beat him to

141

the railway siding and skidded his cycle into the gateway. He turned, dragged out his Colt and covered Jens over the last ten yards. He collapsed behind the gatepost, shaking badly, clumsily chasing a grenade through his overalls as a Militia troop carrier swerved into the road from the bridge. 'Use this!'

The drab-grey Steyr slewed right, gunning its motor to jump the kerb as Erikssen stepped out and side-armed the grenade at its narrow windscreen. The driver stood on his brakes and started to bale out as it went off, slamming the carrier at a stack of sawn timber. It reared up and slowly overturned. The two running men felt the heat flash as its fuel tank detonated above the shrieking Militia trapped behind jammed doors.

'Where now?' Erikssen grabbed and steadied Jens, reeling with hunger. 'Just keep going!' He pulled away, tottered upright and fired his legs for the end of the tracks where a local train was snuffling off, tiredly picking up speed. Erikssen easily outran him, hooked the iron railings on one coach and vaulted aboard, turned and dragged Jens after him. 'Now?'

'There!' Jens dropped his head and bolted across the observation platform into the tiny lavatory. Three minutes on, as the train slowed into its first station, two men rolled off, hit the ballast and sprinted for a goods exit. Their luck held.

Jens knew where he was going. He steered Erikssen into a poor bar. The man serving beers dropped his glass cloth and hurried them to a back room. 'Where's the phone?'

'Over here!' Jens followed him behind the alcove curtain. 'What's happening?'

'Go small!' Jens fed the coin-box with ten øre bits, dialling Sørensen's home number. He glanced back at the bar-keeper. 'Got two caps and different coats?'

'Yes.'

'Fetch.' He faced the mouthpiece as Sørensen lifted the receiver and cleared his throat. Jens cut him short. '*Eggbeater!*'

'Right!' Sørensen immediately hung up and trotted out to the loft where Meyer and Shepherd were hiding. 'You must go at once!' Meyer was on his feet, cradling the transmitter case under one arm, ready to move. 'Things have gone badly.' Sørensen was a frightened man with far-reaching problems to solve in the next handful of seconds. He turned and ran the two Englishmen down to the ground floor. 'Which of you understands Danish the best?'

'I do.' Sørensen looked at Shepherd. 'Excellent. You're my assistant.' He bit his mouth and thought hard. 'Behind that wall you'll find a wardrobe; inside are our coats, scarves and tall hats;

142

start putting on the best fit!' He spun and sized Meyer's body. 'I was right; come here!'

He hurried the man over to an old, glass-sided hearse, originally a glossy black and nobly built for two pair of horses. Now, with the rationing of animal fodder, the shafts had been cut down to take the single hack which Sørensen stabled next to his workshop. 'That's yours.' He pointed to a plain, white-painted coffin waiting to be slid aboard.

'Inside?'

'Yes, and get your stuff in, quickly!' He bedded Meyer down with Shepherd's thrown-off clothes, but stuck at the transmitter case. 'God help us!' Sørensen jumped down and stowed the radio in a locker, behind some lowering tapes and useful black cloths. 'How the hell do I breathe in here?' Meyer peered over the coffin rim. 'I'll see to that; put your head down!' Sørensen climbed up again and began to screw the lid tight, using brass washers to make a slight gap for ventilation. 'Better?'

'Not much.'

'Now listen to me very carefully. We shall be stopped twice on the way out to the cemetery—unless they've changed their search. Both times it's nothing to worry about. Just stay completely still and quiet, understand?' Sørensen jumped off and hurried behind the wall to change himself and to see how the other man was making out.

Shepherd had dressed with skill. His lanky hair was neatly combed to a centre parting; the pointed face was sad and drawn with official, paid grief; a mauve stock joined his neck to the threadbare frock-coat which hung nearly down to his ankles, cased in a pair of grubby spats. He stood ready with a tall silk hat and limp streamers tucked under one frail arm.

'Uh huh.' Sørensen nodded, stripping off his jacket as he began to explain this man's part. 'You're a mute—we use them for mourners and sidemen. You can neither speak nor hear, of course, but you can lip-read which means that you can follow instructions and act on them if you have to.'

'Right.'

'I'm going to try and get you to my mortuary chapel—or, rather, the one I rent—which is next to the Sondermark Crematorium. It's as safe as any place can be for you now, and it's naturally quiet.' He paused to knot his stock and set the angle.

'I shall be acting as your liaison from now on till you go. I shall bring out your friend as soon as he arrives, understand?' He didn't wait for an answer but turned and hurried out to the horse-stall. 'Get those doors opened!'

143

Shepherd obeyed and helped harness up a painfully thin, tubercular mare. Sørensen adjusted her snaffle. 'It's the only reason we haven't turned her into sausage meat—yet. That, and the fact that I don't want to pull the clients myself. So.' he finished and mounted the box seat, 'get the yard gates open now.' Shepherd went ahead and waited for the hearse to catch up and pass before swinging the gates shut and clambering up beside Sørensen, grave and serious, a black-ribboned whip in one hand, the silk hat pulled down over his ears.

The hearse probably made good time to the cemetery, but cycles and fast pedestrians were serious competition. A few of the older people reverently touched their hats as it plodded along the streets, but apart from that no-one cared. Even the troops on duty at the two checkpoints were glad to see it move on.

Sørensen whipped up the mare and reined her through the cemetery entrance, shambling her down a gravelly drive closely planted with cypress trees. They reached the chapel and Shepherd helped him ease the coffin, sliding it along the runners of a bearer trolley before trundling into the small, granite building. Sørensen locked the doors from the inside and deftly unscrewed the coffin lid to let Meyer out. He looked round and tiredly pocketed his screwdriver. 'You'll remain here till something can be done to get you away. You won't open up to anyone unless you know it's me, understand?'

'How shall we know that?' Shepherd stopped peeling off the black frock-coat. 'You'll know it's me when I knock twice and slip a piece of white card round the door-frame. That way,' he added simply, 'if I'm taken by them and brought here you'll know what's happening. A knock without a card means the Germans are with me, understand?' Meyer nodded for them both. 'Meanwhile, let me show you where you can hide.'

Sørensen went over to one of four catafalques built in line, waiting to support coffins before burial. He stooped and dragged away one of the heavy wooden sides. 'Down there, under this floor, you'll find a small vault.' He straightened up. 'It's no longer in use—hasn't been this last eighty years—so you won't be troubled. We store a few things in the niches, including a kerosene lantern and some matches which you can use to make yourselves comfortable.' Sørensen picked up Shepherd's coat and hat as he started moving over to the door. Meyer followed him as he finished off. 'I shall ask my wife to make you some food; I'll bring it over with your friend.'

'Why couldn't we have waited, then all come over together?' Sørensen looked him over. 'Be thankful you're safe, if only for

144

the moment. We got you away while we could.' He turned the key in the door. 'So stay here, out of sight, while I bring in your radio.'

The ride back was a repeat of the one out—slow, watchful and very hard on the nerves, but no preparation for the other end.

Jens had dragged Erikssen into the workshop, head lolling, arms pulled over both shoulders, knees buckling under the load across his back. He'd squatted behind a vat of formalin, covering the door and yard with his revolver while Frue Sørensen worked fast, staunching the venous blood weeping from Erikssen's side.

'What the hell's happened!' Sørensen threw the door shut and ran to the man laid out on a bench among the jars of tinting fluid. Jens tiredly got to his feet. 'Jumped by a Militia patrol in Brocksgade. He dropped a couple. I did the others and carried him into the park like a drunk.'

'How did you get away?'

'Bribed a taxi.'

'To the decorator's?'

'Yes.'

'Christalmighty!' Sørensen was furious. 'You brought him to me, directly!'

'Who else!' Jens flared back. 'You're the only safe letter-box now!'

'How did it go wrong?' Sørensen shouted over his shoulder, hurrying to the end of his workshop and pulling something from under the deep sinks. He ran back with a looted Wehrmacht medical kit. His wife stood ready as he ripped open the brown canvas flap and set to work on Erikssen. She slapped a pair of blunt-nosed scissors across his palm; he began cutting away the man's clothing. 'What happened?'

'They started to pick him up at the checkpoint. He socked one and bolted. We bombed one of their troop carriers at the scrap-yard and broke out on the train to Valby.'

Sørensen wasn't listening any more, he'd just laid Erikssen bare by slitting open the trousers and flannel shirt. He was out of his depth with this mess.

The Militia's cheap alloy bullet had driven an entry three fingers from the nineteenth vertebra; fragmented and dum-dummed out through the man's right side, scooping an exit wound the size of a small orange. Erikssen must have instinctively thumbed in a wad of clothing as he went down; now it was a sludge of bloody rags and pearly white tissue. Sørensen looked away. 'Where's our safe doctor?'

145

'There isn't one.' Jens stood where he could watch the door and Sørensen at the same time. 'Do it yourself.'

'Not this I can't!' Sørensen nervously wiped his mouth along the back of his hand. 'He'll drain the moment I touch it!'

'No doctor!'

'He'll bleed to death!'

'He's doing that anyhow!' Jens elbowed Sørensen aside while he rummaged through the medical kit. 'Spray this over him; it's marked "Adrenalin"; it might help.' He deftly filed open a glass ampoule, holding it at eye level to load a syringe. 'No, give me room, I'm quicker!'

Erikssen shocked awake and began to shriek as Jens aimed the syringe at his side. Frue Sørensen gagged the writhing man while her husband stabbed a morphia syrette in the exposed thigh and knocked him out.

Jens worked fast. He ripped open gauze and crêpe-paper shell dressings from the haversack, packing them in Erikssen's side. He glanced up sharply. 'Linen!'

Sørensen tore a new shroud. Jens bound the strips tight, pinning them over both wounds. He jerked his head sideways at the hearse, still waiting outside the workshop. 'Putting him aboard the Himmel Express?'

'What d'you reckon?' Sørensen moved the light, giving Jens a better view of his work. 'It's the best thing now. Once they get that taxi-driver and put him through the squeezer we'll be washed-up here.' He looked at Sørensen. 'Get another sheet to put under him and we'll lift him in a box while your wife covers our trail from the decorator's.'

They heaved Erikssen's coffin into the hearse, tiredly sliding it along the runners. Sørensen turned and looked appealingly at Jens as he wiped his hands clean on a piece of the shroud. 'Will you come and be my assistant?'

'No.' Jens peeled off his raincoat and looked where Erikssen's blood had splashed down the back. 'No. I'll be more of a liability than an asset. Someone must go back down the pipeline to shut off what might remain after today's stupidity. The Gestapo have at least two tails to pull if they find them—the taxi-driver, and Nils. Both of them know too much.' He paused, softening a little. 'Get that one off your hands and then go into deep quarantine; no more helping these idiots, understand?'

'You're right.'

Jens left the yard by another way as Sørensen climbed up to the box seat, pulled a black oilskin over his knees against the steady rain and set off back to the cemetery. The first check-

146

point passed easily enough, then the second one dragged into view.

'You again?' the young Militia corporal on pass control demanded. 'And where are we going this time, I wonder?' He arrogantly prodded the dejected mare and slowly hitched at the Krag carbine under his cape. 'Well?'

'Alas, I must go back to the cemetery.'

'Without a mate?' Sørensen was all misery, real and simulated. 'It rains so heavily, and Arne isn't as strong as he was in the days when he first came to work for me. We must all grow old with time, my son.'

'So?'

'I allowed him to remain at the cemetery while I returned,' he sighed tiredly, 'while I returned for this unfortunate.'

'Two in one day?' The corporal glanced at the others who'd left their fire and were gathering round to watch the sport. 'Business must be improving.'

'It's the inclement season. Winter is always a busy time of the year for us.'

'Lucky you.' He motioned with the carbine barrel. 'Get down. Let's take a closer look at your load.'

'You would be unlikely to find any black market potatoes while I performed this solemn duty, my son.'

'We're after bigger fish than potatoes,' the corporal snapped. 'Get down!'

'Would you knowingly disturb the dead? Are you capable of such a thing?'

'Why not? They won't mind. We get used to them.'

'So I've been told,' Sørensen stepped down heavily, 'but I very much doubt if you see them in all the infinite variety we must prepare ourselves to face, every day.' They began to walk round to the end of the hearse.

'Let us consider this particular one as an example of what I mean by that,' Sørensen went on, one professional in Death comparing notes with another. 'A mother of five little children, and old before her time. For all that, destined to meet her end when a vat of boiling rubber accidentally exploded at her place of work. A most distressing matter to arrange satisfactorily. *Requiescat In Pace*.' He started to climb into the hearse.

'It is, of course, quite unusual in its severity. It will interest you.' Sørensen had judged his man correctly. 'Come closer, let me see if there is some way in which I can raise the casket lid, judge for yourself.' He gently stretched out his hand. 'Have you a sharply pointed knife? Your bayonet will do . . .'

147

'Get away from me.'

'I must have something pointed, to cut certain things.'

'Don't touch me!' The corporal backed off instinctively. 'Beat it, you old ghoul!'

'Those are harsh words, my son, you cannot mean them.'

'PISS OFF!'

The barrier swung aside and let the hearse clop past, dragging away into the evening murk. Sørensen chocked its wheels outside the chapel, rapped twice and slipped in one of his paste-board business cards. Shepherd pulled the doors ajar and let the man hurry inside. 'What happens?'

'You're the stronger, come here!' Meyer went out and helped wheel in Erikssen's coffin. Sørensen knelt on the lid and savagely twisted the screws.

'What's happened?'

'Shot in the side and dying,' he pushed the top away and felt around for the pulse in Erikssen's neck, 'if he hasn't already done so.' He paused for several seconds. 'No, it's still there, but thready.' Sørensen slowly climbed off and looked round at their two outlines against the fading light. 'I hope you are both happy with your day's work, Englishmen.' No one spoke.

Shepherd walked over and looked in at Erikssen. After a moment he glanced round at Sørensen. 'How do you get a doctor in Denmark?'

'You don't.'

'No doctors?'

'Not for you,' he paused, 'nor for us, either.' He looked from Shepherd to Meyer. 'The so-called authorities have developed a charming custom. They put a watch on all clinics and hospitals whenever there's been a shooting incident. Contact one now and we shall all meet in the cellars of Shell House.' He shrugged. 'In any case, he will die soon.'

'You're sure?'

'I patched the hole!' Sørensen jerked a hand inside his coat pocket and pulled out another morphia syrette. 'Use this if he should regain consciousness before death.' He slapped it on the coffin lid. 'Now I must return to my home, if it still remains.' He bowed slightly. 'I bid you both a good night, and goodbye.'

'Shall we stay here?' Shepherd sounded politely casual. Sørensen's sneer hit them like a wet rag. '*You* may do just whatever you like. Stay, or go, or cut your throats, we simply do not care any longer!' He banged the chapel door shut and left them to follow his advice.

'And I still don't know what happened.' Meyer shaded the

148

kerosene lantern over the coffin and began to calculate Erikssen's chances. They were non-existent.

A dew of cold sweat had already settled across his forehead; the lips were changing colour, twittering, silently forming words; the breathing was becoming more shallow and irregular, bubbling with fluids accumulating in the trachea; his pulse had lost its bouncing rhythm.

'What do you think?' Shepherd had come over to stand opposite Meyer. He shifted the lantern to read his watch. 'He won't take another half hour of this.'

'That long?'

But the Dane had been an obstinate man all his life, and he hung on stubbornly, only giving ground to the enemy when he had to, wrestling with the shades every step back. Finally, at a little before seven in the evening, Lars Christian Erikssen tired of the uneven fight.

Meyer had been saving the lantern's oil, now he turned up the wick and shut Erikssen's eyes. Shepherd handed him a couple of brass, two kroner pieces and made ready to slide the lid back as soon as Meyer had finished emptying Erikssen's pockets.

They walked over to the catafalque, Shepherd pulling the false side shut before following Meyer down into the vault. He paused on the bottom step and tiredly looked around. 'So that's that.' Meyer nodded and hung the lantern from a bracket over one of the coffin niches. He sat down on an empty ammunition box someone had left with the oil and matches. 'How far did he say Sweden was from here?'

'About three hours, *if* you could get the boat.'

'My geography isn't good,' Meyer commented, gently pulling an ear lobe, 'but I've a strong idea the distance is much less—farther up the coast by Helsingør.' He paused. 'What do you think?'

'Think? I think that someone's already pointed that out to the Germans; they're not all daft.' Meyer winced and began going through Erikssen's things. He broke one of the three chocolate bars and passed it over with Shepherd's share of the rations. 'You'd better have this as well.' Meyer held out the Colt which someone, probably Jens, had stowed back in its holster. Shepherd cleared the live round from its breech, sniffing the stale reek of burnt cordite while Meyer sadly turned over Erikssen's papers. He went on speaking, mainly to himself. 'God, how I wish I knew what happened out there.'

'Does it matter now?'

'Perhaps not; perhaps it doesn't matter very much now.' Shepherd bit off a piece of the opened chocolate and let it melt in his mouth, using his tongue to hold it away from a badly filled tooth. After a time he looked up from the floor. 'I suppose Erikssen was well-intentioned—in his own funny way.'

'Mm?'

'I said that he was probably all right in his own way.' Shepherd carefully rewrapped the chocolate and stepped over to get a better view of the paper which Meyer was smoothing out on one knee. 'What've you found?'

'The late Erikssen was not only well-intentioned—he was also true to everything the Army ever taught him.' Meyer looked up and handed the paper to Shepherd. 'Take a look at that survey. Quite fair, isn't it?'

'Uh huh.' Shepherd moved nearer the light and studied the meticulous drawing. After a while he turned it over to see if the Dane had written anything else on the reverse side, then glanced at Meyer. 'What d'you make of the famous defences?'

'I think they want to keep us out.'

'I think they have.'

Meyer grunted something and carefully lit one of Borg's cigarettes off the lantern chimney. He blew smoke away from Shepherd. 'They've certainly succeeded in doing that,' he thought aloud. 'How good are you at swimming?'

'You'd never reach Sweden. To kick off with, the current's too fierce, and the water's too cold.'

'You know the Sound?'

'I know the Baltic, which amounts to the same thing in the end.' Shepherd went quiet as his restless mind took itself for another walk round Erikssen's diagram. After a short pause he looked up again. 'I'll bet there's never been a fortification so perfectly defended against ground assault...'

'You'd probably win.' Meyer drew smoke and coughed gently. 'I like their machine-gunnery in particular.'

'Aye.' Shepherd chewed his lip. 'The way it covers the wiring is brilliant, there's no two ways about it. Of course, with such a small place they can afford to be thorough.'

'Of course.'

'Even so, someone knows his trade.' He paused. 'I thought I'd seen it all at Koivisto. The Ivans put everything into that sector —mines, machine-gun nests, tanks, artillery, the whole bloody shoot.'

'So?' Meyer was studiously impartial on the subject of Shepherd versus the Red Army. The little man shrugged. 'So this

150

fascinates me too, in a way.' He sombrely folded the sheet of paper. 'I'd give a lot to try it with the right equipment.'

'A nice day-dream.' Meyer blew smoke down his nostrils and stretched out his legs. 'I think you would give a lot if you were to try, regardless of the equipment.' He grinned ironically. 'At the very least you'd give your life.'

'That'd be some hardship.'

'You speak of your life?'

'Aye.'

'Very curious.' Meyer drew on the cigarette. '*I* was brought up believing it to be the most precious thing one had to lose.'

'Just wait.' Shepherd was bitter. 'See what you think of it later on.'

'What's the matter?' Meyer narrowed his eyes. 'What troubles you?'

'Nothing you'd understand. Nothing but the certain knowledge of what's waiting for me if I'm fool enough to survive the next few years.'

'The next few hours, more likely.'

'All right. Even that's not such a bad thing.'

'What?'

'I said you'd not understand; how could you? You don't have the horror of an old age to be spent alone. Embrocation, long flannel underwear and the Old Folks' Home.' His voice turned flat and hard. 'I've had a gutful of Homes and Institutions; I shall never go in another.' Meyer nodded and slowly looked up. 'You were quite wrong, my friend, I can understand.'

'Thanks, but it still remains.'

'True enough, I'm very sorry.'

'You've no need to be.' Meyer ignored the vicious tone. 'I *am* sorry because, at least I have the hope of reaching Palestine one day, whereas you haven't.' He paused. 'You are more of a wandering Jew than I shall ever be—and that's very bad.'

'I'll beat it yet.'

'With a bullet?'

'If I have to.'

'That's no solution.'

'I think it might be.'

'You're wrong, I'm afraid.'

'Am I?' Shepherd sneered. 'While you sit there handing out aspirin tablets for the world's ills—remember where we are now. We may be unloved, but we're certainly not unwanted.'

'That's one way of putting it.' Meyer took the hint and gave up humouring Shepherd. The little man scratched his neck and

151

chest. 'Though I stink like the bottom of a dog basket, we've a sketch of Mercur; that should amuse London if ever we get back.' Meyer nodded and pulled out his ration of German cigarettes, nipping one in half and lighting up from the lantern. He sat back and watched Shepherd restlessly move around the vault. 'I'm glad you mentioned that.'

'The factory?'

'Yes. I've been thinking of it myself.'

'Oh? Which part?' Meyer took his time. 'The thought of reaching Sweden doesn't worry me—I think we'll do it quite easily.'

'Easily? That's nice to know. What the hell's it got to do with the factory?'

'A great deal. Very soon after we get to Sweden they're going to start questioning us—interrogating us, if you prefer it that way.'

'You're repeating yourself, we went over all this earlier today. Because of it Erikssen went out and stopped one.'

'I know.' Meyer smoked hard for a couple of seconds. 'I also know that things are going to be difficult for us unless we both have an agreed story. You know what they're like in London.'

'Let's get there first.' Meyer shook his head. 'We shall never have a time like this again, we'd better agree now on what we have to tell them.'

'While I admire your motives, I'm buggered if I can see why we have to fret over it now!'

'Let me put it simply, maybe you will then,' Meyer grated. 'London sent us to sabotage this factory.'

'Wrong. London sent four men to sabotage this factory; we're what's left!' Meyer was patient. 'As I was saying, London sent us to sabotage this factory, and it hasn't been done. They're not going to like it very much.'

'Small bloody wonder.'

'One moment!' Meyer dragged on his cigarette, 'Let me finish!'

'Go on.'

'What I'm interested in hearing.' He puffed smoke and coughed. 'No, let me put it another way. A few seconds ago you said you'd like to attack this factory.'

'With the right equipment!'

'By the living God!' Meyer roared. 'Just let me finish off one sentence!'

'Go on, then!'

Meyer chewed smoke and squinted at the little man through the grey haze. 'For the last time of trying—how would you attack Mercur, eh?'

'Are you serious?'

'I've never been more so—*I* can imagine the grilling we shall be put through once we reach London.'

'Uh huh.' Shepherd shook his head. '*If* we reach London.'

'We shall.' Meyer sounded oddly confident. 'I've a few ideas over that particular problem.'

'Then it's a pity you can't stretch them to include the factory as well!' Shepherd began irritably pacing round the vault. He stopped short and slowly looked back at Meyer from the opposite corner. 'Could you be right, I wonder?'

'Depend upon it, I am.' Meyer was very terse. 'That's the one good reason why I'm listening to all you have to say.'

'Is it now?' Shepherd didn't hurry as he unwrapped a bar of chocolate and gnawed off a corner. He licked his fingers clean and carefully unfolded the sketch diagram. 'All right, if that's the way you want it, let's play at make-believe,' he began walking across, 'let's pretend to attack Mercur.'

'How?'

'Follow me closely and you'll see.' Shepherd pulled up another empty ammunition box and sat down, facing Meyer. 'As Morgan would have said to the chaps, there exist but three ways in— underground, by air, at ground level.' He paused to smooth the paper. 'Numbers One and Two are beyond us now, which leaves us choice number Three—the ground attack.'

'Tactically brilliant!'

'Save the humour. Remember, you're the one haunted by fears of London, not me, so pay attention!'

'Very well, prove me wrong.'

Shepherd sucked his teeth and decided to be patient for a little while longer. 'The only sensible way inside Mercur is where it's always been—through the front door like gentlemen, not farting round the wire like Morgan.'

'Miraculous.'

'Jesus wept!' Shepherd held on to his temper's coat-tails with difficulty. 'If I had to get inside such a place, you know what I'd do? I'd pinch a flat hat, hammer the door down and demand to read the canteen gas meter!' Meyer's laugh wasn't kind. 'You don't believe me, do you?'

'Frankly, no.' Meyer took off time to elegantly jet smoke at the lantern. 'I think you are a little mad.'

'Fortunately for us both, I know I'm not!' Shepherd flicked the drawing with a fingernail. 'Try using that high voltage intellect of yours for once and look at Mercur through my eyes.' He paused. 'Inside that celebrated wire they've stuck Christ knows

153

how many troops, all with one purpose in life, stopping us. Imagine them, if you can. Scores of trigger-happy humans, all milling round; all getting under each other's feet; all full of pep-talk; all waiting for hundreds of sinister men with darkened faces to come creeping through the undergrowth.' He paused to check the drawing for a sudden idea.

'As I was saying, under those conditions they're seeing spies behind every tussock of grass. I wouldn't mind betting they're getting casualty reports every morning as guard plugs guard in the dark.' He paused moodily. 'Yet they wouldn't spare a second thought for the gas-meter inspector.' Meyer dragged on his cigar-ette and carefully picked a crumb of tobacco off the tip. He looked up after a moment. 'You have the gift of words; you make it all sound so easy.'

'Oh no, I don't! You're the one who wants a likely story in the unlikely event of us returning to London.' He paused, checking the diagram for something else.

'They won't buy it. The Army can't demote you, but it can lock you in an observation ward—that is the right expression, isn't it?'

'It is, and thank you.' Shepherd went back to analysing the diagram while Meyer carried on smoking. He looked up angrily. 'That bloody Roumanian tobacco stinks even worse than you say it tastes! Either put it out or go upstairs!' Meyer sighed and carefully ground out the butt, saving it for later. 'And while I'm about it, let me tell you something else, something that'll show you what I mean about using the obvious when all the usual gambits fail.'

'Tell me.'

'Pay attention because, like all my little anecdotes, it'll be told at the expense of your Ivan pals.'

'Of course.'

'Remember, too, that in Finland we were always out-numbered, out-bombed, out-gunned.' He scowled at the memory. 'Against those slight disadvantages we did hold a few tricks—mainly because we fought in our own back garden for most of the time, and because we used brain power.'

'Zum Beispiel?' Meyer was chilling fast.

'Like this time, for example.' Shepherd pushed the diagram aside and crouched farther into the light. 'We'd infiltrated the Ivan advance by several dozen kilometres—or they'd overrun our position, whichever way you care to look at it. Anyhow, the company lay holed-up in the forest either side of an arterial road down which rumbled convoy after convoy, all going to the front.

154

We just lay there, infested with body lice and nigh on frozen to death, watching torrents of armour, guns, lorried infantry, the whole works stream past without stop. At first we thought about ambushing a few with a home-made landslide before breaking to the west—but it was too crude, and unlikely to hurt them enough. Then a particular mate of mine—another Sergeant, from Tampere—had an idea, started to use brain power.

'We both went down to the road and waited for a chance to catch ourselves a couple of fresh Ivan MP's, the sort which rushed up and down on motor-bikes every so often. The uniforms were scruffy and only fitted where they touched, so we both looked every inch a Russian Liberator. Anyhow,' he went on, 'we chugged along the road to a point about nine hundred metres above our bivouac where a large forestry trail wound off to the left, aiming itself at endless Karelian lakes and trees.

'Even if a convoy just ran up it they'd be stuck for hours before they could reverse clear again. But,' Shepherd added, 'there was one bonus feature which Arvo, my mate, thought up for Ivan. It was turning spring and the thaw was well under way. I don't suppose you know what a Finnish thaw is really like?'

'No.'

'You've not missed anything. Melting ice, slush, biting easterly winds, grey skies, loneliness on the big scale and mud, always mud. However, as I was saying, the thaw was well under way, loosening everything it touched. At the same time, during the winter, this forestry trail had been laid on logs and run across a sizeable, frozen swamp. To the careless it looked rock solid, good for a thousand years.' Meyer nodded, following the story like a connoisseur.

'So we parked our motor-bikes, took out a "Diversion" placard from the MP's kit and set it up in the middle of the road. Very soon the next convoy rushed into sight—lorries piled high with stores, five or six tractor limbers towing howitzers, even a squadron of medium tanks.' He paused, smiling oddly. 'I thought they'd never stop. At the last moment the commander's staff-car braked hard, damn near running us down. "What the hell's the matter now?" he shouted out at us. "Road thaw and earth-slip, comrade Major!" Arvo snapped back, saluting like an MP should. "Such a diversion isn't marked on the issue map," he was an above average Ivan, "explain yourself!" "Newly pioneered, comrade Major!" I cut in glibly. "It crosses firmer ground and rejoins the highway at kilometre 400."' Shepherd paused, thinking.

'In the end they believed us and sank through the mud with-

155

out trace—just some oil slicks and ration boxes on top. We watched them go under. About half a dozen tried wading back through the ooze. I put an end to that.' Meyer coughed and slowly glanced up. 'I suppose the moral of your tale is, "never trust a copper?"' He began picking his teeth with a matchstick. 'You've proved your point, so did the Trojans. But it wouldn't work—even if London put in another team, with explosives and so on. *That's* your real problem, I think.'

'Not for me it isn't.'

'I don't understand?'

'You don't have to. Once inside that place and I'd send it sky high.'

'Without your explosives?'

'Simple.'

'How?'

'I began sweating my guts out in an ordnance works on the morning of my thirteenth birthday. By the time I finished I'd built more bombs and shells than you've had hot dinners.'

'So?'

'So there's no big mystery about explosives, it's the first trade I ever learned. There's not a self-respecting chemist shop in any town that doesn't carry enough stock to rip out the entire neighbourhood, when it's correctly proportioned.'

'You can actually *make* explosives?' Meyer was becoming quietly excited. 'Make them as well as use them?'

'Of course.'

'Can you make dynamite?'

'No.' He paused and enjoyed Meyer's disappointment. 'The Nitro element is too tricky for kitchen-sink armourers; the glycerine has to be blended with the acids round coils which circulate chilled brine, for one thing. But if you're really hard up for ideas, you can always fall back on benzine or simple sugar for energisers.'

'Sugar?' Meyer sneered.

'Yes, sugar!' He paused irritably. 'Icing sugar and sulphuric acid is the base of a dandy incendiary compound. While ordinary loaf sugar and stuff like sodium chlorate will go off very nicely. It's criminally unstable and quite highly rated for power.' He paused again, stepping back in time. 'And if you add fifteen per cent of aluminium or magnesium dust, the power generated goes up seventy-five to eighty per cent over normal, weight for weight and under Standard Test Conditions. A few ounces will knock over a small house.'

'You're not joking, are you?'

156

'Don't be a prat all your life!'

'I'm sorry.'

'All right. But those are only easy examples—there are fifty or sixty others even more unpleasant to use. A major drawback with this sort of explosive is the mess it can make of your hands; they generally come off at the elbows.' Meyer was the first to pick up the talk again. He coughed and scratched himself, 'You could replace the explosives we lost, if you had to?'

'After a fashion,' Shepherd began to sound cagey, 'yes.'

'And you've outlined a way of getting inside Mercur, if you had to?'

'Oh no!' Shepherd chopped the air between them with the cutting edge of his hand. 'You can put that idea away! We're much better employed thinking a way back to England!' He paused. 'Those clever dicks in London have the rank, they have the pay and they have the prestige. So far as I'm concerned it's their pigeon, not mine!'

'Only a few minutes ago you said you'd like to try!'

'Nuts!' But Meyer wasn't paying attention any longer. 'You know,' he said, coming back from some private and invisible point in time ahead, 'I believe the original plan can still be done!' He smiled radiantly. 'What a beautiful attack it could be; what a masterly partisan stroke; what perfection.'

'Go to it, wonder boy!' Shepherd jeered unpleasantly. 'Practice as much as you like for the New Jerusalem—count me out!'

'No,' Meyer was still smiling to himself, 'you're necessary. You've talked too much about brain power, I've been convinced. You were right all along.' He paused ironically. 'Where's your problem?'

'The problem, cloth ears, is to be found in the slight difference between me giving you a pleasing story to tell London and having to prove it personally! For us, as we are, to attack this Mercur—if we survived that long—is too much like ramming my arm down a shark's gullet. Easy to get in, impossible to pull out.'

'Easy, you say?'

'So far as it goes, yes. The factory could be done my way,' he admitted grudgingly. 'After all, people must be running in and out of those gates at all hours of the day and night. It's the old, old story—you just have to be born the right sort of people to get anywhere in this world.' Meyer squinted thoughtfully. 'Who do *you* think stands the best chance?'

'Batman.'

'I am serious!'

'Then more fool you.'

157

'Shepherd, listen to me very carefully!' A new Meyer crouched into the light. 'If there remains but a single chance to destroy that place, *I* shall take it!'

'Again, more fool you.'

'I can remember why it must be done—even if you can't!'

'You were twerp enough to believe that Brigadier?'

'No—but I believed what he had to say.'

'I suppose there's a difference.'

'Yes there is, you damned thick-headed Englander!' Meyer bit his tongue. 'I know what my nation can do to its own people; I don't wish that on anyone else.' He paused to become more subtle in his tactics. 'Your approach to the problem was right; I was wrong to disbelieve you.'

'Thanks.'

'I remember the time I learned English. Part of the course was a short story by your G. K. Chesterton—one of his Father Brown series, I think.' Shepherd rolled his eyes to heaven. 'In this particular one a corpse is smuggled out from an apartment building, right past the porter or janitor. It was carried in a sack by the postman—yet afterwards the porter testified to the police that no one had passed that way.'

'Very roughly what I told you in the first place.'

'Quite,' Meyer seemed pleased, 'because there are some classes of person the world takes for granted. One never notices them, they're always there, part of the furniture.'

'Still my idea.'

'I know, I know!' Meyer brought his temper under control. 'So, can you tell me who the world takes for granted the most?'

'RE Sappers for one; Signals Corporals for another; us.'

'Very, very unlikely to work in this case.'

'If you don't like that, why not a policeman?'

'Could be an answer.'

'Or a smart soldier-laddy?'

'No.' Meyer knew he was being incredibly patient.

'There's always your famous postman.' Shepherd sarcastically clapped his hands. 'Just imagine, I could not only make a parcel bomb—but deliver it too!'

'Hold your mouth!' Meyer broke at last.

The anger and cursing flared up, then died back as they viciously nagged each other over Erikssen's diagram. Nobody led the thinking, and nobody followed. Two unusual talents had agreed to co-operate for a short while; it was the best they could do; it would be enough.

Towards midnight, Meyer tiredly got up and refilled the lan-

158

tern with kerosene for the third time round. Shepherd struck a match and gave him light to trim the wick. Meyer sniffed and stood aside. 'The ventilation is atrocious in here!'

'Small wonder—if you think about it a moment,' Shepherd commented, lighting up and reseating the glass chimney. Meyer climbed the vault steps and pushed open the false side to let some fresh air seep in. He ducked round and slowly came back. 'Anyhow, as I was saying, the final decision to attack can only come once we've heard from London—and that raises the problem of a good transmission site.'

'That's the bit I won't buy at any price.'

'You don't think the Underground will co-operate?'

'Not them so much, but London. I don't like being too dependent on non-existent goodwill.'

'What of the Danes?'

'They're not the most enthusiastic of our fans, either.' Shepherd went on fiddling with the lantern's flame. Meyer frowned. 'Please?'

'They don't like us.'

'I see. Yet only a little time ago you said you'd be able to handle them,' he was terse, 'why the sudden change of heart?'

'Up till then you hadn't decided to rope in London.' He sat down on one of the boxes and tiredly bunched his fists. 'You know my views. This job has to be done quickly, if at all. I don't see London co-operating within days, let alone hours. I'll play at silly buggers and carry on with the attack just so long as it's a matter of bullying the underground people—that I can do.' He paused thoughtfully. 'But for us to rely on London giving their all, quickly and on time, simply isn't good business in my book.'

'What if I guarantee it, what then?'

'Can you?'

'Yes.'

'How?'

'I'll be enciphering the telegram; they'll come running.'

'Hm.'

'Can you guarantee so much from the Danes?'

'No.' Shepherd toed one of Meyer's old cigarette ends across the floor. 'The only thing I can promise is, there won't be any hanky panky. They'll be whispering behind their hands, of course, but I'll be listening.'

'*If* they come back for us.'

'They will,' Shepherd learned forward confidently, 'it's the only certainty we have left in this life. Wait till their tempers cool, they'll come back. They'll come back either to push us over

159

the Sound, or pack us off to heaven.' Meyer frowned. 'You look surprised, you shouldn't be. Only one or the other makes sense to me now. Alive in Sweden, or dead in Denmark, we comb the Germans from their hair.'

'I agree with that, yes.' Meyer was smiling again. 'Frankly, in their place I shouldn't go to the trouble of looking for a boat. Two bullets and a word to the police will be quicker and cheaper.'

'Glad we're gradually coming round to look through the same end of the telescope.' Shepherd left the cigarette ends in peace and glanced up. 'In fact, I'd go so far as to say we both have nasty, suspicious minds.' Meyer almost grinned. 'Of course, my friend, I never thought otherwise. We're different from most people. Neither of us could have survived till now if we hadn't been very careful with smiling strangers, eh?'

It was well into the early hours when Jens returned to the chapel, working past the military patrols by taking to the sewers and drains under the city; coming up in a side road near the crematorium and cutting across the deserted cemetery. He thumped the door twice, slipped a card inside and waited. He had to thump again before Meyer let him in. Jens brushed past and climbed down into the vault where Shepherd sat waiting. He looked up in surprise. 'Hello, Jens—this is unexpected. What can we do for you?'

The Dane was breathing hard and stank of sewer damp as he slumped on one of the ammunition boxes. He sensed Meyer standing guard behind him, but quickly recovered his poise and even managed to smile a little. 'It has been decided that you both come with me now. We shall get you away from here.'

'To Sweden?'

'Of course,' he hesitated a fraction too long, 'where else but Sweden?' Jens didn't see Meyer pucker his mouth and silently nod across to Shepherd. The little man gave smile for smile. 'I just wanted to be sure. Thank you, Jens, you're a real pal.'

'Come on then, we haven't all night you know, there's a lot to be done.' He began getting to his feet again. Shepherd wagged his head. 'That's where you're wrong, friend, so please sit down again.' Jens' good humour began breaking apart from the inside. 'What the hell do you mean by that?'

'I mean we aren't going with you,' he paused delicately, 'to Sweden I think you said?'

'It's your only chance of survival!'

'Precisely.'

'But if you don't come quickly, the Germans will take you!'

160

'Instead, you'll take us? To Sweden?'

'That's what I said!'

'I believe you. We both believe you, but we're not going any-where tonight. We've changed our minds, we're going to stay here with you. Hard to please aren't we?'

'Gentlemen!' Jens nervously studied his fingertips. 'I am offering you the only chance you will ever have.'

'Thanks.'

Jens was an exhausted man, exhausted beyond human limits. He felt lost and alone in the hidden cross-currents of this ridiculous dialogue. He looked round at the ugly German, then back to the little rat. 'I simply cannot understand either of you.'

'It's really very easy—let me explain.' Shepherd was the soul of sympathy. 'My colleague and I have decided to attack the Mercur factory after all, but we're going to need a little help from you to make it successful.' Jens waited for Shepherd to finish off the joke. There was an awkward silence till it registered. 'YOU ARE INSANE.' He didn't shout, he just spoke very loud and very clear. 'YOU ARE BOTH INSANE, THE PAIR OF YOU.' Shepherd politely raised a hand and cut him off. 'Wrong. We both know exactly what we're going to do, and we also know what you're going to do, as well.'

'I doubt it!' Shepherd abruptly halved the distance between them. 'Just tell me if I'm guessing! You're about to leave and arrange for me to see a member, or members, of your Liberation Council.'

'NO!'

'I'm sorry you persist in seeing things that way, but it isn't going to make a scrap of difference! You will go, and you will get me that rendezvous.'

'NEVER!'

'You've no alternative, wrong again.'

'What makes you think that!'

'This. If we don't destroy Mercur from the inside, then certain unpleasant men in London are going to order its destruction from the outside. Of one thing you may be sure, Jens, it will be destroyed eventually. Don't fool your time away by thinking they won't, I can promise you they will. Unless we sabotage Mercur, and soon, the RAF will come instead. The bombers aren't going to stop while one brick stands on another. They'll have orders to flatten that factory, turn it into rubble and concrete dust.' He paused. 'And now we've reached the whole point of my tale, for, by the time they've done that to Mercur, very little is going to be standing in that part of Copenhagen either. Not every bomb hits

161

its target, you know. Very often they scatter all over the place—something which a lot of your friends are going to have reason to know from bitter experience unless you change your mind, and change it soon.' He let the other man catch up again.

'I hate having to remind you of this just now, but it's in everyone's best interests to work together from here on—you do understand me?' Jens had aged a lot in the past few hours; he was no longer the man he had been. 'It's not possible the RAF would do it to us, we're allies.'

'This is your unlucky day—wrong for the third time!'

'I can't tell you anything,' Jens' eyes watered, probably with the smoke drifting from Meyer's cigarette. 'I must speak with others about this.'

'That's all I asked for in the first place,' Shepherd gently chided him, 'we're not unreasonable men, really.'

Meyer escorted Jens up to the chapel door and showed him into the night. 'Mind you remember my friend's words,' he said, jutting a bony hand for the other man to shake. 'It would be very unwise if you forgot them, or let someone else talk you into changing your mind again.'

162

CHAPTER FIFTEEN

JENS came back a couple of hours before daybreak. Shepherd let the man step inside, turned and carefully followed him down the vault steps. 'Well, what's happening now?' Jens tiredly hunched his shoulders. 'You have a rendezvous with two men from the Council.'

'Good.' Shepherd twitched his raincoat off the pile of old sacking he'd used for a bed. 'Where're they now?'

'Waiting outside.' Jens glanced at Meyer on another pad of sacks. 'You're to come as well.'

'Oh no I'm not.' He coughed sleepily. 'I like it down here.' Jens didn't argue. He turned and wearily climbed back to the mortuary chapel.

He led the way between dank shrubs and trees, cold and wet in the windy darkness before dawn. They branched left up an unseen gravel path which ran at a large tool-shed by one of the cemetery walls. Two silhouettes moved round the corner as they approached the shed. They all came together in its doorway, the blackest part of a very black night. 'This is one of the Englishmen,' Jens opened in quick-fire Danish.

'Where's the other one?'

'He doesn't trust us; he won't come.'

'I see.' The silhouette stepped closer. 'Then ask this one what the devil he wants.'

'I want you.' Shepherd's staccato Norwegian abruptly cut out the middleman. There was an empty pause at this surprise move. The silhouette coughed discreetly. 'I didn't realise you, uh, spoke Danish.'

'Small matter, I only want your help.'

'For Mercur's sabotage?'

'Correct.'

'You sound very sure of yourself, Englishman,' the second man interrupted. 'What if we choose to disagree with you?'

'You won't.'

'Oh? What makes you think that?'

'Smiler,' Shepherd pitched his voice sideways at Jens, 'told you all about the RAF coming?'

'He mentioned it.'

'Now you know. You'll see things my way in the end. We work together on this attack, or you can stand by and watch your city get knocked around—take your pick. One thing though,' he added, 'don't delay too long, that's all.'

'I see,' the first man picked up after a very unpleasant pause. 'Why Mercur?'

'London wants it doing.'

'I'm sure of that!' the second man snapped vindictively. The other one carried on unemotionally. 'We shall have to know why before we can consider acting.'

'I haven't the time. Just accept that Mercur has to be lifted out, and quickly.'

'No.'

'Don't get clever with me!'

'Have you any idea what the defences are like now?' The second man chopped in again. 'Do you know what it's really like out at the Mercur, eh?'

'Yes.'

'That being the case, even you must see how absurd your request is!'

'It isn't, and this is no request.'

'You'll never get past those defences, never!'

'Wrong. I shall pass them, so shut up and pay attention!'

Neither man pretended to understand at first. They made him go over the main points again, underlining the things he expected them to put into the attack. It took the better part of twenty minutes' wrangling to convince them that he wasn't bluffing, and another ten to sketch his timetable in full. It was uphill sledding all the way. They turned him down with contempt on an average of once a minute, but he didn't listen and he didn't care. Win, lose or draw, they were bound to him and his attack plan—and in the end they knew it too.

There was a hostile break while the two men drew off a good few yards and began quietly raging at Jens in between arguments over the Englishmen. After a lengthy time they bunched up and trooped back to the dripping porch where Shepherd huddled, wriggling his toes against the biting cold. The first one delivered their verdict. 'Very well, we'll work with you—but for your own sakes be careful.'

'Thank you, we shall be.' Shepherd had never once taken his hand off the Colt inside his coat front. 'So now you can tell me when we get the transmission site?'

'Tomorrow. Today, that is.'

164

'Good. And the other stuff?'

'If you can keep your part of the bargain, we'll keep ours. Everything will be made ready for tonight.'

'Good again. I want the explosives, too. At least twenty kilos of hexogen, dynamite or blasting gelatine.'

'And for the last time, there isn't any left!'

'So you keep telling me—start looking.'

'Sweet God!' the second man detonated. 'Only an imbecile like you could keep baying for the moon! Don't you ever take "no" for an answer?'

'That's right.'

'Well, understand once and for all, London never sends us enough material! We're not yet important to the British Empire!' The first one deftly took over again. 'You'll get no explosive, and that's final. Every last gramme went on the Hillerød sub-generating station last month.'

'All right,' Shepherd grudgingly let go, 'but I'll want the sugar and chemical salt by early this afternoon.'

'The sugar you ask for will be very difficult to obtain.' The first man sounded angry. 'There's a war on.'

'You're making life very difficult for yourself.' Shepherd aimed low. 'I want it, and I want it by three this afternoon, so you haven't much time!'

'Very well,' the first man drawled acidly. 'DSK's warehouses will be raided for you. After all, what's one extra impossibility among allies?' He dragged his collar against the slanting rain and turned to the other man. 'Come!'

Shepherd went back to the chapel, bolted the doors and climbed down to the vault where Meyer lay flaked out on the sacking; he slowly blinked open one eye. 'Go all right?'

'They're on our side now.'

'Good.' Meyer let the other eye swim into focus. 'Arranged the transmission site?'

'Yes.'

'Good.' Meyer started to doze off. 'Explosives?'

'No.'

'Uh huh.' Shepherd dowsed the lantern and made ready to catch up with sleep.

They were both awake and impatient to move a good couple of hours before Jens came for them next morning. Shepherd nervously cruised round the small chapel, nibbling bits of chocolate while Meyer enciphered their telegram. After a short time he gave up and went back to see how the man was getting on. Meyer was sitting astride a box under the light, drafting groups on a

165

thin pad of rice paper. 'Give me three nulls.' Shepherd sat on the bottom step and thought for a moment. 'A, B, C.'

'Quite original! Imagine anyone finishing a group with A, B, or C—the monitors will have them quicker than the clerks in London.' He looked back at the papers. 'Try again f'Godssake.'

'All right—F, X, S.'

'Better.' Meyer's pencil tip continued to delicately pick over the encoding grille. Shepherd tiredly scratched his chest. 'What method are we using now?'

'A Double Columnar Transposition variant,' he looked up, 'can you use it?' Shepherd nodded. 'It's been keyed to the Army's ranks with a twenty-four hour change on three hundred hours, starting at Field-Marshal and working down to Private.'

'Sounds so typical it must be true,' Shepherd bitched sourly. 'Still, it marks a great improvement on the Lord's Prayer recited backwards, or the Oxford Book of Verse, the standard key systems since Christ knows when.' He paused, thinking of his empty stomach. 'Who do we sign the telegram?'

'Morgan.'

'Good plot.' Shepherd nodded in agreement. 'They'll turn out the band for a Lieutenant-Colonel, dead or alive. We'd be lucky to get a raspberry.' He got up and slowly walked across to look over Meyer's shoulder. 'Going to mention Erikssen to them?'

'No.'

'Good plot again.' He straightened. 'Tell London everything's just wonderful; the chaps are well and happy and obedient; Mercur is going to be a simply topping piece of cake.' Shepherd knew the form. 'Strewth, but am I hungry!' He forked the idea over in his mind. 'You know, if they've left that oil and lantern down here, I wonder what else might be hidden?' He started with the nearest coffin, carefully running his fingertips along the brittle, soldered seams.

'Either get out of my way or sit down! Can't you see I'm trying to do a job of work!'

'So am I,' Shepherd commented blandly. 'I'm beginning to wonder if I shall have to make that powder after all.'

'How do you mean?'

'I'll bet they store other things apart from bloody lanterns; finished with that light yet?' Meyer nodded reluctantly and helped Shepherd pull himself up to the highest level of granite niches, four coffins above the floor. 'Hand it up here...' Meyer gave him the lantern and stood back to watch while Shepherd half lay on the slab. 'See anything?'

'Aye, just as I thought, Gudren Thorvaldsen 1781–1820 had

166

visitors recently.' He wrestled with something out of sight. 'A neat bit of carpentry; could be friend Sørensen's by the style; there!' Meyer heard the side fall away. 'What's in it?'

'An old Hotchkiss gun packed in rags and a box of cartridge strips. And a cleaning rod.'

'Try the others.'

Two coffins later, Shepherd found that Ragnar Rasmussen was now host to some medical stores, a carton of British airborne rations and three bottles of mineral water, but no explosives. 'You can start serving breakfast, if nothing else,' Shepherd called down as he pushed the side back in position. He dropped to the floor with a couple of the bottles and some of the ration blocks. 'Maybe they were telling the truth.' He sounded unhappy at the thought. 'Perhaps they haven't any blasting mix after all.'

'Will it make so much difference?' Meyer stopped uncapping one of the bottles. 'Too true it will.' Shepherd ripped the waxed paper off a ration. 'I'd rather use certified materials any day, they will at least fire when you tell them to, not like this schoolboy prank I've been stuck with.'

'You think there's a chance it won't explode?' Meyer worried, crushing a piece of peanut toffee between his teeth. Shepherd glanced up. 'Oh, it'll work, it'll go up with a beautiful wallop. The only problem is, when?'

'You tell me.'

'Wish to God I could!' He chomped a fig bar and rinsed it down with some of the mineral water. 'Most probably a split milli-second after I begin sifting the elements together—so keep well back. And don't go fooling about with the charges once I've got them packed, if I get them packed, the Instability Rating must be close to that of boiling nitro-glycerine.' He savaged another chunk of the bar. 'The quantity Muggins volunteered to make will scrape the ground clean for a hundred yards in any direction; I must need my head seeing to.'

Jens finally came for them at a little after nine and led them out through a side entrance of the cemetery to a parked lorry. He waved them into the hold and went round to the cab. A minute or so later he came back. 'You see those overalls?' He pointed to some dumped across a stand of pickaxes and three coils of co-axial telephone cable. 'Start getting them on.' He paused, mentally working out something else. 'The men in front are going to take you to our safest transmit site, now. Apparently there's a way round the roadblocks they've discovered. Don't be surprised by what you'll see. Afterwards they'll take you to the next

167

rendezvous.' Jens turned abruptly, leaving the Englishmen to stew in it if they liked.

The Post Office lorry bowled along several quiet side-roads, bumped across a private yard and drove into the exact centre of Copenhagen, weaving through the skimpy civilian traffic to park on a small, reserved grid a few yards from the Town Hall's massive clock tower. The driver and his mate slowly climbed down and strolled round to the back. 'Keep out of sight till we say so,' the shorter one ordered as he scrambled aboard and started handing out bits of their gear.

Within ten minutes they'd set up a telephone repair tent on the pavement inside a hedge of bold red lamps. They sauntered back to the lorry and the taller one of the pair spoke this time, in passable English. 'Behind that screen you'll find we've opened up the junction box—it's an inspection chamber quite big enough to take one man and a transmitter.' He paused to see if they understood him.

'Good. Now, about three metres back is the foot of the clock tower, see? And coming down at that point you'll find the Town Hall lightning conductor—ninety-seven metres of pure copper rod, and most of it going straight up into the sky.' Meyer had begun to grin like a cut melon as the Post Office engineer went on chatting casually.

'That meterage should give you all the range your set can use and more than makes up for the flat scenery in this part of the world. It's aligned on England, too.'

'What about the D/F vans?' The man looked puzzled; Meyer searched around for another word. 'The radio locators?'

'Oh, don't worry too much about them!' It was the man's turn to grin. 'At the last count we heard eight of them snooping around; we'll see the raid they order, if we're not fast about it.'

'You've tried all this?'

'No problem, friend. That conductor's a beautiful aerial to use —and if you're worrying about the Germans, don't.' He winked at Meyer. 'Have *you* ever thought of clandestine transmissions from a public square, in daylight? No, and neither have they. This remains the safest and best site we have, so go over and use it.' He turned to the other man. 'We'll stay here and watch that nothing goes wrong.'

Meyer swung over the tailgate and Shepherd passed him the transmitter before jumping down. No-one noticed another couple of Post Office engineers go into the tent and pull the flap shut. Shepherd gave Meyer a lift to climb into the narrow, con- crete chamber. He crouched over the set for a moment, then handed back the extension antenna—a thin, ten-metre wire and crocodile clip. Shepherd poked the antenna under one wall, went out and snaked it across to the lightning conductor.

'Excuse me, madam, just routine testing, I'm sorry to disturb you.' The two women stopped chatting, glanced down without interest at the shabby little man in overalls, then moved off as he knelt on the pavement and clamped the antenna to the conductor. He ducked back inside the tent and squatted, watching the top of Meyer's head. 'Ready when you are.'

'Good—three minutes to go.' He screwed the accumulator terminals tight and watched the voltage come up; a dull red guide bulb faded out. Meyer settled himself comfortable and flexed his fingers across an imaginary piano octave before pulling up the earphones from round his neck. 'Still ready?'

'Still ready.'

'Anyone near?' Shepherd looked out. 'No.'

'Hold that thing where I can see it, then.' Shepherd steadied the small pocket torch over Meyer's shoulder, lighting the encoded signal form. 'OK there?'

'Thanks.' Meyer wiped his damp fingers on his trousers and started flailing out their call sign in three, closely packed bursts. He paused a fraction, then hammered down their five letter groups before flipping to Receive. London's operator tuned to his frequency was class, there was no call to repeat. Instead, a brisk twitter confirmed the transmission.

Meyer stuffed the scrap of paper in his mouth, chewed and swallowed; ripped off the headset and began stowing it away. 'Die Antennenleitung—schnell!' Shepherd twitched the wire free as Meyer reeled it in. 'Catch this!' He dragged the set through the hole and steadied Meyer's elbow as he scrambled clear, tucked the case under one arm and slicked down his ruffled hair. 'Come!'

They'd jumped aboard and were moving out as the first SS and Militia patrols raced past, sirens howling, going in the opposite direction. Shepherd flinched back from the tailgate. 'Jesus, but that's quick.'

'Isn't it?' the shorter man commented sourly, fondling a loaded Sten, watching the hostile streets unroll astern.

CHAPTER SIXTEEN

'KNIGHTSBRIDGE?'

'Yes, sir.'

'Have it brought in at once!'

'Sir!' Deane snapped down the speaker extension, crowded over his desk and scooped up the red telephone. 'Reserve me the next open line to the Deputy-CIGS. Then get him out of conference; ring me back immediately!' He settled all argument by tossing the receiver back in its cradle as Major Pierce rapped the beaver-board partition and stepped round in the same hurried scramble. 'Well?'

Pierce force-landed his classified signals file on Deane's cluttered desk; the phone's startled jangle caught him before he'd time to comment. 'Yes, Deane speaking.' The Deputy-CIGS frowned at his tone. 'Explain yourself.'

'You asked me to keep you posted about the Knightsbridge affair, sir.' The Brigadier snapped his fingers. Pierce moved the file nearer. 'They're the operation originally constituted under Special Cabinet Memorandum SEC/41, dealing with that factory in Denmark, sir.' The General rapidly filled in the rest from memory; his voice warmed; became cautiously eager. 'What's happening to them, Deane?'

'Morgan has made contact with the Resistance people, at last. They've established a working liaison, and reconnoitred a way into the building.'

'Excellent!'

'Yes, sir, I knew he'd succeed.' Deane paused. 'There's only one snag, as I see it.'

'What's that?'

'He's asked for the RAF to arrange a convincing diversionary raid, to muffle him.'

'The RAF?'

'Yes, sir.'

'That's not so good, is it?'

'No, sir.'

'When does he want this thing laying-on?' Deane breathed out very softly. 'Tonight.'

170

'I see. Tonight. That's bad.' There was a lengthy time lag while the General delicately balanced considerations one on the other. He coughed in Deane's ear. 'The Air Force isn't going to be happy about this.'

'Then bugger the Air Force, sir!' His future career, or what remained of it, wasn't likely to suffer much. 'Amen,' the General murmured dryly. He hesitated a moment, thinking aloud. 'Luckily for us the Chief of Air Staff is still in Washington and won't be back till the eighteenth—while obstacle number two's been given the MEAF in Cairo.' He paused, thinking hard. 'Deane?' The voice sharpened. 'I want you over at Horseguards within the quarter hour, understand?

'Leave this to the Kingsway people and you'll never get your raid, not the way they're behaving nowadays. I shall back you all the way with the Old Man. You, for your part, had better have some really convincing arguments ready for me to use.' He rang off, leaving Deane with a dead line.

However, none of his arguments was used—the Old Man had been standing Godfather to this operation right from its birth. They awakened him to initial what amounted to a blank cheque, outbidding all human opposition, giving Knightsbridge an absolute priority in men and equipment.

Joint-Service planning departments were feeling the lash, sullenly falling into line as a briskly tailored ADC tried hustling Deane into the CIGS' quarters under Horseguards. The Brigadier put up a stiff salute and cagily eyed a tight cluster of Air Force officers grouped round the General. 'Come closer!' he was terse to the point of personal rudeness. 'Tell these—gentlemen— what it is you need!'

Deane turned slightly and felt the near visible wave of hostility slap his face. The RAF was represented by tired men, all with valid reasons for refusing him the little they had left. For a short moment he wanted to attack them with spiteful complaints, demands and facts. Instead, he managed a kind of smile.

'Gentlemen,' he began simply, 'at this very moment there are four men hiding in Copenhagen. Tonight, if against all the odds they're still alive, they'll attempt something which the rest of us have written off as impossible.' He glanced round, gauging the probable effect of this line. 'They knew it before they went, yet they're carrying on right to the end. They've only asked us for one thing, your help when they go in, tonight.

'They'll be dead, or worse, dying by the hands of the enemy in only a few hours from now, that's almost certain. They must have

171

realised this will amount to a suicide raid, yet they're still going on with it. They're going to give everything they have, let us do the same. We couldn't fail them now, gentlemen, not now.' His voice lost something. One of the Air Force men finally broke the short, awkward silence. 'Tell me, Brigadier, what exactly *do* you require from us?'

'They, not me, sir. They need a diversion in force against the Luftwaffe at Kastrup.'

'Tonight?'

'Yes, sir. In the first hours of the morning, while the darkness lasts.'

'Thank you.' He turned to a cold-faced Air Commodore. 'What's the squadron availability, Hallam?'

'Very meagre, sir.' Hallam opened a plain cardboard file and thumbed some sheets of paper. 'Eleven Group has the U-boat pens at Brest and L'Orient; we could poach from them if it were really pressing.'

'No. What else is there?'

'Eight Group drew the Caproni works in Milan as well as the Porto Marghera refineries—one or the other could be pruned, or put off again.'

'No.' Hallam searched his file. 'That being the case, sir, I'm afraid it only leaves us with the odds and sods.'

'Tell me about them.'

'There's not much to say, sir. It's either the Whitleys which Coastal Command are scrounging, or the two re-forming Wellington squadrons.'

'You don't offer much. Where are the Wellingtons now?'

'Gransden Lodge, sir.'

'Group Captain Andrews, commanding?'

'Yes, sir. One squadron's largely RAF, the other's all New Zealand.'

'Very well, move them.' He paused and slowly faced the two Army officers again. 'You can tell your men they'll get their bombers tonight.'

Curtains of bitterly cold rain drifted across beet fields; a pair of tired rooks tacked against the dull wind; fen drains brimmed with surface water; Cambridgeshire.

There'd be no flying today, and there'd be none while this dirty weather lasted. Some of the aircrews were still going through the motions of Dry Dinghy Drill in One Hangar; others dozed through a lecture from a Ministry of Information team in the station cinema; everyone gathered urge for a thrash in Cam-

172

bridge—the first house of a new Deanna Durbin film, dinner at the Blue Boar, then opening time. It should have been memorable, but something went wrong.

Abruptly, at a little before three-thirty, Service Police began shouldering hurdles across all access roads on to the airfield; no one and nothing could leave the area now; a total security clamp would isolate them till the bombers came back next morning. Then the Tannoy began passing out orders.

Cursing mechanics, mittened and padded against the groping cold, manhandled the aircraft from their sandbagged dispersal areas. Diesel tractors chugged long trains of bombs back from the dumps hidden out in the woods; sweating armourers winched each charge into the empty bomb racks. Specialist NCO's zigzagged their cycles round the airfield, whipping the groundcrews to move faster, to do more, and to do it in less time. Endless belts of sombre .303 cartridges clinked along the magazine tracks, feeding the hungry Brownings. A river of fuel spilt from the waiting bowsers—1,030 gallons of 100-octane spirit and forty-seven gallons of lubricating oil to each aircraft. Pair-by-pair the Pegasus motors shook alive, peaking at full power before gradually shutting off. The rain and darkness fell together.

Nearly a hundred and fifty intent young men waited on hard chairs and faced Northern Europe, the grubby half-million air map pasted across one end of their badly heated and badly ventilated Nissen hut. Black wooden models of German, Italian and British aircraft hung from the rafters, gently twirling on short threads as warm air and stale tobacco smoke slowly climbed past. The crews numbed their stomachs with talk and laughter, both too loud and too high; with cigarettes whose taste, if they had any, no one would remember; with collections of comic strips. They were glad when the end door thumped open and the Station Master breasted in with his Wing Commander (Flying).

'Please be seated.' The Group Captain peeled off his gloves and deliberately laid them in his cap on the table. He cleared his throat and faced the unnaturally quiet room. 'Your target for tonight will be the installations and supply facilities at Kastrup airfield, Copenhagen.' He waited for the puzzled shuffling of feet to stop. 'I realise this must seem an unusual target after the Ruhr, and somewhat unexpected in view of the weather, especially as we're only just coming up to strength again as squadrons. However,' he looked round reassuringly, 'they've given us a soft target, to play us in so to speak.

'Now, as to the actual place itself, Air Intelligence have at last

173

identified Kastrup as being a vital link in the GAF's air defence system—offering servicing and refuelling to their night-fighters, as well as doing much the same thing for the Focke-Wulf Kuriers flying north-about on Atlantic shipping patrols. Apparently it's recently gained even greater importance as a staging area for Norway and Russia: it's time we paid them a visit.' He turned to the younger man seated behind the bare, wooden table. 'Carry on, Wing Commander.'

'Thank you, sir.' He stood up and came round to the front of the stage, instinctively testing the crews' mood. He stuck one hand in his hip pocket and shared a wry smile. 'On the face of it, this all sounds rather hairy—especially that mention of night-fighters. But I think it may well turn into a milk run. I'm basing this bit of wishful thinking on the fact that Kastrup is well to the north of our usual excursions—something which should add a dash of surprise to our sudden appearance. Another thing, their home-based fighters are going to be tied up by the sad weather creeping in from the south, they'll be clagged solid by the time we come along, so no joy for the Luftwaffe over Germany to-night. As a result,' he went on with assurance, 'this *is* going to involve some tricky navigation all the way there, since we'll be flying right into it. However,' he turned and beckoned to a middle-aged Flight Lieutenant, 'I think Met have a ray of sun-shine to offer us.' The nervous tension blew away in a gale of ribbing, sardonic laughter as the solemn man uncovered his weather board and tried to begin. He flushed, and patiently waited for the Wingco to call them to order.

'There is a deep depression centred to the east of Iceland,' the Wing Commander's one free hand murdered a harsh, braying laugh as Met hurried on, 'with an associated front slowly moving across Scandinavia, here.' He carefully drew a blue chalk round part of his board. 'This front should give rise to unsettled weather conditions in North and Central Germany, the Baltic region and Western Poland, probably covering the target area by the early hours of tomorrow morning.' The room had grown very cold and watchful again; the Met officer ran on, gaining con-fidence from their hostile attention.

'Heavy Nimbo-Stratus, capping at ten thousand plus, will spread and cover the entire region, possibly causing some mag-netic flux to affect compasses and radio reception.' He paused. 'There's also a very strong possibility of intermittent snow showers everywhere—so pay particular attention to icing which might occur anywhere above three thousand feet.' He paused again, absent-mindedly playing with the piece of chalk; there

174

would be rows of empty seats by this time tomorrow night. 'I'm very sorry.'

The Wing Commander took over again. 'Bombing Leader?'

A short, tubby man got to his feet and bustled over. 'We'll be taking them a generous assortment of incendiary caskets as well as the five-hundred-pound fragmentations. These have been set with delays of up to half an hour—just to keep the pot boiling after we've gone.' He brusquely uncovered a large blackboard diagram.

'I shall commence the run-in from this point, here,' his right hand slowly crabbed up the board, fingers spread wide. 'Allow for a mean altitude of eight hundred feet over the fuel dumps, here; the three main workshop hangars, here; the barracks which you'll find at the top of your photographs, here and here.' He looked up again.

'Use this canal and particularly this railway spur for your final drift check and to identify the target area—*don't* wander over here and confuse this housing development for these stores buildings.' He glanced along the rows of faces. 'Be very, very sure of your aim-off, and remember there'll be cameras in B-Beer, N-Nuts and K-King.' He paused again. 'Any questions so far?' Within a few minutes it was the Gunnery Leader's turn to take the stage.

'Don't be too surprised if we meet some Me. 110's and, of course, our old friend the 88. They're known to be based at Skagen and Kristiansand where the weather probably won't hamper them so much as the others farther south. I don't consider it unreasonable to expect a few roving around, looking for trouble.

'We can certainly bank on a big flap over the target itself. They'll be very cross and may well put up some 109's from the air gunnery training flight they keep there—a second showing of the surprise packet some of us remember from Essen. However, we've plenty of SAP, Incendiary and Explosive, so don't feel shy about squirting them, or the flak and lights grouped round this small factory a bit to the north of Kastrup if you stray into it by mistake. And don't forget the airfield dispersal areas, either.' He looked round. 'I'm told they're stuffed with new machines which should burn quite nicely. And remember the Luftwaffe barracks here, here and here. They'll show up as the darkest buildings once this fuel dump, here, gets it.' Then the Navigation Leader began summing up in a familiar, plodding voice.

'Navigators. Our initial course will be zero-three-zero, crossing the coast at Cromer—remember the two railway wishbones and correct for a heading Cromer–Dogger. In this weather I'd certainly recommend you allow for Dead Reckoning all the way there and back.

'After a timed run, vector zero-seven-zero to make landfall north of Sylt, here, at the mouth of this small creek—note the lighthouse, here. I'm hoping this arrangement puts the wind up Hamburg Air Defence Command, if no one else, and scrambles their communications while everyone enjoys a cold night in the shelters.' He smiled at some intensely private joke.

'From there it will be a straight run to Copenhagen, calculating an ETA at 02.15 hours.' He marked the map with his index finger. 'There ought to be a couple of good chances to get drifts and new winds over these fairly broad channels—the Little Belt, here, and the Great Belt here, between Fünen and Zeeland.' He paused, a benignly detached smile embracing everyone and everything in the room.

'Meanwhile, be wary of freakish changes in wind direction and strength—under these weather conditions anything can happen, and most probably will. I doubt if we'll have much opportunity to use Astro, so keep a really frequent plot going. If you should get into trouble over the target, steer zero-nine-zero and try for Sweden—leave it for the diplomats to argue the toss about neutrality.

'Now, on the way back, keep a sharp lookout for friendly naval forces round the Friesian Islands. The Navy's sending out a flotilla of MTB's to finish off a convoy the Canadian Tor-Beaus jumped earlier this afternoon, so everyone concerned is going to be very nervous of aircraft. Our colours will be four greens and our callsign APPLETREE.' He watched the indelible pencils work across the Navigators' wrists.

'Repeat, four greens and APPLETREE. I think it better if we started anticipating Bandmaster sending us up to Cranwell, Woodhall Spa or Coningsby if the weather really clamps down here—they should stay reasonably clear till morning. Old hands will tell you it's not too hard to find the Wash, no matter how unpleasant the atmospherics may be; after that you simply turn right for Boston and follow the LNE Railway in the general direction of Lincoln; nothing could be easier.

'Now, when you join circuit, be leery of Eight Group's Stirlings who'll probably be working along with Bandmaster as well. Remember that Ju. 88 Intruders may have followed them home, or been sent over from Holland, so keep an eye open—especially as the Stirling gunners will be tired and jumpy, too. Nobody's going to wait to notice the difference between a Junkers and our

176

Wimpeys; all twin-engined machines will be bogeymen tonight. As Confucius says, accidents are caused, they don't just happen.'

'Thank you, David.' The Wing Commander got to his feet and started to wrap up the briefing. 'There you have it. Fingers out and it won't be nearly so gloomy. At the risk of seeming to bind a little, you must be very sure you've properly identified the target. Don't be fooled by any convenient bonfires on this open farmland between Kastrup and Amager; even the most experienced crews fall for it now and again, and the enemy is getting particularly skilful at burning cardboard cities. Similarly, once you *have* found the target, stay inside the limits and don't go outside them. We can't afford any damage to civilian property, so go round again if the first run aborts. If you are hit and have to jettison bombs, for God's sake remember to do it over water if you can— either of the two channels will do, or the Sound between Denmark and Sweden. If you don't, then there's a surprisingly good chance you'll not only strain Anglo-Danish relations but scatter yourselves all over the sky as well.' He let the point make itself quite clear.

'Group have reasons of their own why they want this target to be clobbered just now. To be clobbered hard, accurately and above all, on time.' He paused. 'That's why they came to us in the first place.'

From the draughty locker rooms, into the waiting lorries and out to the loaded Wellingtons was only a short ride in time and space, it just seemed to go on without end. The sodden tarpaulins slapped and strummed in the darkness, keeping some of the rain off the crews squatting inside on their parachutes, ration bags clenched between their knees to hold the Thermos jugs upright.

Six-by-six the men jumped down as their drivers braked and shouted back each aircraft's squadron letter, leaving them to stand alone in the streaming night, watching the tail-lights fade round the peri-track.

Each Pegasus began draining current from its battery trolley; firing the ring of cylinders; rolling back the silence as their throttles wrestled the clamouring motors. Then the hydraulics gasped, throwing off the brakes, turning the bombers free.

The Wellingtons started their tired waddle; dragging themselves into line; dourly waiting a turn to aim down the mile and a half corridor of dimmed runway lights. Each machine crept forward, bomb heavy, exhaust stubs exploding blue flame, carefully trimmed for the lumbering gallop at the sky. On time, to

177

the second, a green Aldis lamp began its lazy stare from the Controller's caravan, waving off the first to go.

In the end, twenty-one bombers lifted away from the threshold and started the shake-down into formation. Only B-Beer stayed behind when her starboard motor suddenly shed power. The staggering Wellington reaped a fir plantation at eighty knots, bleeding fire as she went straight in. The numbing blast of her tightly packed bombs and their rippling flashes slit the night, jerking the machines in circuit overhead.

The cheerful glow of burning woodland marked their track astern on the first leg out to the coast.

CHAPTER SEVENTEEN

'WHAT's the GMT?'

'Please?'

'What's the bloody time!' Meyer patiently tilted his watch at the shaded light. 'A quarter before nine—they haven't even begun the news bulletin yet,' he looked down at Shepherd, 'so just take it easy and leave the radio to me, eh?' Meyer gently shook his head as Shepherd reluctantly went back to probing out a grenade primer with the wrong end of a pencil. A flurry of sleet lashed the metal roof and leaked through some rusted nail holes.

'You think the RAF can make it?' the little man nagged again. 'That sounds very rough to me.'

'I wouldn't know.' Meyer stepped closer to get a better look at Shepherd's technique. 'The only time they had me in one of their aeroplanes, someone ordered me to jump out, and the same applies to you.' He paused moodily. 'What're you doing now?'

'This is the arming pistol—you'll find one in most kinds of bombs and grenades.' Shepherd had an eager apprentice, he didn't mind doing a step-by-step explanation.

'Why go to the trouble of pulling one out?'

'So I don't waste my time with fuze matches once, or if, we get inside that factory.'

'I see. Where does it go?'

'There, on top.' He pointed briefly. 'I'll wire one to each charge. When the striker, here, pips this cap, here, it'll initiate this train of slow-cord to the penthrite-wax gaine, see?'

'Uh huh.'

'That, in turn, will flash off the picric tablets and get the main charge going.'

'Uh huh. How long?'

'A very bare five minutes.' Shepherd eased the striker spring and visually checked that it coiled without snagging. Meyer frowned. 'Why that time particularly?'

'It's just long enough for us to get clear, if we shift; it's too short for anyone else to find and disarm each charge in turn. One or the other will send the lot up.'

'Does it always?'

179

'Always what?'

'Burn for exactly five minutes.'

'Length for length, yes, generally.' Shepherd got up and walked over to the first charge, delicately loaded into one of three twenty-kilo spun-steel drums originally filled with vitamin-C extract from the Swiss Red Cross. 'Of course,' he continued the lecture, 'you must always snip off a few inches and time their burning for yourself. Never trust *anyone* else is the motto of all long-lived armourers.'

'I see.' Meyer squatted beside him and steadied the cocked mechanism while he gently fixed it in place. Shepherd twisted and cut the tie-wires. 'How's your radio going on?'

'There's still plenty of time—relax!'

'Well, mind you don't miss it, that's all. I'd hate to arm these efforts only to hear there won't be a raid after all.' He paused and carefully teased the stiff fuze-cord into place. 'I'm shitting bricks just doing this—I refuse to dismantle them for anyone!'

'All right, all right! The RAF *will* come.'

'Next time I ask, say it with more conviction, I might believe you.' Shepherd taped the slow-cord to the primer and gently slid it down a rolled paper tube to the explosive's core. 'Give me that bit of Plasticine, on the box lid, that's right.' Meyer obeyed and cleared his throat. 'Very well, let me put it another way, I wish I could be as certain of the Danes coming tonight.'

'And the snippers.' Shepherd pointed again. Meyer handed them over with a touch of irritation and slowly looked round the decorator's shed. It was dirty, cold and very draughty. It had also hidden them for the better part of the day. The taxi-driver had remembered his duty after all, and said nothing. 'You know,' he looked back at Shepherd, 'they've got every reason for staying clear of this rat trap.'

'No more than I have!' He looked up from his work. 'Stop bleating and keep still. I drop this now and nobody'll ever know there was a street here, let alone a bloody shed! Push off and play your radio; find some music; do something useful for once!' He went back to measuring the next striker's clearance with a spill of folded card. 'The Danes will be along, sooner or later, mark my words.'

'I wish I shared your confidence!'

'You don't.'

Shepherd was right this time, they came. Jens swung an old Berliet fire-truck through the yard gates, braking hard as two of his men dropped off and ran back to heave them shut again. The rest slowly dismounted and ducked under the blankets hung

180

round the shed's doorway, leaving the first pair to stand guard outside.

'Well?' Jens tiredly stripped off his driving gauntlets and threw them at a bench. 'Are you still going?'

'We're still going.' Shepherd finished wiping his hands on a scrap of towel. 'The BBC used our code-phrase; the RAF are already on their way.' He dropped the towel. 'How did the ride go?'

'Three routine checks.'

'No problems?'

'None, apart from you, of course.' Shepherd thought it best to ignore Jens for the moment. Instead, he looked round at the others. The Danes had kept the last part of their bargain, rounding up seven extra men from the Auxiliary Fire Department to come along and man the truck. 'Thank you, friends.' He began to shake hands. 'Please make yourselves comfortable, but go outside to smoke if you must.' He nodded at the three drums, armed and standing in rope carrying slings. 'They're the sensitive ones, they might cough suddenly.' It wasn't much of a joke in Norwegian–Danish either, but the firemen gradually started to loose a taut line round their mouths.

'You *are* still serious?' Jens slowly pulled off his dull brass helmet and dumped it with the gauntlets. Shepherd frowned. 'About the factory?'

'Yes.'

'I've never been more so.'

'You must be mad.'

'I've been told that many times.'

'I tell it you again.' Jens wearily massaged his face and temples. He looked up after a while. 'But wherever you go, we must go. If you go to Mercur, then we go to Mercur as well. That was our agreement. Let us finish like colleagues if not as friends.' He put out one hand. They both shook it with unexpected warmth.

'Who are the rest of your men?' Shepherd asked, dropping his voice. Jens blocked the question. 'No names, no regrets afterwards, we prefer things to be that way. But one thing you ought to know—they all volunteered to come with you tonight.' He read Shepherd's face. 'Oh yes, they did, and they knew what was involved, too.'

'I didn't think it possible. Not after last night.'

'Neither did I, Englishman, but this is a life full of surprises.' Shepherd nodded and glanced up. 'I can't say I expected to see you here again. Why did you come?' Jens shrugged his shoulders.

181

'Someone had to arrange this from the inside, and I happen to be a Captain of Fire Volunteers. It seemed logical, I suppose.'

'Hm.'

'I could ask you the same question,' Jens loosened his uniform collar, 'not your German colleague, but you personally.'

'Why count him out?'

'I recognise the type—there are quite a few German Democrats, Progressives, Patriots, call them what you like, fighting this war. But I can't place yours, forgive the expression. I'm really curious to know what made you decide to stay here, to attack Mercur of all places. After all, you aren't a Dane, or a German for that matter, there's no logical motive.' Jens searched critically for the right words. 'What do you get for doing it?'

'Six bob a day.'

'I'm sorry, I don't understand you?'

'I wouldn't let it fret me.' Shepherd fell back slightly as Meyer came over to join them. 'Did you find the right uniform?' Jens nodded. 'It's in the locker under our hoses. I had it wrapped in brown paper with one of ours, for your friend.'

'Good.' Meyer went outside to fetch them. Shepherd picked up again. 'While we're still in the mood for answering questions, did you find a machine weapon that actually fires?'

'There we have been lucky.' Jens brightened up. 'Someone had a new Bren delivered from England a few months ago, and they've agreed to loan it with ten things of explosive shot.'

'Sounds very promising,' Shepherd agreed. 'Where do you intend mounting it?'

'The railway workshops modified our turntable with some welded steel sheet; it might protect the gun from small arms fire.' Shepherd nodded as Jens went on. 'I'm driving the Berliet myself this time; I'll position the gunners where they can cover the hut and gate.'

'Good. They know that if things go wrong they're going to have it all to themselves?'

'They know.'

'What about the other stuff?'

'The tools you asked for—the bolt-cutters, sledgehammer, wedges and crowbar—have all been put in a webbing roll. You'll find it in the crew's cab.'

'What make of bolt-cutters?'

'Eskiltuna Bahco, just as you asked for.'

'What else have we got?'

'An additional three Stens were negotiated which brings our number up to five all told—fortunately there's plenty of 9 mm to be stolen from the Germans. We've also a recently acquired Schmiesser carbine, our revolvers and a self-loading shotgun.'

'Uh huh.' Shepherd thought aloud. 'Horrible as they are, I'd prefer more Stens round the place—nobody could possibly mistake them for anything else in the darkness.' He looked up sharply. 'Keep that Schmiesser out of sight unless it's really needed, agree?' Jens agreed; it was good advice. 'Did you find any smoke?'

'A dozen phosphorus grenades came with the Stens.'

'How many fragmentation have you left?'

'Eight.'

'How about the PIAT?'

'Nothing doing—I'm sorry.'

'No more than I am. I'm counting on some heavy artillery.'

'We'll have to rely on Molotov cocktails instead.'

'And the best of British luck.' Shepherd chewed his lip. 'What about the beach? Has that worked out?'

'Yes, the launch will be standing offshore. It'll come in, using the bombing noises to cover its motors.'

'That's something to look forward to.' Shepherd stamped his feet to keep the blood moving round. 'What's the signal?'

'A pair of sodium candles ten paces apart on the foreshore.'

'Who'll be carrying those?'

'Me. But in any event the launch will come if groups of three bursts are fired straight up in the air.' Shepherd looked properly sceptical. 'Nobody's going to hear a pipsqueak automatic tonight. You and those candles stay close to me.'

'I'm sorry. It's a risk we've had to take.'

'I still don't like it.' They both turned as Meyer came back. Jens nodded. 'You found them?'

'Where you said they were.'

'I hope you won't mind the darning across the back; it was the only way we could get you one in time.' Meyer carefully studied an SS Hauptmann's freshly brushed and cleaned tunic. 'Looks as if it will be a tight fit.'

'We hadn't much choice.' Jens moved nearer the light to get a better view. 'You'll probably find it more comfortable if it's left undone till we go.'

Everyone watched with cool interest as Meyer began turning himself into a recognisable German again. He stood up and wriggled his toes. 'The boots are narrow, too. His feet must have been unusual.' He stopped and unholstered the late Hauptmann's Walther.

'It's loaded, I saw to that myself.' But Meyer still broke the

183

action, slapping home the magazine, tugging the cocking slide before taking his own Colt from the heap of discarded clothing. 'You don't intend being short of fire, do you?'

'Not in this uniform, not tonight,' Meyer grated, holstering the second pistol under his tunic. Jens understood. 'How goes the time?' Meyer fingered back the cuff. 'Half over twelve.' Jens clicked his tongue. 'I must go and change the guard at once.' He turned and detailed two other men. They pulled their fireman's oilskins tight against the weather and trooped outside.

The first pair walked through the blanket light-trap and tiredly shook off the rain. Jens followed them a few moments later with some packets of food and a small petrol stove to heat three bottles of ready brewed chicory which his wife had made up earlier in the evening. Shepherd coughed and pointed at the armed charges. Jens warmed their drinks at the far end of the shed.

The rain belted down with sullen indifference, flinking in the gutters, puddling under both doors. Jens changed the guards again—but nothing else happened, and no-one spoke without good reason. The long night slowly humped over and started to become tomorrow.

'What time did you tell them to come?' Jens asked, sitting on a box opposite Shepherd.

'Two-fifteen when, you said, the last watch changes on the barrier.' He shivered and tucked each hand under an armpit. 'Of course, I can't say they'll arrive dead on time, to the minute.'

'If they arrive at all.'

'All right! *If* they arrive at all!'

It began to seem that way when half past two gonged across the canal from Sankt Nicolaj's church. Jens fidgeted uncomfortably and went out to look at the truck. He came back after a while and peered round the blanket. Shepherd came over and joined him under the leaky eaves. They leaned against the wall and quietly listened to the watery silence. Sankt Nicolaj's struck another quarter.

'Thirty minutes!' Shepherd turned on Meyer. 'What's up with them?'

'Patience, my friend.'

'Patience be buggered!' Meyer shrugged easily, then suddenly cocked his head on one side, knocking the high-peaked cap askew. 'Hear anything?'

'When?'

'Just now.' Shepherd frowned and listened to the night for a few moments. 'Wind!' He was wrong.

184

Far out in the suburbs beyond Valby a lonely siren began screaming for help. Fire-watchers scrambled to their posts among the chimneys as more sirens came in. The first brilliant pencil of arc light shot away, nervously groping among the cloud banks. A Command Bunker telephone shrilled. Someone answered, turned and sprinted topside. 'Feindeinwirkung!'

'FEINDEINWIRKUNG!'

'Zwanzig Grade! Fünf Tausend Meter!'

'Achtung Kononieren! Achtung!'

'Fliegerschutz—FEUER!'

Someone tramped down hard on a flak cannon's firing pedal, angling off vivid indigo and red tracer at the droning aircraft. More searchlights blazed, fumbling around, drifting apart, pinching together, coning on their first accurate predictor bearings. Camouflaged batteries of 88's gorged mounds of fuzed shells; spitting back the smoky cases; long barrels cranking; violet muzzle flames biting the sky; range settings closing fast.

Abruptly, something started to burn high above the horizon, haemorrhaging liquid fire as it fell. Twinkling jewels of cannon shot scampered upwards, racing each other to get there before the fun was over. The blinded Wellington detonated, splashing its own ghastly sunset. The remaining bombers closed up and butted the flak curtains.

The Berliet slowed and wheeled hard right along the street. Jens wound the motor full out and toed down the Klaxon contact. 'Next left, the bridge!'

Meyer stood up in the open cab, gripping the windscreen frame, ready to bawl a way through the first roadblock. Waving Militiamen hurled the fire brigade past without stopping their mercy dash.

'Slower!' Shepherd felt the clapped motor start overrunning on the down grade. Jens pulled off an inch of throttle, swerved left and revved up Vermlandsgade.

'Three hundred—get ready!' Meyer wrenched up the doorcatch and kicked it into the slipstream.

'Two hundred!' He swung out and straddled the runningboard, hanging from the ladder brackets.

'One!' The first steel barrier charged backwards up the headlamp beam. Meyer dragged out a wad of quite useless paper from his tunic as the Berliet skidded unevenly over the last ten metres of free road.

An SS Unteroffizier ran at the driving cab, cutting a rigid salute at the Hauptmann standing head and shoulders above him. 'The factory's struck! Clear the way, idiot-dunghead! This

185

is Reich Priority!' Meyer all but gouged out the unfortunate NCO's eyes with his impressive fist of papers. The man's stunned face dropped open as the rearing bombers hit their primary target—twelve million litres of aviation fuel not a couple of miles away. 'JAWOHL!' He fled, shooting orders left and right. Jens heeled in the clutch and knocked flat a pair of SS guards having trouble with one of the obstacles.

Meyer drew his Walther at the second barrier. 'Move! Dirt! Filth! Oxbrains! Clear my way!' He beat a sleepy Feldwebel with the pistol barrel. The Berliet jerked away and raced through, taking the last stretch of road to the factory gates.

The SS Duty Officer doubled over from the picquet hut, pulling on his black steel helmet and leather field equipment. Flecks of Meyer's spittle dotted the lad's face. He obeyed by instinct while the night jellied with concussions; choking banks of cordite smoke hung across the road and factory like a fog; glowing fallback seeded the earth; a drumfire barrage exploded overhead; he obeyed.

His men ran to obey in their turn, one of them saving time by blowing off the second gate's lock and chain. He sprang clear as the fire brigade lumbered past and bounced towards the boiler house.

Jens swung the tail and gave their Bren a clear field of fire. 'Out! GET TO IT!' Two Sten-gunners jumped clear and dashed up the high coke heap. Shepherd bundled after Meyer and swerved round the truck to hand down their first charge.

'CAREFUL!' He glanced at the gateway. 'Next pair!' He shoved the first two men and their bomb. 'Now you!' He snatched up the tool kit, turned and started running with Meyer, lurching the heavy charge between them.

The others had already started an attack on the outer door, ripping out the panels with their axes. Shepherd elbowed them, drove a crowbar through the uprights and threw himself against the lever, eyes squeezed shut. The door crashed inwards. The bomb carriers surged after Meyer's torch.

'Next left!' Shepherd charged the Laboratory's single cruciform lock; his bar jumped off the thin metal sheeting; he screamed with rage.

'STAND BACK!' Jens knocked him away, levelled his Schmiesser and chewed out the lock and upper hinge with point-blank fire. 'NOW!' Meyer booted down what still hung together, trampling the door flat, slashing the darkness with his torch.

Surgically clean instruments and equipment, fragile and precious beyond price, marched down the hall; benches of partly

186

assembled components and glassware caught the jerking light beam.

'There!' Shepherd jabbed at the helium store. The bomb carriers doubled after him across the assembly hall. London's model had been right in every detail; armour plate sealed the valve chamber; an over-sized padlock and toughened hasp kept it shut.

Shepherd dropped the tool kit and grabbed at the bolt-cutters, forcing the jaw arms apart, biting the metal. His stringy sinews cracked under the load; he sagged over the jammed cutters: 'Oh Christ!'

'Set the fuzes!' Meyer dragged Shepherd off. 'SET THEM!' He clenched the cutters; neck corded; teeth bared; air roaring up his nostrils. Very gradually the jaws began to move again, squeezing blood between his fingers.

Abruptly, someone pitched a grenade across the yard. The Bren immediately felt back, probing the dark with mean little bursts, jigging excited sparks where the bullets struck. The two other men, prone on the coke heap, nervously lit the rag stoppers in their quart bottles of creosote, benzene and minced tyre rubber; viciously overarming at the running Spandau gunners; sending them up like a hayrick with the wooden hut.

'HURRY-F'GODSSAKE-HURRY!'

A blizzard of shots blew from the Bren, sawing from side to side; cutting down the first Storm Party to rush the narrow gate; swiping them into the barbed wire. Fangs of yellow tracer whipped down from the rooftop nests. Another flock of stick grenades twiddled over the fences, chiselling up stone splinters and gravel. Someone began to shriek on one high note. The Sten-gunners wrenched out their empty magazines, slammed in reloads and took the next rush from the side, silhouetting them against the blazing hut.

Meyer didn't notice. He braced, nearly motionless, fluttering his pectoral muscles, fighting the cutter jaws through nickel steel. TLINK! He collapsed with the metal. Shepherd levered over the heavy armour plate, ducked inside and twisted round. 'First charge!'

He held the drum, crouched low and wriggled into the freezing chamber; working between the frost-rimed valves and pipes; ribboning his skin and flesh as he gently settled the explosive under a complex of junctions and high-pressure gas lines.

'Where's this go!' Meyer squatted with the next charge. Shepherd flagged him to the left. He crawled away along the wooden

187

inspection track, through cobwebs of asbestos fibre, breath clouding the lamp glass, frosting his beard stubble.

'Ready to arm?'

'Ready!'

'NOW!' Shepherd tugged out the first arming pin, synchronising it with Meyer, sprawled by a globe of liquid oxygen.

They broke surface as Jens skidded back from the yard. 'OUT!' His gun stabbed at the remaining bomb carriers. 'MOVE! Support Hansen! GET!' He spun. 'Hurry, English!' Jens latched a fresh magazine under the Schmiesser, turned and ran out with reinforcements.

A third assault of Deathshead SS threw itself at the gateway, heads bent double under the storm of counter-fire. Flying metal and puddles of fire blocked the gap. They still came on. The surviving Spandau had been pulled clear of the flames, swung and trained through the fence. Its gunner leaned on the triggers, hysterically whirring off a half-belt raking the Berliet, sieving it from end to end. Hansen tumbled his dying mate over the side, craned their Bren at the tempest of Spandau fire and blew it out with explosive shot, still holding a jerky aim as the fuel tank split under him.

The two saboteurs were alone in the hall. Shepherd smashed down the master vacuum pump's glass wall; Meyer delicately lowered the third charge between its impeller housing and the reduction gear. He sprinted after Shepherd for the corridor, coming up short at the yard.

There was little cover left outside now. The exploding truck outlined the gate and everyone who tried it from inside. Slews of assault fire moaned like wasps, clearing the way for another attempt. The SS had manpower. They were using it without counting the cost, breaking wave after wave over a perfect defence system which no one planned could be worked in reverse.

Jens had collapsed behind the boiler chimney, shot through the groin, holding his life with difficulty. Tmp! Someone panicked with a 60 mm mortar. Tmp! Tmp! Tmp! A flight of bombs curved over, bursting ahead of the bunched troops. They straightened up and charged on the command. Jens and the two remaining gunners crawled from cover and hacked them down. The attack faded out in a fresh litter of dead and dying.

'Try it now?' Meyer bawled sideways at Shepherd.

'With phosphorus!'

'Right!' They bobbed round the doorway and set off along the shadows to the boiler house.

'Go!' Jens gagged on his chewed tongue, vomiting blood over

188

Meyer as he dropped beside him. Two men cascaded back down the coke slide. 'Go.'

Meyer didn't argue. He dragged off the satchel of grenades and reloads, crouched and snatched up Jens' carbine. Shepherd looted the chokeless automatic shotgun and half-empty bandolier of shells, thumbing five along the tube as Meyer thrust round the smoke canisters. 'When I say so, hit the gate!' He paused. 'NOW!'

Four gusts of burning phosphorus spewed over the wire, blanketing the gap with white smoke. Meyer went through fast, snap-shooting from the shoulder, flicking away crowded black uniforms.

'Here!' Shepherd swerved after Meyer's shout. They stumbled into the weeds and rubbish, crossing the railway tracks well clear of a flak wagon tossing up long chains of green bubbles at a bewildered Wellington. The last two alive were safe while everyone fought the air battle. Meyer quickened and grabbed at Shepherd. 'Move faster! The beach!' They started to cover the final hundred yards of low sand dunes and factory debris.

'Halt!' Lumpy shapes broke the faint skyline; SS posted to hold the seaward flanks against Commando attack.

'HALT!' They started fanning out, clearing their automatics. The two running men went left, hunched double, racing the encirclement. Someone aimed a parachute flare and wiped away their darkness.

'LOS!' The hunters ranged in, hosing short bursts at the men scrambling over to the narrow beach and muttering sea. Another flare popped.

Meyer stumbled as the bullet took him in the lower spine. He sat down heavily and slowly rolled over to face the attack. His right hand dragged the bolt on a fresh magazine; the eye aimed itself; the finger jerked; the SS hit cover.

'HURRY!' Shepherd turned and shambled back through the glacis of empty bottles and junk. 'Start the signals!'

'Take them yourself, little man! Take them; go on alone!' Shepherd ran the satchel down to the shore and touched off each sodium candle with the flame from his Colt's muzzle blast, stabbing them upright in the loose shingle. He dived as the SS let fly from the left.

His aim was shaky, but a sawn-off shotgun isn't too critical. He pumped out three loads of goose pellets, mauled the flanking attack and jackknifed up the slope to Meyer.

He'd knotted his hands under Meyer's chest and started to crawl him away when a wobbling grenade pitched short. He kicked over, slowly elbowed clear and put two shells into the

189

troopers rushing the counterscarp. Meyer swept off a ragged spatter of bullets. The SS went down again.

'Get away! GET AWAY FROM ME!' Meyer screamed foully. 'Get down to—the launch!'

Shepherd wasn't listening. He strained the darkness, watching the factory's outline waver against a trellis of flak and searchlights, bursting bombs and swirling fires. He couldn't hold it off much longer.

He didn't have to. The nibbling fuzes bit, proving his work. The western horizon recoiled in one belch of orange and blue light; ton slabs of walling and masonry shook free, tumbling away in an expanding cyclone; the thudding shock waves ran ahead to Sweden.

Shepherd tiredly rolled on one side and faced Meyer; the Colt weighed down both hands; it was time for them to be going. 'We really showed those bastards how to live, didn't we?' He threw up rich, arterial blood. 'Now—let's—show—them—how—to—die.'

The lunging troopers heard two dull shots and eased to an angry walk over the last few yards of dirty shingle and weeds.

Copy 1

Kelly, Michael
Assault.

WITHDRAWN